MURDER-BY-MONTH MYSTERY SERIES

December Dread

"Lourey pulls out all the stops in this eighth case." —*Library Journal*

"Lourey creates a splendid mix of humor and suspense." —*Booklist*

"Lourey, who keeps her secrets well, delivers a very breathtaking finale."
—*Publishers Weekly*

November Hunt

"Librarian/sleuth Mira James is smart and resourceful…This light novel keeps the reader engaged, like one of those sweet, chewy Nut Goodies that Mira is addicted to."—*Boston Globe*

"Jess Lourey skillfully navigates her way along the razor's edge of the traditional mystery. A masterful mix of mayhem and mirth…[and] a fun read all the way through."—Reed Farrel Coleman, three-time Shamus Award–winning author of *Hurt Machine*

"Lourey has successfully created an independent, relatable heroine in Mira James. Mira's wit and fearlessness enable her to overcome the many challenges she faces as she tries to unravel the murder."—*Crimespree Magazine*

"A good story told well, with solid writing." —*Ellery Queen Mystery Magazine*

"Clever, quirky, and completely original! This taut and compelling mystery—with a twist on every page—is edgy, entertaining, and irresistible." —Hank Phillippi Ryan, Anthony, Agatha, and Macavity Award–winning author

October Fest

Shortlisted for a Lefty Award from Left Coast Crime

*"Lourey has cleverly created an entertaining murder mystery…Her latest is loaded with humor, and many of the descriptions are downright poetic."—*Booklist* (starred review)

"Funny, ribald, and brimming with small-town eccentrics."—*Kirkus Reviews*

"I loved Lourey's quirky, appealing sleuth and her wry yet affectionate look at small town life…I hope Mira's misfortune of stumbling over a dead body every month lasts for many years!" —Donna Andrews, *New York Times* best–selling author of *Stork Raving Mad*

September Fair

"Lively."—*Publishers Weekly*

"An engaging novel with pathos, plot twists, and quirky characters galore... Beautifully written and wickedly funny."—Harley Jane Kozak, Agatha, Anthony, and Macavity Award–winning author of *A Date You Can't Refuse*

"Lourey has a talent for creating hilarious characters in bizarre, laugh-out-loud situations, while at the same time capturing the honest and endearing subtleties of human life."—*The Strand*

August Moon

*"Hilarious, fast paced, and madcap."—*Booklist* (starred review)

"Another amusing tale set in the town full of over-the-top zanies who've endeared themselves to the engaging Mira."—*Kirkus Reviews*

"[A] hilarious, wonderfully funny cozy."—*Crimespree Magazine*

"Entertaining."—*Library Journal*

Knee High by the Fourth of July

Shortlisted for a Lefty Award from Left Coast Crime and chosen as a Killer Book by the Independent Mystery Booksellers Association

"Mira... is an amusing heroine in a town full of quirky characters."—*Kirkus Reviews*

"Lourey's rollicking good cozy planted me in the heat of a Minnesota summer for a laugh-out-loud mystery ride."—Leann Sweeney, author of the Yellow Rose Mystery series

June Bug

"The funny, earthy heroine is sure to stumble her way into the hearts of readers everywhere. Don't miss this one—it's a hoot!"—William Kent Krueger, Anthony Award–winning author of the Cork O'Connor series

"A funny, well-written, engaging story... readers will thoroughly enjoy the well-paced ride."—Carl Brookins, author of *The Case of the Greedy Lawyer*

"Jess Lourey is a talented, witty, and clever writer."—Monica Ferris, author of the best–selling Needlecraft Mysteries

May Day

"All the ingredients for a successful small-town cozy series are right here."
—*Publishers Weekly*

"A likeable heroine and a surfeit of sass."—*Kirkus Reviews*

"*May Day* is fresh, the characters quirky. Minnesota has many fine crime writers, and Jess Lourey has just entered their ranks!"—Ellen Hart, author of the Sophie Greenway and Jane Lawless Mystery series

JANUARY
THAW

JANUARY THAW

A Murder-By-Month Mystery

jess lourey

MIDNIGHT INK
WOODBURY, MINNESOTA

First Edition
First Printing, 2014

Book format by Bob Gaul
Cover design by Ellen Lawson
Cover illustration by Carl Mazer
Editing by Nicole Nugent

Midnight Ink, an imprint of Llewellyn Worldwide Ltd.

Library of Congress Cataloging-in-Publication Data
Lourey, Jess, 1970–
   January thaw: a Murder-by-Month Mystery/Jess Lourey.—First Edition.
      pages cm.—(A Murder-by-Month mystery; #9)
   ISBN 978-0-7387-3875-8
  1. Murder—Investigation—Fiction. 2. Minnesota—Fiction. I. Title.
  PS3612.O833J36 2014
  813'.6—dc23
                    2013027483

Midnight Ink
Llewellyn Worldwide Ltd.
2143 Wooddale Drive
Woodbury, MN 55125-2989
www.midnightinkbooks.com

Printed in the United States of America

DEDICATION

To Catriona, for being such a gallus besom herself.

A special thanks goes to the Prospect House & Civil War Museum for letting me set major portions of the novel in their amazing mansion and on their grounds. A special thanks to Jay Johnson and Abby Bizzett-Johnson for the private tour. They have allowed me to cherry pick from the history of the Prospect House (and a little bit from their personal lives) and twist where necessary to fit my narrative. Everything good I wrote about the Prospect House and the dedicated, incredible people who care for it is true; everything dark is entirely a work of fiction. If you are in the Battle Lake area, I encourage you to stop by and visit this impressive piece of history. Heck, I think you should make a special trip just to check it out. It's that cool. Find out more at their website: www.prospecthousemuseum.org.

ONE

THE WORLD WAS SAFELY tucked in under blankets of snow. I navigated Battle Lake's well-lit main street, pushing against the weather with hands shoved deep into fleece mittens and chin tucked into my neck. I could have driven the eight blocks from the library to the Fortune Café, but this was my favorite kind of snowfall—the flakes drifting down lazy and white like dandelion fluff. The outdoors felt cozy, the air scrubbed clean by ice crystal ions, all sound muffled in soft white snow.

Earlier today, Jack Bloom had mentioned that a January thaw was on its way. I believed that about as much as I bought into the covers of the pulp fiction books he checked out weekly. It was currently six below, not counting the windchill. The glittering Christmas garlands had been removed from the light posts just a week earlier. Plus, this was Minnesota. If the thermometer topped zero in January, we referred to that as a "warm snap." I didn't expect to see above-freezing temps until March. That was fine by me—winter is a magical season, if you have the heart for it.

I took another step, admiring how the snow dusted up like smoke. If you'd told me a year ago that I'd be living in Battle Lake, Minnesota, population 747 and dropping, spending an evening walking and admiring the weather, I'd have laughed in your face. But sometimes, life steers and all we can do is hang on. For my part—

"Are you writing a book in your head or just trying to hold in a fart?"

I glanced over at Mrs. Berns. I'd almost forgotten she was with me. *As if.* She was in her eighties, sharper than me on my best day, and my closest friend. She also possessed a wicked tongue, blended in nowhere, and courted trouble with the same single-minded focus she used to chase men.

"Because if it's the latter," she continued, "I suggest you let 'er rip. The only people stupid enough to step outside in this weather wouldn't complain about the extra heat. That includes me, by the way. Remind me again why we're walking?"

"It's a gorgeous night." I kicked up another puff of snow. "And you didn't have to come with, you know."

My plan for the evening had been to close up the library and grab a bowl of Sid's famous firehouse chili and an olive cream cheese–slathered bagel to go. I could visit with Nancy while Sid readied my order, then shuffle back to the library to grab my car and head on home to enjoy a quiet dinner with my cat, dog, and TV. I normally enjoyed cooking, but the library had gotten so busy today that I'd had to skip lunch and work well past normal closing hours. My stomach was burbling like a tar pit. When Mrs. Berns, who was also my assistant at the library, heard of my evening plans, she suggested we head to the Fortune Café together.

She loved Sid's homemade bagels almost as much as I did. They were chewy on the outside, soft on the inside, and the perfect vehicle for cream cheese salted with thick olive slices. Turns out the food was only one of the unexpected rewards of moving to Battle Lake, the teeny-tiny town I'd relocated to last March. Previously I'd been living in Minneapolis, a grad-school English major dropout paying the bills with tips from my waitressing gig at a Vietnamese restaurant on the West Bank. My boyfriend at the time was a bass player who turned out to be a little too free with his "music." On top of all that, I was regularly drinking too much. On that fateful day when Sunny, a friend of a friend, asked me to house-sit for her in Battle Lake, I'd gotten flashed by a vagrant whose business looked like a sad little green bean that had sat in the microwave for too long. *Voilà*. The scales tipped.

What was supposed to be a few months of house-sitting had grown into an open-ended appointment. Despite having lived in Battle Lake for nearly a year, however, I was and always would be "not from around here." Plus, I'd developed a distasteful habit of discovering one corpse a month since May. A lesser woman would think herself cursed. I'd been raised by a codependent mother eligible for sainthood and an alcoholic father who'd killed himself and the occupants of an oncoming car in a drunk-driving accident when I was a sophomore in high school, and so I had a different perspective on life. I was, of all things, an optimist, though one who was always waiting for the other shoe to drop.

The inaugural dead body appeared about the time I landed my first job in town. Both the job and the corpse were located at the Battle Lake Public Library. When the head librarian disappeared shortly after the murder, I'd been promoted to fill in for him until someone qualified could be found; a budget cut plus the fact that I kept "losing" applications kept that possibility at bay. The most recent carcass had almost been mine. Three weeks ago, an honest-to-goodness serial killer—nicknamed the Candy Cane Killer by the press—had hunted me like an animal, stalking close enough to leave scars that I'd carry for the rest of my life, inside and out. I hadn't slept a full night since, though I refused to reveal that when anyone asked how I was. Admitting it out loud would make it too real. Besides, to whom could I confess that I'd started sleeping under my bed instead of on it—that every evening before I drifted off for an hour or two, my nose inches from the box springs, I wondered if I'd gone too far to ever feel safe again?

And so I kept my mental state to myself. I worked, I laughed, I played, and I watched the shadows.

On a positive note, I'd discovered more about myself since moving here than I could have imagined. My drinking was mostly in check, I had begun to repair my relationship with my mom and make peace with the memory of my dad, I was pursuing my PI license based on the belief that the Universe was telling me it was that or become a mortician, and I'd even fallen in love with a guy who walked upright. His name was Johnny Leeson, and he was a horticulturist and lead singer for a local band.

Tall, with strong hands, a great smile, and wavy blonde hair, if Johnny was food, he'd be chocolate. And if he was drink, he'd be a rare red wine. I still didn't entirely trust that somebody as amazing as him was all mine, but I was willing to work on it. We'd been dating exclusively, more or less, for a few months. And over Christmas, the file I'd started on Johnny had finally gotten indexed, if you know what I mean. It was everything I'd imagined, except for the location: my childhood bedroom. He'd been busy since then starting the spring seedlings at the local nursery and playing gigs all over the Midwest with The Thumbs. Subsequently, we hadn't gotten to repeat the glory we'd first discovered under the Jimmy Page and Leif Garrett posters my mom still kept up in my room, though we did have a date planned for tomorrow night.

"You're thinking about Johnny now, aren't you?" Mrs. Berns said, interrupting my thoughts for the second time. "You better not take up poker. You're easier to read then a comic strip. With large print."

I realized I'd been smiling as I walked through the fairy snow, and that made me beam even wider. "He's pretty cute, isn't he?"

"You could do worse."

The occasional car burred past us as we briskly covered the eight blocks, but it was almost seven at night and all the businesses except for the Apothecary and the Rusty Nail were closed in accordance with their winter hours. Theodora, manager of the Apothecary, glanced up from rearranging her Valentine's Day window display as Mrs. Berns and I strolled past. She waved, and we returned the gesture before crossing the street. We'd nearly reached the end of the block, encased again in our own thoughts and body heat, when I heard what sounded like a child crying to my right.

I stopped and cocked my ear. When the snowflakes get this big, they sometimes warp sound.

"Hear that?" I asked.

Mrs. Berns kept walking toward the intersection. "My feet crying out from the cold? My stomach growling from starvation? Yep and yep."

"No, it's definitely something." I pointed at the alley entrance between the post office and an abandoned building that used to house a movie rental store. "From down there. I can't tell if it's a person or an animal."

Mrs. Berns returned to my side to listen with me.

The plaintive cry repeated itself, high and whining, at a pitch that thrummed a deeply instinctual fear chord. The six below temperature suddenly felt ominous, and my blood turned sluggish. The leering face of the Candy Cane Killer returned to me, unbidden: handsome, banal, deadly. Familiar. I forced myself to breathe regularly, repeating like a mantra the fact that the police station was only two blocks away.

"Should we run for help?" I asked. I was grateful that my voice worked.

"Excellent idea," Mrs. Berns said. "Nothing Chief Wohnt would prefer to do tonight than check on a rabbit stuck in a snowy alley. Unless you broke a nail? Because he'd want to hear about that as well."

I realized I'd been holding my breath. I released it in a sharp gush. Mrs. Berns was right. The Candy Cane Killer was in a maximum-security prison in Chicago. He couldn't get me. There was nothing horrible down that alley. It was only a hurt animal. And I'd feel like an ass if I called out the guards for a rabbit, not to mention Chief Gary Wohnt and I didn't have the best relationship. Ultimately, though, what spurred me to check on the sound was this: I was tired of being so afraid. I'd been wearing it like a shock collar since the Killer put me in the hospital, and I could already feel the conditioning settle in. *Don't take chances. Stay in your routine. Don't step out of line, and you won't bring any more bad on yourself.*

I glanced around. Theadora was still busy in the Apothecary display window down the block and across the street, though she looked far away and pieced-up through the falling snow. The Fortune Café was three blocks ahead, the streets mostly well-lit. A rusty Ford pickup with a snowplow wedge mounted on the front drove past, the snow muffling the engine's rattle. The driver honked a greeting at Mrs. Berns and me. I held up a hand. He kept driving.

I sighed. It felt like now or never: confront my fear or forever wear the yoke. If the boogey man was down the alley, I could yell and Mrs. Berns would have someone here in two minutes. If it was an injured

6

animal, I could carry it back to my car and drive it to the emergency vet. If it was a scared child, or worse, an injured one, I was a monster for even debating this long.

"I'm going in," I said. "You wait here."

I held my hands loose at my sides like I'd learned in a recent self-defense class and strode resolutely down the alley.

And right into the devil's paw.

TWO

"HEY, WHATCHU DOIN' WALKING down alleys? Didn't your mama warn you?"

My heart was pounding on the back of my throat, looking for escape. Even in the dim light, I could see that the brute was younger than me, maybe early twenties, an ogre of a man with a heavy forehead and eyes that squinted under the weight of it. His jean jacket was far too light for the weather, even with the hoodie underneath. I sensed another person behind me, certainly male. I couldn't see him, knew he was blocking my escape, but I was too scared to turn away from the ogre. The man behind me made a sound, a replica of the mewling that had drawn me into the alley in the first place.

"He breathes like that when he gets tweaked. Says he can't hear it himself, but I tell him he sounds just like a damn trapped kitten." He reached forward and plucked my hat off my head and shoved it onto his. "And that's exactly what I feel like. This weather is inhumane, you got that? It's like someone left the goddamn freezer door open in this state."

White spots floated across my eyes. I wanted to look at who was behind me but couldn't drag my eyes off the immediate threat. I prayed fervently that Mrs. Berns wouldn't follow me down here, that she would instead intuit I needed help and take off for the police station. I considered yelling, but I knew she'd come if I did, and the only thing that would make this situation worse was if there were two of us stuck in it.

The ogre stared me down. I knew if there'd been more light, his flat black shark eyes would have just reflected it back at me. I could barely see around his hulking form, the back wall of the post office on one side of him, the three-story wall of an apartment building on the other. Behind him was the alley leading to the opposite street, a street light flickering at the end through the deepening snow, forty eternal feet away.

"How 'bout those mittens, baby? They look like they'd be mighty warm to slide into."

Behind me, the soft animal cry took on a wheezing quality that made my stomach tighten. I was aware of each hair on my head.

I slipped off my mittens, every nerve in my body keening. I needed to escape. The guy behind me might be small enough to run through, but I couldn't seem to pull my eyes off the beast I was facing. My best bet was to run through the ogre, but I'd have only one chance. I held the mittens out, visibly trembling. As he reached forward, I pretended to drop them. He bent down, and I charged to his right. I made it all of two feet before the person behind jumped onto my back and crashed us both into the icy ground.

The fall knocked the wind out of me and twisted the newly healed knife wound in my right arm. The pain burned all the way to my teeth. I so wanted to play possum until all this went away, until the bad guys were gone and I was back safe on a well-lit street, but I didn't have that luxury. The man who'd dropped me rolled off, and I gasped for breath, taking stock of my ribs and wrists, feeling for breaks. The ogre toed me with his boot.

"Where were you going, baby? Doncha know there's nothing to see around here? This place is about as interesting as bread. Everyone looks the same, nothin' to do."

I winced as I pulled myself into a sitting position. In a different life, I might have agreed with his assessment. I tried out my voice, not liking how small it sounded. "What are you doing here if you dislike it so much?"

"She talks!" said the ogre. "You hear that, Ray? She's got a voice."

My back to an apartment dumpster, I finally risked a look at the ogre's partner, Ray. He was lean and hungry-looking, also under-dressed for the weather, with a lick of a tattoo showing on his neck. Where the big one looked like he was from eastern European or Russian stock, Ray appeared Hispanic. Rather than answer, he kept glancing furtively down the alleyway behind him then over the other guy's shoulder, as if expecting someone. Jumping on me had ramped up his baby-animal noises, and he seemed ready to crawl out of his own skin.

I pushed myself to my feet. My hands were ice-scraped from trying to brace my fall, and likely my knees were as well, but I was alive. From this angle, I noticed the crowbar and duffle bag at the ogre's feet, and I added that to what I knew. That meant I now had three bits of knowledge, the other two being that the man who had pounced on me was quick and that running clearly wasn't going to work. Which left talking. Mrs. Berns had surely gone for help, right? I just needed to keep them from hurting me until the police showed up. It was a long, desperate shot, which felt just about right.

I rubbed at the palms of my hands, checking for ice shards and gravel. "I have plenty of other hats and mittens. I could bring you some if you like."

Ray's fidgety glance stopped on me for a moment, then kept traveling.

The ogre tried to stretch one of my mittens over his meaty paw. It covered three fingers. "Naw, baby, I don't think your winter gear is worth crap. What else you got that might be worth somethin'? You got a purse? Why don't no ladies here carry purses?"

It was true. When the temperature dropped, Minnesota women tend to store everything close to their body. It just made sense. My money was housed in the interior pocket of my down jacket, along with peppermint lip balm, keys, and three pieces of cinnamon gum. I could live without any of it.

I held up my cold hands. "I've got about thirty bucks. You're welcome to it. It's inside my pocket."

I started to reach in, but before I could unzip my jacket, Ray had me pinned to the icy ground again, this time flat on my back. Sharp air rushed out, scraping my lungs. And here I'd just gotten the hang of breathing again. I willed myself to keep calm, to ignore the hot trickle of blood that had begun seeping out of the freshly opened wound on my arm. If I didn't have my wits, I had nothing.

"I don't like this, Hammer! I don't like her, I don't like this town, I don't like any of it." The mewling was coming rapid, like a heartbeat.

The ogre named Hammer seemed unsurprised by his partner's jittery outburst. "Do what you need to, man."

"Wait, what?" I asked. "No one has to get hurt here."

Ray leaned in. His shivering pupils were so dilated that his eyes looked like two bullet holes. His breath smelled cough-syrup sweet. His exact intentions were unclear, but he wore his unhinged state like a sign. A distant part of me could not believe this is how I was going to go, in a small-town alley, one block and a million miles away from friends and warm food. My eyes felt hot, but I was going to fight rather than cry.

Gathering my strength, I punched Ray's stomach and twisted my hips at the same time, hoping to unbalance him and then buck him. The force of my thrust knocked him off, but he landed on his feet and clenched, ready to pounce back on me.

"What the goddamned hell is going on here?"

All three of us froze and turned to the voice.

It was Mrs. Bern. She was alone.

My heart plummeted.

Ray glanced from Mrs. Berns to Hammer, his eyes agitated, his fingers curled into claws. Mrs. Berns stood her ground, one hand on her hip and the other stuffed in her pocket as if she might be hiding a gun. She looked like the angriest grandma you ever met. Why had she come down here? Had she gone for help first?

"Run!" I yelled to her.

Too late.

Ray pounced.

THREE

I LURCHED FORWARD, MY strength superhuman. It's one thing to hurt me, but it's a whole 'nother to hurt my friends. I flew at Ray, who had Mrs. Berns's beautiful bony arm twisted behind her back. I fully intended to take a pound of flesh. Before I had a chance, though, he was yanked backward, a shocked expression on his face. Free of his grip, Mrs. Berns fell forward and into my arms. I pulled her close.

Another man, a new one, had Ray pushed against the rear wall of what used to be the video rental store, his forearm against Ray's throat. This third man wasn't large, but Ray's feet weren't touching the ground. My eyes raced between the three strangers as I inched Mrs. Berns and myself toward escape.

"Whachu doin', Maurice?" Hammer asked, not moving from his original position. "We were just having some fun."

The man named Maurice shot me a dismissive glance, not letting go of Ray. I recognized him immediately. He was mid-twenties, African American, a cap pulled tight over his head. His jacket, gloves, and boots looked warm. He'd been in the library maybe a half dozen times in the past two weeks, spending a lot of time in the local history section but never checking anything out.

"Stupid whangsters," he said. "I told you to sit tight. Why you have to make trouble?"

"Shit, we was only playing," Hammer said, his voice whiny. "Killin' time. When did you get so soft?"

Maurice stepped back. Ray dropped to the ground, his hand on his throat as if he hoped to reinflate it. His mewling returned to a steady rhythm, but his eyes grew busier. Hammer's heavy brow drooped even farther.

"Go," the man named Maurice ordered us. He flashed me another look, his expression indecipherable.

We didn't need to be told twice. I pushed Mrs. Berns toward the light at the end of the alley, leaving my hat and mittens behind.

FOUR

"Tell me again why the two of you went down an alley alone."

I didn't care for Battle Lake Police Chief Gary Wohnt's tone of voice any more than I liked the way his deep blue uniform hugged his chest and arms. When Gary and I'd first crossed paths last May, he'd been paunchy, crabby, and perennially concealed behind mirrored sunglasses. We were instant enemies. I didn't like him because he was arrogant and seemed always on the verge of catching me with my hand in the cookie jar. I had no idea why he disliked me.

I had him perfectly pigeon-holed until he left town with a born-again lady, got dumped, and returned to Battle Lake lean, dark, and handsome. My brain and heart knew the score. I was working on the other parts. When he made me this angry, though, all I wanted to do was fry him like an ant under a magnifying glass.

"Like I said, we thought we heard a hurt animal. Or a person. I went ahead to check, and when I didn't come out after a few minutes, Mrs. Berns came in after me."

"Definitely sounded like a baby," Mrs. Berns hollered from the other side of the room, where the new deputy was examining her arm. He'd sworn there was no need for her to remove her sweater, but she'd demurred, arguing it was better to be thorough. She'd recently joked that her boobs were now 32 longs instead of 32 Cs, but they looked pretty good in the lavender silk bra she was wearing. It didn't hurt that I'd already checked out her arm and knew it was fine, if a little bruised. My arm would also be all right. The fight had ripped the last scab off the scar, but the rest of the stitched skin had stayed intact. The only casualty was the tattered remnants of my personal security.

"That Maurice guy saved our biscuits," Mrs. Berns continued loudly.

Gary ignored her and studied me over the steeple of his fingers. His eyes were inky, and they gave away nothing. They also made me want to blurt out the fact that I had stolen two pencils from work today and didn't always wash my hands after using the bathroom.

"Look," I said, when the silence became painful. "Am I the one on trial? Because last I checked, going down an alley intending to help the vulnerable is a *good* thing. It's attacking people and stealing mittens that's the crime."

He leaned forward, grabbed a pen and a slip of official-looking paper off of his desk, and began writing. Finally, he was going to take me seriously. I sat forward.

"You say they stole your mittens," he said with gravitas, "but were you able to get away with your lunch money intact?" He didn't pause in his writing.

Was that a smile tugging at the corner of his mouth? I wanted to hit him so badly. But then, suddenly, I just wanted to cry. "The one guy was *huge*. The second one jumped me from behind. He was all hopped up, making the noises. Who knows what they would have

16

done if that Maurice person hadn't shown up? Do you really want these guys walking around in your town, robbing people or worse, right under your nose?"

He laid down the pen and paper, and his jaw clenched in a gesture I was familiar with. Any levity that might have been present was now completely erased. "I have all your information. Is there anything else?"

I studied him, noting the abrupt change in his demeanor. "You already knew about them, didn't you?"

He opened a drawer, dropped the pen in, and closed it. "Like I said, is there anything else you want to tell me? If not, I've got work to do."

I reflected on the men's clothes, and the street rhythm of their language. They weren't from this area, maybe not even from the Midwest. Hammer and Ray had *gang* written all over them, but Maurice seemed cut from different cloth. He'd still been rough around the edges, no doubt, but he'd saved us when he could have just as easily walked away. I shuddered to think what would have become of us if he hadn't shown up when he did. "You're watching them, aren't you? Who are they? What are they doing in Battle Lake?"

He grabbed a brochure off the top of his desk and began reading it.

I leaned forward. "Minnesota Fishing Regulations? Fascinating. You're not going to tell me anything about the hulk and his sidekick, are you?"

No answer. I scowled. I sat there for another full minute watching him pretend to read, then my stomach growled. I sighed. I knew Gary well enough to realize I wouldn't get anything out of him that he didn't want me to know. I also knew I would get even less sleep than usual unless I had some reassurance that he already had an eye on the bad guys. "Fine. I won't tell you about their tattoos, then."

"Hammerhead shark across the back and shoulders of the large one, stingray on the neck of the other."

I grinned. I'd only been guessing about the ogre having a tattoo and hadn't gotten a good look at Ray's. "Thank you."

He never removed his eyes from the brochure he was pretending to read, but a brief, rare smile moved across his face. "You're welcome."

———

Despite his apparent nonchalance, Gary had immediately sent a car to check the alley as soon as Mrs. Berns and I spilled into his station, out of breath and jabbering all at once. I was sure the thugs were long gone, and my hunch was confirmed when the police car rolled into the parking lot just as I exited the station without Mrs. Berns, who said she was going to stay and practice some "stretches" with the new deputy.

I waved at the officer to stop and jogged over. He rolled down his window as I approached. "Did you find anyone?"

"Nope. Just these." He held up my hat and mittens. "Yours?"

I nodded and accepted them gratefully. "Gary seems to know the culprits. Have they been causing trouble around here lately?"

The officer, a bearded man named Victor who was the middle guy on the three-man force, glanced over my shoulder toward the cop shop. His breath puffed out in tiny cumulous clouds.

"Let me guess," I said. "Gary told you not to tell anyone?"

He shrugged apologetically. "He specifically warned against saying anything to you. Said you stumble into enough trouble all on your own."

I held up my hands. "I don't go looking for it."

All he had for me was a smile. I sighed. "Thanks for my hat and mittens, anyways."

"Be safe." He rolled up his window and pulled out of the lot.

I glanced toward the sky. Snow was still falling, but it had lost its magic. I was cold and tired and hungry. The library and therefore my car were nearer than the Fortune Café, and my craving for a bagel and chili had been replaced by a strong desire to be home, behind locked doors, under my bed with my cat and dog. I should have asked Victor to give me a ride to my car. It was only four blocks away, but in my current state of mind, that felt like four miles.

"Yoo-hoo!"

I immediately recognized the voice coming from the far end of the parking lot. I scrunched my shoulders and hoofed it in the opposite direction, toward the library and the relative safety of my car, following the tried and true axiom, "if you can't see them, they can't see you."

"Mira James! I can see you plain as the nose on my face. Now turn around and say hi to my new sidekick."

So help me, I was powerless to deny Kennie Rogers's command, such was my complete submission to curiosity. I'd met Kennie about the same time I'd been introduced to Gary Wohnt—which was no coincidence, as they'd been dating at the time. Both were in their forties and graduates of Battle Lake High School. Neither had escaped their hometown, Gary becoming police chief and Kennie mayor. Their past was sordid, as far as I could suss out, and since Gary had left Kennie cold when he'd skipped town with his Jesus-loving floozy, their relationship had been strained, to say the least.

They had to work together, though, and both were masters of the passive-aggressive game, a skill most Midwesterners come by naturally but that the two of them elevated to an art form. It was funny, almost, to think that they had ever been a couple. Gary was stoic and Kennie pathologically outgoing with an intermittent Southern accent, despite being born and raised in west central Minnesota. Gary favored dark colors and Kennie was hard-pressed to leave the house without a tiara. Gary possessed all of two facial expressions—annoyed and suspicious—whereas Kennie wore make-up like a wedding cake wore frosting. My natural aversion to Kennie had been nearly as strong as my dislike of the police chief, but god help me, the woman had grown on me. She was a fighter, and I liked my women strong.

So I stopped.

And I turned.

Which is how I came to be face to face with Kennie jogging toward me in a sequined pink snowsuit, a wiener dog wearing a matching sweater trundling along behind her, his stubby legs pumping like pistons in the accumulating snow. The wiener dog also wore a pointy elf hat fastened under her neck, her ears poking out of the pink yarn. Her eyes were impossibly big, wet, and brown.

"Awwww," I said. She really was that cute.

"Thank you," Kennie said, stopping a few feet away. Her breath was short—it can't be easy to jog across fresh-fallen snow in pink stiletto boots—but she covered by fluffing the crispy platinum hair that curled around her ear muffs. "I just got it done."

"I was referring to the puppy. When did you get her?"

"Him," she corrected. "His name is Peter. He's been living with me for two weeks."

"You named your wiener dog 'Peter'?"

She ignored the question as Peter pitter-patted over to sniff my ankles. "I adopted him from the Humane Society. I stopped by to see if they had any teacup poodles because they're the latest must-have fashion accessory. Lord knows if I don't keep pushing the fashion envelope in Battle Lake, who will?"

I shrugged. It was one of those questions.

"Well of course they didn't have anything cute and small, but then I met Peter. I didn't think much of him at first, until he had one of his spells. That was when I heard The Calling."

The capital letters were audible, but I stuffed fingers into curiosity's ears and lalalala'd. Kennie was notorious for her start-up businesses, from coffin tables that could be converted to your place of eternal rest, to Come Again, her online used marital aids company. Just two months ago, she'd sold me questionable vitamins that had nearly destroyed my dating life. No thanks to finding out about her latest business, I say.

Instead, I knelt to pet Peter. "Hey, sweetie, come here. That's right. Aren't you a honey? Aren't you a doll?" I started scratching his ears, and his back right leg thumped in joy. I reached under his chin to get at the sweet spot that my foster dog Luna loved. Peter's eyes rolled up in ecstasy. I was smiling when he fell over on his side, stiff as a stick.

"Oh my god!" I put my hand on his chest, feeling for a pulse. "Did he have a heart attack? Did I kill your dog?"

"No, silly," Kennie said, kneeling down to scoop him into her arms. "I was trying to tell you. I was in the kennel with Peter when he had a spell. He's narcoleptic. That's when the Lord came down and called me to help. He said I was to help the silent by becoming an animal and plant psychologist."

"Animal *and* plant?" I asked, suspicious, and probably about the wrong thing.

"He works in mysterious ways," Kennie said. "Who can explain His thoroughness?"

I suspected the dual-career idea had more to do with Kennie's constant marketing machine than divine intervention. "Doesn't that require some training?"

"Turns out it doesn't," she said. She whispered into Peter's ear, and he began to wiggle. He blinked twice, and then sat up in her arms and began thumping his back right leg again, rejoining us exactly where he'd left off.

The mini-miracle gave me pause. Had Kennie finally discovered her real deal? Could she actually be an animal whisperer? I gave that line of thinking a full twenty seconds. Nope, not possible. Surely Peter had woken up on his own.

"How's business?" I asked.

"That's what I wanted to talk to you about. Can I put some flyers up in the library tomorrow? You know, spread the word?"

"Sure," I said. It wouldn't cost me anything.

"Can I also use you as a referral?"

"But I haven't used your services."

"Not yet, but I am offering you a free consultation." She dug into her front pocket and came out with a business card that appeared printed from a home computer. The word *Serenity* was scrolled across the top in an ornate script, and below that in increasingly smaller print, *Pet and Plant Psychologist*, and underneath that, *Kennie Rogers, PHD.*

"You don't have a PhD."

She drew herself up. "I don't *have* a PhD. I *am* a PHD. 'Plant/Pet Helper and Doer.'" She winked. "So what do you say? I'll come by tomorrow morning, maybe around eight? I can visit with your pets, perk up your plants a little? While I'm there, I could give you make-up tips, too. You look like a potato farmer on a death march. That's just my two cents, of course."

I wanted to tell her I had change for her, but suddenly I was exhausted. The full stress of the evening had finally caught up with me, landing on my shoulders like vultures, digging into my flesh and pushing me into the ground. "Can I get back to you on that? It's been a long day."

"Fine. I'll mark you down as 'appointment pending.'"

Looking back, I still wouldn't be sure if allowing her to come by that next morning would have made any difference, as the pawns leading to the latest and most brutal murder I was to uncover were already in play.

FIVE

"You got anything on Battle Lake?"

It was a week earlier, and I didn't yet know I'd soon be meeting this man in a dark alley. I was kneeling at the bottom shelf of the "H–Ki" shelf of the fiction section, where I'd been scraping fossilized gum from the metal racks. If Stephen King's *The Stand* was shelved, I couldn't see the gum, but the book had been on a steady check-out for three weeks, and I was sick of looking at the liver-colored blotch.

I turned toward the voice, paused just for a nanosecond, and then answered, "The history of Battle Lake, you mean?"

I'm not proud of the pause, as short as it was, but the truth is that in this part of Minnesota, nearly everything was white: the food, the weather, and especially the people. I could count on one finger the number of people of color who'd come into the library, and I was looking at him. Early- to mid-twenties, five-foot-nine maybe -ten, skin the color of pecans, eyes a dark brown, his tight hair cropped close to his head.

"Yeah. The history."

He said it matter-of-factly, though his stance was uncomfortable, his hands shoved deep into his pockets.

"Mmm-hmm."

It was the sound of a deliberate cough. I rose to my feet, leaving the butter knife and paper plate of bubblegum shards on the floor. I tipped so I could see around Maurice to the throat clearer.

"Yes, Jack?" He was a regular in his sixties who knew everything about the weather, trains, and guns, and loved to read pulp fiction.

"Everything okay here?" Jack asked.

I was momentarily puzzled, until he pointedly looked at Maurice, then back at me. Maurice kept his hands shoved in his pockets, his back to Jack. I guessed he'd been through this before.

"I'm fine. Just helping a patron."

Jack stood his ground for a moment, his eyes on Maurice, then pursed his lips and stepped away.

"Sorry." I wasn't sure who I was apologizing for. "The local section is right over here."

He walked behind me. The library had maybe fifteen people in it. With the exception of Jack, and maybe a stray glance or three, they all kept to what they were doing. We reached the back of the library, and I pointed at the two shelves I'd devoted to Battle Lake materials.

"Any specific time period you're interested in?"

"Hey, it's about Battle Lake. It's all got to be interesting."

It took me a beat to realize that he was joking. I smiled. "This must be your first time to the area."

He shrugged, and the gesture was oddly endearing. "Naw. My grandma used to rent a place near here. A cabin. Stopped by and it's nothin' but rotten wood now, but I used to come when I was a kid, a couple weeks each summer."

He looked like he was going to say more but stopped himself. I stood a moment longer, giving him a chance to continue. He didn't.

"If you need anything, I'll be scraping gum."

He flashed me a lopsided smile. It was quick, but brilliant. I smiled back before returning to my dirty chore.

Maurice came in four more times, always walking straight to the local shelves, sometimes with a camera, other times carrying a shabby, spiral-bound notebook and a pen, never checking anything out. A couple times he'd make light conversation with me, but mostly he worked like a man on a mission. I was used to giving people space in the library, so I never asked any questions. After last night's altercation, I wished I had.

At least, that's what I told myself, as I drifted in and out of uneasy sleep, curled against the wall under my bed. I'd altogether slept forty-five minutes, every muscle in my body aching from the uncomfortable position and the aftermath of the previous night's adrenaline clench. I finally dragged myself into the murky sunlight a little before 7:30 AM, my hands, knife scar, and knees sore from the attack in the alley. Luna rushed in through the bedroom door when she heard me moving, licking my face and wagging furiously. She didn't like that I was sleeping under the bed, whined at the edges of the mattress when I went in, and acted like it was Christmas in January when I came out.

"Hey, sweetie. How're you?" She wagged some more and followed me around the house as I poured fresh food and water for her and Tiger Pop and prepped myself for work in a blur. The healing knife wound and my left knee needed salve and a bandage. The rest of my body would be fine after I washed down a handful of ibuprofen with yesterday's strong coffee heated up in the microwave.

I was out the door in under thirty minutes. When the sound of the ice cracking on the lake made me jump out of my hair on my way to start my car, though, I headed back into the house and slipped my fully charged stun gun into the back seat of my car. If I didn't have the library to go to this morning and instead had to be alone with my thoughts, I don't know what I would have done.

The library was its own kind of church to me, and I wasn't the only one. However, thanks to budget cuts all over the state, the library's limited Saturday hours meant I was off at noon. I was already working at slave wages, and Mrs. Berns made even less. Of course, she didn't do much work and shamelessly stole office supplies, but you get what you pay for.

I loved working at the library. The books were wonderful, of course, and I'd stuffed juicy, leafy green plants in all the windows and corners when I took over last May and was currently keeping up the Christmas twinkle lights past their season, but it was the people who walked through the door that made the job such a perfect fit.

They were mostly quiet, first of all. Second, they liked books, so they were guaranteed smart, though I was discovering that was a wide net. I had romance readers who reread the same book a dozen times and could remember every character's name in a ten-book series, fans of nonfiction who regularly checked out books thick enough to press flowers and who would tell me everything I didn't want to know about history if I stood still for too long, and literary fiction readers who always wore a secret smile. My favorite of all were the kids. I read to a regular group of them every Monday, and without fail, they were a squirming, burping, giggling pile of warm puppy love.

The library was my life raft. The only upside of our slashed hours was that it gave me more time for my second job, which I'd landed shortly after being hired by the library. I was a very part-time reporter for the *Battle Lake Recall*, an essentially one-man show known for its coverage of local church happenings, updates on city council meetings, high school sports scores, and my food column, "Battle Lake Bites." When I'd started the column, I was feeling a tad passive-aggressive about living my nowhere life in another small town—I'd graduated from a very similar one twelve years earlier—and I'd vowed to take editor/layout supervisor/sales director/owner Ron Sims's suggestion that I find dishes representative of central Minnesota. Hence deer pie, Twinkie sushi, and phony abalone, among others.

In addition to that column, Ron occasionally tossed me articles, including the latest: he wanted me to follow up on a report that Gilbert Hullson's miniature poodle had accidentally slipped into an ice-fishing hole last week while Gilbert was looking the other way. According to the rumor, Gilbert had leapt forward to save his dog, but his reflexes weren't what they used to be, and she disappeared. Distraught, he stumbled out of his fish house just in time to see Jiffy pop up out of an uncovered hole thirty feet away like a mop head shot out a geyser. She was reportedly a little shaken but happy to be topside.

Being as it was a rare heavy news week, Ron also had me covering this weekend's Winter Wonderland festivities, Battle Lake's premier cold-time celebration. Day one of the two-day festival included the grand opening of the Prospect House's Civil War Museum, Darwin's Dunk on West Battle Lake, and ribbon cutting at the ice castle situated near the Dunk. I still couldn't get my head around the idea of jumping into a frozen lake in nothing more than your swimsuit and a smile, but that's Battle Lake for you.

The library was on the south end of town and the Prospect House and the section of West Battle Lake where today's Winter Wonderland was held were on the north end. Since a mile separated the two (and since yesterday's walk hadn't panned out so well), I'd decided to drive from work to the event I was covering for the paper, even though it was another postcard-perfect winter day. The temperature hovered around ten degrees with a crisp lemon sun shining heatless rays off a world of snow crystals, lighting up the landscape like a pirate's treasure. The air smelled like cold metal with the tiniest hint of green in it, and I wondered if there really was something to that talk of a January thaw.

I'd only driven half a mile before the traffic started backing up. Parking would be a bear. It seemed like this area held some sort of major festival every other month, but they were always well-attended. I guessed it was a holdover from the agricultural days when we really were all in this together, and we had to make our own fun.

Just ahead at the corner, a white four-door pulled out and I thanked the Universe and glided the Toyota into the spot. The Prospect House was still two blocks up, but I was lucky to have parked this close. I stuffed the newspaper's digital camera into the pocket of my puffy jacket, pulled my hat down tight over my ears, and hopped into the stream of festival-goers.

In my preliminary research, I'd discovered that the Prospect House was a Battle Lake original, an eighteen-room Georgian mansion built in 1860 by Barnaby Offerdahl, a man whose family came by money via the railroads. Barnaby, who'd never earned a blister a day in his life, lost his wife to childbirth in 1862 and decided to join the North's fight in the Civil War, enlisting with the 1st Minnesota Light Artillery Battery and leaving behind a newborn daughter. He didn't return, and she died under mysterious circumstances at age eight. After that, the Prospect House and its surrounding acreage passed through various hands, falling into disrepair, until recently. Carter

Stone, a local historian, bought the mansion and its carriage house, minus most of the land, at auction the previous year. He and his wife, Libby, moved into the carriage house and spent countless hours restoring the magnificent estate next door. In doing so, they uncovered many of the original furnishings along with an extensive collection of Civil War artifacts. Carter had applied for nonprofit status, and today he and Libby were hosting the grand opening of the Prospect House and Civil War Museum.

I was excited to tour the mansion, which perched on a hill on the edge of town like aging royalty, hidden behind ancient hardwoods and thick, gnarled ivy branches, closed off from the public for decades and fodder for tales of hauntings and buried treasure. The official press tour wasn't scheduled for another hour, so I made my way to the lake across County Road 78 from the Prospect House, enjoying the buzz of a large crowd, the monolithic noise occasionally punctuated by laughter or an enthusiastic greeting.

The West Battle Lake beach became the public ice rink in the winter, and its gray-blue surface was already packed with families enjoying the sunny day. The warming house door was constantly opening and closing, letting in and out smiling people who were exchanging skates for boots and vice versa. Beyond the skating rink, the Battle Lake ice castle soared toward the sky, her two gorgeous spires catching the sunlight and reflecting it back as a deep, crystalline cobalt blue. It was not much larger than a three-bedroom bungalow, but its glowing ice and delicate turrets made it enchanting, drawing skating children to it like moths to a flame, despite the yellow tape marking its perimeter.

This was the first year the town had an ice castle. The structure was sponsored by O'Callaghan's, the microbrewery that had recently opened outside of town. They'd hired the workers who'd taken eight days to build the hollow castle replica, using plans drawn by an architect from St. Paul and enormous ice blocks cut from the center of the lake. The official lighting ceremony was tonight, and I bet the castle was a million times more magical glowing with twinkle lights. If I didn't have a date with Johnny, I'd have been in the front row. As it was, I couldn't wait to be in his arms. Maybe I'd finally be able to sleep.

Even farther behind the ice castle and to the left was a roped-off area designated to be the site of tomorrow's Darwin's Dunk. O' Callaghan's was also sponsoring this feature of the Winter Wonderland, though the Dunk was an annual tradition. It had been jokingly developed as a direct rebuttal to naturalist Charles Darwin's theory of evolution of the species. Participants signed up for a time slot in which to jump into a hole carved in the 26-inch-thick ice of the lake, and then leapt out about as fast as I imagine Jiffy had after she'd slipped into her little ice hole. The jumpers raised money for the charity of their choice, and the Dunk motto was "Survival of the Littest." To that end, O'Callaghan's had installed a walk-up bar between the roped-off Dunk area and the ice castle. I'd heard it would be open up for business an hour before the lighting ceremony began, after the children had cleared off of the ice but well before tomorrow's annual Dunk.

The closer I got to the ice rink, the stronger the smell of hot chocolate grew. I smiled, captivated by the clean, slicing sound of hundreds of skate blades against ice and the sight of people gliding along at various levels of skill.

"Mira!"

I glanced toward the warming house. Jed, a local friend, had popped his head out. Jed was a harmless stoner, the local Shaggy always in search of Scooby Doo. His parents owned the Last Resort on the edge of town, and Jed was the local handyman. He'd tried to get a glass-blowing business going in November, but that hadn't panned out as expected. Since then, he'd gone back to working odd jobs. This must be one of them.

"You're running the warming house?" I asked as I walked toward him.

"Just for the Wonderland." He smiled his wide grin and nodded agreeably, the tassel on his Nordic winter cap bobbing. A riot of black curls exploded from the base of it. He seemed to be trying to grow a beard and mustache, though both were wispy with more than a little Fu Manchu to them. "Are you gonna skate?"

A father and his daughter teetered down the carpeted path from the warming house to the ice. "I don't know," I said. "I'm not very good. It's been years."

"If you can walk, you can skate," Jed said, motioning me into the warming house.

The blast of heated air and the heavy scent of wet wool were impossible to resist. Within ten minutes, Jed had me suited up and hobbling toward the ice. At least fifty people were already on the lake, which reminded me of a saying in these parts: *You know who walks on water? Jesus, and every Minnesotan in the winter.*

I tentatively stepped onto the ice. I was shaky at first, sticking to the edges so as not to mow over children and the elderly. As I gained confidence and grew less wobbly, I swirled in and out of people, remembering my father teaching me how to skate when I was eight. He'd brought an old kitchen chair onto the ice for me to balance with. We spent a whole afternoon on the slough behind the farmhouse, and when we were done, I was bruised but happy, not to mention a decent skater. The memory was bittersweet—more sweet than bitter, as I'd recently started to let go of resentments toward him and accept him as the whole, flawed man he'd been when he was alive.

The mental shift was hard, and I figured it would be an eternal work in progress, but it turned out to be a lot easier to love his memory than to judge it. Go figure. And once I opened up all that real estate where before I'd been holding anger and regret, I found a lot of things were simpler than I'd made them. Up until a few weeks ago, I'd been able to escape the cage of my thoughts and appreciate the moment more often. I'd even considered taking up meditation.

"Oh, sorry!" I said, narrowly missing a teenaged couple holding gloved hands as they skated. They rolled their eyes at me, but I didn't care. Skating felt like total freedom. I could almost hear the stress of yesterday fall away. Sure, it revealed another layer of stress immediately below it, but it was a start. I didn't even mind when I took a spill to avoid colliding with a chain of skaters playing Crack the Whip.

"Whoops!" They yelled as they flew past.

I shrugged and smiled, getting to my knees so I could hoist myself up using my hands and the toe of a skate. It was from this position that a flash drew my attention. I looked up, across the road, and toward the Prospect House. This was a perfect angle from which to see the mansion a few hundred yards away. The grounds were crawling with people dressed in red, blue, green, and patterned parkas, but what had caught my eye was higher. I followed the grain of the house to the second floor, and then to the attic. There it came again, a flash from the round window below the chimney, like a piece of jewelry had caught the glare of the sun. I squinted. Were people up there?

Then, like a jack-in-the-box, a face appeared in the window, staring directly at me.

My heart jumped. Surely I was imagining that she could see me in this crowd, but the girl in the window seemed to be gazing right into my soul. She had the round cheeks of a child, and something about her stare left me icy inside.

"Beep beep!"

My attention broken, I glanced around. The voice making the honking noise sounded familiar. Mrs. Berns?

Before I could locate her in the crowd, my attention was drawn to the roar of a giant engine firing to life. I twisted around toward the ice castle and swallowed my own tongue.

SIX

Mrs. Berns was rolling toward the skating rink on a Zamboni that lumbered as steadfastly as a dinosaur. It must have been parked behind the ice castle. She had one hand on the steering wheel and was pumping the air with the other, a grin of pure joy on her lovely lined face. She was wearing an old-fashioned aviator's cap and goggles, and a white scarf unfurled in the wind behind her.

"Mrs. Berns!" I yelled, scrambling to stand and waving my arms at her. "Put on the brakes!"

Her eyes landed on me, and her smile grew even wider. She stood, pumping both hands in the air. The words "I'm the Zamboni queen!" drifted above the grumbling roar of the giant machine. Because she was directly on top of the beast, I could hear her, but she couldn't hear me.

Families were gathering up their children as a mass exodus began toward the relative safety of land. A few people screamed as the Zamboni began to methodically eat up the 200 yards of ice between the castle and the rink. I skated away from the crowd, trying to lead Mrs. Berns to an unpopulated spot.

"Turn it off!" I yelled over my shoulder.

She cupped a palm to her ear in the universal gesture of, "I can't hear you," but at least she steered the Zamboni toward me.

"I'm just going to clear a wider rink!" she yelled back. "Get everyone off of the ice!"

I glanced toward the shore. The sensible people of Battle Lake were taking care of that just fine by themselves. When I turned back toward Mrs. Berns, the Zamboni had grown uncomfortably close.

"Turn it off!" I screamed.

She nodded and reached below the steering wheel. Then her head shot back up. Was that a look of panic in her eyes? I kept skating away, and the Zamboni kept drawing nearer. The ice was rough out here, covered in crusty snow, and I went from skating to high-stepping, trying desperately to put distance between me and her. This lasted all of four steps until the toe of my skate caught on an ice shear and I pitched to the ground like a four-legged creature who'd been putting on airs. I levered myself back to a standing position and took mad, mincing steps away from Mrs. Berns. Whichever direction I went, though, the relentless, hulking Zamboni seemed to follow. In the periphery, I spotted two men in winter overalls running across the ice toward Mrs. Berns. Would they make it here in time?

I fell again, and the Zamboni continued to rumble toward me.

"Move!" Mrs. Berns hollered. "I can't figure out how to turn it off!"

"Can you figure out how to steer it?" I hollered, crawling forward as fast as my cold knees could take me. The caution ropes surrounding Darwin's Dunk were straight ahead. I scuttled under the rope and found myself gliding down the indent toward the center of the Dunk, where the Dunk crew must have begun the time-consuming work of cutting the hole the night before. My heart hammering, I swiveled, still on my knees, and tried to return to the safer ice, but gravity was pulling me toward the thin center.

My soft mittens and wet knees gave me less traction than a long-nailed dog. I kept my eyes on the Zamboni, hoping against hope that it would stop and that last night's fresh ice would hold.

I slid to dead center of the Dunk and held my breath, thinking light, light thoughts.

The Zamboni growled closer.

The ice under me made a gentle cracking sound, and I spread myself as flat as I could, my eyes closing involuntarily.

I waited for the inevitable impact of the Zamboni or the icy rush of West Battle Lake in January.

And then the world grew quiet.

I opened one eye. The Zamboni was on the edge separating the thick lake ice from the prepared Dunk ice. A man in overalls was laying stomach-down across Mrs. Berns's lap with the expression of someone who'd just swallowed a goldfish. Mrs. Berns, on the other hand, looked completely exhilarated and ready for Round Two.

I opened the other eye and breathed in the heavy, oily scent of diesel, grateful I was still around to smell. "What were you doing? You almost killed me!" I didn't know if she'd be able to hear my shrill voice above the pounding of my heart.

Mrs. Berns rested her hands on the man on her lap. "You're the one who kept skating into my path."

The man on her lap raised the Zamboni keys into the air. His hand was shaking. "Got 'em," he said weakly, sliding to the ground.

I shook my head, fear turning to anger. I gently pulled myself onto my knees, intending to very carefully hoist myself up and off the ice so I could go give Mrs. Berns a piece of my mind. I was balanced on all fours, the roar of the Zamboni still echoing in my head, when a motion under the ice caught my eye.

I glanced down and into a dead man's eyes.

I was suspended above his frozen corpse, his blank gaze staring into mine, his open mouth and clutching hands mirroring my gesture, only a thin skin of ice separating us.

SEVEN

"You were just ... skating along." Police Chief Wohnt stated. The disbelief sounded like it had less to do with the veracity of my story and more to do with the sheer variety of ways in which I had discovered bodies.

I was sitting on the bumper of his car, my head between my knees. I hadn't stopped shivering since I'd been pulled off of the dunk hole. Jed was standing to the side, where he'd been begging me to drink hot chocolate for several minutes. Mrs. Berns was on the other side shooting me the stink eye, a cross between "don't tell him about the Zamboni" and "really?!? *another* dead body?"

I sat up. The blood rushed to my head. The ice had blurred the corpse's face, but not so much that I couldn't stare right into his brown eyes, his mouth open in a silent cry. It was impossible to make a positive ID, but he looked an awful lot like Maurice, my recent library regular and the guy who'd rescued us just last night. My stomach had been greasy since, my brain on overload.

The entire lake had been cleared, the mood gone from festive to shocked, children quickly herded to cars, conversations dropped to whispers. Only twenty or so people remained, milling on the edges of the lake, a handful talking to the waiting EMTs as the police were cordoning a wider area around Darwin's Dunk in preparation for removing the body.

"Did he drown?" I asked Gary, ignoring his question.

He glanced over my shoulder, his breath showing up big and bold in the frozen air. He was wearing a trim blue winter coat and a fur-lined cap. His face was free of sunglasses. "We'll do an autopsy," he said.

"But what do you *think*?" I asked. The horror of that sort of death—being trapped and suffocating under the ice with freedom so close by—was overwhelming. It didn't help that I had liked Maurice, at least what I knew of him. My shaking grew so strong that I had to tuck my hands into my armpits to contain myself.

Gary's jaw clenched. "I think you should go home."

He strode off toward the lake, leaving me to wonder why he'd interviewed me in the first place. One of his deputies could have handled the duty. His absence also left me wanting Johnny, though I didn't want to think too much about that. I didn't like the idea of being dependent on someone. I knew I loved Johnny, though I hadn't told him yet. Since we'd slept together, I was feeling even more vulnerable, and if I was honest with myself, we hadn't seen each other lately as much because I'd been avoiding him. At this moment, though, I felt cold and scared and wanted him here. I dragged in a deep breath, relieved to discover that I wasn't shivering as much.

"I can see your hard-on," Mrs. Berns said.

"What?"

"You. Remember you've got the poker face of a kindergartner? Are you thinking about Johnny or the Chief?"

For a moment, I thought she meant Chief Wenonga, the 23-foot-tall fiberglass statue that resided just over the hill from our present location. He was shirtless and sculpted, and in my lower moments, I'd harbored some adult thoughts about him, but I'd thought I'd played those cards closer to my chest. A full-on blush was warming my cheeks—a relief from the horror—before I realized who she was really talking about. "Gary Wohnt?! I'd sooner eat a toe."

She nodded sagely. "I know how confusing it can be to the lady parts when we realize an officer of the law is one of the hottest cookies in town."

"Please," I said. I stood and turned, just catching sight of Gary's back before he disappeared into the ice castle with a deputy. What were they doing over there? Darwin's Dunk was a good hundred yards away.

"Is that a request?" Mrs. Berns asked, smirking.

I shook my head. "I'm begging. I need to get out of here, take a shower, and wash the dead body juju off of me."

"I recommend steel wool for that," Mrs. Berns said, patting my shoulder before tipping her head toward Jed. "Since you're in good hands, I'm going to leave you and go find out some more about that Good Samaritan who saved you from throwing yourself under a Zamboni. Like, his phone number."

She strode off before I could reprimand her for driving the Zamboni in the first place. A shudder ran down my body as I thought of Maurice's silent, screaming face again, and more details came to me, like his one shoeless foot.

"You sure you don't want the hot chocolate?" Jed asked worriedly.

I realized he'd been standing next to me in the cold for nearly a half an hour, leaving his post at the warming house, and desperately wanted to do something for me. "Thank you," I said appreciatively. I took the hot chocolate, but it was his friendship that I was grateful for.

"Do you want me to drive you home?" He was focused on me, but I could tell he wanted to check back at the warming house. There wouldn't be any more skating today, and maybe not for a while, but he'd still need to clean and lock up. At this very moment, a gaggle of adults were milling around the door of the little hut, unreturned skates in hand. The children and most everyone else had been cleared off the lake. I could feel those who remained staring at me.

"I'm fine. Really."

"You positive?"

I smiled reassuringly. "Positive."

It wasn't true.

EIGHT

Although I'd told Jed I was driving directly home, I was too unsettled to be confined to my house. I'd probably make Luna and Tiger Pop crazy with all my nervous energy. I wasn't quite ready to tell Johnny I'd skated upon a dead body, either, though I'd have to come up with a story before our date tonight. He'd always been sympathetic to my bad luck, but even someone as amazing as him must have limits. It's not like I needed to quit smoking or snore more quietly. I had to stop finding *dead bodies*. It was honestly a surprise I had friends left. Or, I mused as I drove, maybe the safest place to be was close to me, like inside the calm eye of a hurricane.

Who was I kidding? I was Typhoid Mary, and that was almost more distressing than the memory of Maurice's wide eyes and final frozen scream. I shuddered. It was like he had a secret he needed to tell me, something that only the person who'd killed him and the fishes who'd swum with him would ever know.

I pulled into the library parking lot out of habit, realizing that I'd assumed Maurice had been murdered. I surveyed the mental image of his body under the ice. Except for the missing shoe and the fact that he was dead, there were no signs of violence. For all I knew, he could have been out walking on the ice, fallen into the Darwin's Dunk pre-cut hole, and been too disoriented to save himself. I liked that story a whole lot better than the alternative.

I exited my car and walked toward the library. Since I didn't have a computer at home, this was as good a place as any for me to be. I still owed Ron an article on the Winter Wonderland and this week's recipe column. Maybe writing would help to organize my thoughts.

I locked the library's front door behind me and left the lights off, relying on the window-filtered light of the setting sun. How had the day gone so quickly? And horribly? Seated at my desk, though, I felt incrementally more comfortable. This was a spot where I had some control. I fired up the computer, sucking on the end of a pen as I wondered what spin I could possibly put on the Winter Wonderland article. "Plenty of Room on the Skating Rink at this Year's Winter Festival"? "Darwin's Dunker Sets the Bar High"?

I swallowed past the oily lump in my throat. Sarcasm was my defense against any extreme emotion, and I couldn't move past the sensation that I'd played a part in Maurice's death. It was guilt that I was trying to bury. What if letting me and Mrs. Berns go had turned the two thugs against him? They could have strangled him and stuck his body in the dunk hole, assuming it wouldn't be found until spring. Or they could have forced him into the hole while he was still conscious, slammed a chunk of wood over it, and sat on the edges until his desperate cries for help and finger-scratching stopped.

I slammed my fist on the desktop. I needed to corral my slippery mind. It was sliding toward ugly worst-case scenarios. Time to focus on something else. But I knew better than that. My mind was a hungry, busy thing, and it wouldn't rest without answers. Who was Maurice? Who were Ray and Hammer? I had little to go on. Well, that is, if "little" actually meant "nothing."

I pulled up Firefox and typed *Ray and Maurice* into Google. I searched ten screens in and found nothing. I added the word *ogre* and found a couple bizarre baseball stories, but nothing else. Gary had given me blessedly little to go on, except for—

My fingers flew across the keyboard. I typed, *hammerhead stingray tattoo gangs*, and hit the Enter key. The first four screens were consumed with tattoo parlor links and ads, and the fifth, as were the sixth, but on the seventh, I found it—an article published the previous year:

"Sixth Suspect Arrested in Gang Activity"

CHICAGO, Ill. —Chicago police arrested a sixth suspect on suspicion of gang-related activity that includes gun and drug trafficking.

The Fugitive Task Force arrested Scott Rayman Monday morning.

Local and federal authorities made five arrests Sunday as part of a seven-month investigation called Operation Sea Monster, named after the sea-creature tattoos the gang members are required to have. The operation included undercover officers buying drugs, as well as tips from the public.

Police still have arrest warrants for three other gang members.

Chief John Lart said the suspects are some of the highest-ranking leaders in the Sea Monsters, one of Chicago's most notorious gangs.

I printed out the article and searched for anything else that fit. Dead ends, all of them. That's when I realized I hadn't even toured the Prospect House today, the central feature of the article I was to write. My head fell into my palm. What a waste of a day.

I felt crazy laughter burbling in my throat. I would have released it if I hadn't just then caught sight of a neon green child's super ball that had rolled near my chair. Somebody must have lost it during last Monday's reading hour. I stooped to retrieve it and remembered the child I'd seen in the attic window of the Prospect House, the little girl with the plump cheeks and wide, haunting eyes. I'd glanced back at the window a couple times after I'd first seen her, and no other faces had appeared. She must have gotten separated from her tour group. Or maybe I'd imagined her. Given how little sleep and how much stress I'd had, hallucinations would not be unexpected.

Well, I'd have to work with what I had. I opened my email and shot off a brief note to Carter Stone requesting a private tour of the Prospect House at his earliest convenience. I didn't know him personally but had heard he was a nice guy, if a little eccentric. Surely he'd understand why I hadn't made today's tour. Next, I conducted deeper research on the Prospect House. I should have probably done this before today's scheduled tour, but I'd figured I already had the basics from asking around and paging through the library's copy of *After the Battle*, a thorough softcover history book of Battle Lake.

Preliminary online research didn't tell me any more about Barnaby Offerdahl and his mansion than what I'd already gathered from local sources. I clicked into the database I'd subscribed to after I'd decided to pursue my PI licensure in October. Once I'd discovered that a private investigator license in Minnesota required six *thousand* hours of work under a licensed PI, with a police department, or for a law firm, I almost quit the dream. But with a firm nudge from Ron at the newspaper, I'd taken my certification class last month in Willmar, near my hometown of Paynesville. I'd since lined up a handful of tiny jobs through a local law firm. Investigative work, surprisingly, was not much different than running a library. I looked stuff up online and listened to people.

My current Prospect House search was running into another dead end, which was the way the day was going in general. I discovered that Carter Stone didn't actually own the Prospect House but had rather bought it through a nonprofit organization he'd created called Preserving History. I also found out that over half of the lots skirting the Prospect House and a big, tear-shaped tract of undeveloped land behind it belonged to Gregory Offerdahl, presumably a descendant of Barnaby's. I didn't see how any of those two pieces of information would flesh out my article, though. People wanted to know about the Civil War Museum hours and the cache of 1920s jewelry and flapper dresses Stone had reportedly discovered in the attic, not who owned what land parcels when.

I sighed. I wasn't going to uncover anything more today. I decided to think about it tomorrow, which seemed like a really good attitude to take when things weren't going as planned, which was most of my life. *I'll worry about it tomorrow.*

Still not ready to go home and mentally exhausted, I decided to do something I knew I'd be successful at: track down a recipe for my "Battle Lake Bites" column. In the past, I'd used the search term "weird Minnesota food" when looking for recipe inspiration. You'd be unsurprised at how many hits that turned up. Since I'd started on my journey of personal growth, though, which included really seeing and appreciating Battle Lake and its people, I'd been reluctant to toss Cool

Whip on top of, or cream of mushroom soup into, something that was already gross and calling it an original Battle Lake recipe. In fact, despite today's gruesome discovery or maybe because of it, I felt like serving up something truly delicious to the town. And what could be better than Nut Goodies?

Nut Goodies have been produced in Minnesota since 1912 by Pearson's, better known for their Salted Nut Roll. It would be generous to call the Nut Goodie a candy bar. It is more of a candy pile. Its base is a creamy maple center topped with unsalted Virginia peanuts, and the whole mass covered in milk chocolate. It's so sweet it'll give your future children a toothache if you eat it, but it is also heaven, particularly if consumed when frozen. Sometimes I wondered if the Nut Goodie was jealous of the Salted Nut Roll's success, if it dreamed of finally fitting in and no longer being a Rorschach blob in a chocolate log world, if it wondered what it'd be like to play all the major vending machines. But in the end, it was the hardest-working, humblest candy I'd ever met, and I loved it for that very reason. Why not share that joy with Battle Lake?

I searched for "homemade nut goodie" recipes and received over 406,000 hits. Holy crap. I gravitated toward the ones with photos, of course, salivating as I read. In the end, I chose the simplest and most honest recipe, giving it a new name and a personal twist so I couldn't be sued for plagiarism.

MMMM-PIES

Ingredients
Fondant:
3 cups powdered sugar
½ cup sweetened condensed milk
½ teaspoon maple extract

Topping:
1½ pounds milk chocolate broken into 1-inch squares
¾ pound Spanish peanuts (not cocktail peanuts)

Mix the fondant ingredients together until well-blended and stiff. Roll into ¾-inch balls. Place the balls 2 inches apart on a wax-paper covered cookie sheet. Flatten the balls with the palm of your hand, keeping them around ⅛-inch thick.

Melt the chocolate in a glass bowl in the microwave in 20-second increments, stirring between each, until the chocolate is smooth and melted. Be careful not to burn. Drop the peanuts in the melted chocolate. Stir. Pour the peanut and chocolate mixture over the fondant, allowing it to crawl lusciously just past the edges. Cool. Flip, spooning just enough of the chocolate peanut mixture onto the bottom to cover the remaining fondant. When cool, turn over and store in the freezer. Remove and ingest as needed, particularly in moments of extreme stress.

I spell-checked the recipe and emailed it to Ron, feeling good about my work. I glanced at the clock in the lower right screen of my computer, wondering if I had time to shelve books before going home to prepare for my date with Johnny.

Despite my mental and physical exhaustion, I got a warm buzzy feeling thinking about a repeat performance of our previous night together. I didn't know if it was a result of the day I'd had, but for the first time in weeks, I was considering whether or not holding him at arm's length was good, or even necessary. When he was around, I was happy. I desperately needed that right now.

He was honest and kind, and man, those hands of his. He'd slide them gently under the curve of my rear and pull me in for a long, deep kiss that left my knees trembling. He might be The One. Maybe it was time to let myself be vulnerable to him and to try to see in him what he saw in me.

My eyes went misty from my hot daydream, and it took me a couple seconds and a few blinks to process the time. How could it be six o'clock already? My eyes darted to the windows. It was dark outside. Johnny would be at my house in half an hour! He said he would bring the dinner and the movies, but I'd hoped to at least have the house and myself picked up before he arrived. Crap. It'd been so long since I shaved that it looked like a homeless Mediterranean had taken up residence in my underpants, and speaking of undergarments, it was laundry day tomorrow and I wasn't exactly wearing the starting lineup. White bra with the puckered cups that was just too comfortable to throw away? Check. Dangit!

I jabbed my finger at the computer's power button, forcing a shutdown, tugged on my coat, and hightailed it out the door, barely remembering to lock up behind me. My car had cooled down along with the night, but I didn't have time to let her preheat. I slammed the gear stick into Reverse and tore out of my parking spot.

I hit rush-hour traffic on the way home, or at least Battle Lake's version of it. Pickup after pickup drove painfully slowly in front of me. Even though the skating rink had been closed for the day, I imagined the Prospect House had stayed open, probably drawing even more visitors as news of the nearby tragedy spread. They were scheduled to close for the day right about now, and all the vehicles crawling in front of me suggested they were right on time.

I pounded on the steering wheel. I didn't ask for a lot out of life, but after the last twenty-four hours I had, I was worried about my mental state if this night with Johnny crashed and burned.

My brain scrambled to make the best of my current circumstances. If I could make it home in ten minutes, and Johnny wasn't early, that would give me exactly thirteen minutes to retrieve my machete and have a go at my legs before switching into the peach-colored, lacy push-up bra I'd bought in Alexandria last week. It made me look as though I had B cups, which was arguably a bait-and-switch if tonight went how I hoped it would, but nobody expects the real thing to drive like the display model, right?

I finally passed the clogged traffic and careened a sharp right onto the gravel. This was a shortcut in terms of miles, but since I usually drove half-speed on the back roads, it took longer. Not today. I squealed around corners, sliding across the ice and staying shy of the ditch with the help of spit and luck. As I turned into my nearly mile-long driveway, I saw I had carved two minutes off my best drive-home time. Excellent work! I might even be able to apply lip gloss and empty the bathroom garbage so as to hide that I had bodily functions.

I was even beginning to smile as I turned the final corner and pulled into the circle loop in front of Sunny's doublewide.

That smile lasted right up until I spotted Johnny's truck.

He was early.

NINE

SUNNY'S PLACE WAS BEAUTIFUL—A double-wide trailer plopped near a pristine little lake nestled in the middle of a hundred acres of untouched hardwood forest. Her sweet red barn and matching sheds stood like comfortable sentries, and her cozy doublewide with its gray siding and maroon shutters faced the frozen water. Normally, living here made me feel both connected and independent, carving out my existence on some of the prettiest land in the Midwest. At the moment, however, it was the last place on earth I wanted to be. I considered turning right around and driving back into town, buying a pack of disposable razors at Larry's, and shaving myself in their bathroom.

That still left the granny bra.

Curse words!

When I'd decided that it was time to make myself more open to Johnny, I didn't mean open to revulsion. Of course he'd be too kind to say anything, but when he pulled off my shirt or slid his hand down my pants, it'd be written all over his face. Horror. Doubt. Curiosity as to when things had gone so undeniably wrong in his life.

I pulled alongside his 1971 Chevy truck, rebuilt from a junker to a beauty. It was solid and stable, just like Johnny. I sighed. No way could I leave him alone in my house and worrying about me as the hour grew later, even if the alternative meant exposing him to baseline me. I turned off the car, got out, and dragged my feet up the walk to my front door. Normally, I loved this short walk. Right now, it felt like the green mile.

I opened the door, in the back of my mind still hoping for some way out of this. That's when it came to me. I could just dart into the bathroom, right? Tell Johnny that I wanted to slip into something more comfortable, and once the bedroom door was closed, I could sneak into the bathroom to shave my legs, switch out my bra, and hide the brush cleanings and Q-tips in the garbage under some clean but strategically crumpled tissues. It'd be perfect! I opened the door with a smile on my face.

I was greeted by Johnny, with an equally large smile on his.

Unfortunately—given my present circumstances—a smile was all he wore.

TEN

JOHNNY WAS STANDING IN the kitchen, the living room and a center island the only thing separating us. The smile fell off my face and landed with a thud at my feet (which, by the way, would benefit from a run-over with a shaver, too). Luna hurried up to sniff my hand but I was in too much shock to pet her. Tiger Pop, my calico kitty, was draped across the back of the couch so as better to witness my humiliation, I imagine.

"Too presumptuous?" he asked, coming around the kitchen counter.

I was immensely relieved to see that he was, in fact, wearing low-slung Levis. The denim hugged his lean hips perfectly, showcasing his sculpted abdomen dusted with a light trail of hair. His chest was perfection, broad and muscled, and his rippled arms made me want to drop my own clothes. He held a bottle of champagne and two glasses in his beautiful, strong hands. And oh dear god, had he used the word *presumptuous*? I was used to dating men who didn't use a hand towel let alone four-syllable words.

"You look delicious," I said.

He kept walking toward me, his lip quirking. "What?"

Had I said that out loud? "It smells delicious! *It*. It smells delicious. What are you making?" I glanced at the chopped vegetables and herbs gracing my counter, a swirl of reds, greens, and oranges. It really did smell amazing. "And how long have you been here?"

He glanced at his wristwatch, and I swear my pants melted a little. Something about a naked-chested man wearing a watch drove me crazy. "About an hour. I knew you had a double-shift today, the library and then the paper. I wanted to surprise you with dinner. I picked up the kitchen and living room, too. I hope you don't mind."

I glanced around the plant-filled living room, searching for the camera crew. Somehow, I could get my head around having a hot, shirtless man offer me champagne and home-cooked dinner. It was the picking-up comment that made me finally realize that Johnny was a robot planted in my life six months ago to study the *Dorkus Allthetimeus* in her natural habitat.

"For real?"

His smile grew wider, and now he was near enough to smell. I didn't know if he actually wore cologne or if his natural scent was clean and spicy, like fresh-ground cinnamon. He locked eyes with mine, his so blue I swear I could see fish swimming in them. His smile changed into something a little more animal, and his eyes dropped to my mouth.

My heartbeat picked up. He leaned forward and placed his mouth on mine, warm and confident. My back arched and I leaned into him, feeling the impossible heat of his hard body against mine.

He held the two champagne glasses in one hand and the unopened bottle in the other. My hands, however, were free. I unzipped my jacket and let it drop to the floor. Then, I touched his chest lightly, trailing my fingertips down, around his waist, up his strong spine, and then back down to hook into his jeans and pull his hips tight against mine. I was trying to remember why I'd ever thought it'd be a good idea to hold him at arm's length. It felt so much better to have him close.

His kisses grew deeper, and I sent one hand to his thick hair and the other to his tight butt. He made a low sound in his throat, like a growl. I ground my hips ever so slightly, and he almost dropped the champagne glasses.

"I need my hands," he said huskily.

I couldn't agree more. He set the bottle and glasses on the living room table. His body was only gone from mine for a second, but the loss of heat felt like an ache. I was back in his arms in a moment. He wound one hand into my hair and the other at the base of my back and was kissing me like his life depended on it. I felt his hips swivel, followed by a gentle push as he steered us toward the bedroom, not pausing in his passion. I was completely wrapped in his strength and his scent and his heat. I would have taken him right there by the front door, but at least one of us was hanging on to their wits. Nothing like glancing up to see a cat and a dog watching like they're taking notes to kill the moment.

He closed the bedroom door behind us. The room was dark, a pair of dirty workout shorts on the floor. I suppose I could have excused myself to quick shave my legs, but it'd be like cleaning your house when it's on fire, and who does that?

He pulled back, and even in the moonlit room, I saw the intensity of his gaze. "I want you."

I nodded, though it seemed like an understatement. I wanted oxygen. In that moment, I *needed* Johnny. We fell toward the bed in a tangle of undressing, kissing, stroking passion. He ended up on top, which was just the way I liked it.

"I've missed you," he whispered into my ear, unlatching my bra with one deft move. Thank god. The white cloth reflecting the glow of the moon was bright enough to read by.

"I've missed you too," I said, grabbing him by the ears and pulling his mouth to mine.

"We should do this more," he said. At least that's what I think he said. I couldn't stop kissing him long enough to let him speak.

The taut length of his body melted into mine, his weight making me feel deliciously protected. My fingers dipped with the curve of his muscles when I ran them down his back and arms. We were both still wearing jeans, and suddenly, nothing seemed more urgent than being completely naked.

Right now.

Johnny was reading my mind because he pulled back to undo the top snap of my button-fly Levis. His eyes were the color of storm clouds in the dim room, his gaze penetrating as he ran it along the length of me, lingering on my mouth, then landing on my eyes.

"You're so beautiful."

The breath caught in my throat. I could feel my blood-hot pulse in every inch of my body. He leaned over to kiss my neck, undoing the second snap on my jeans.

"There's no place I'd rather be right now," he whispered. The kiss moved to the sweet spot under my ear, and I shivered.

The third snap came undone.

"I can't stop thinking about you." His mouth traveled to my collarbone, his tongue teasing me as it ran along the edges.

The fourth snap popped open.

His mouth moved to my breasts, warm and wet.

There was only one snap left.

A growing heat tickled the edges of my senses. I thought I was going to lose my mind if he didn't rip off my pants and take me right now. I was about to tell him that exact thing when the phone rang in the kitchen.

"Forget it," I said. Passion made my voice deeper than usual.

He didn't even slow to respond, his hot mouth driving me closer to ecstasy. My chin shot up as the growing heat began to vibrate inside of me.

The phone rang again.

"The machine will get it," I whispered, tossing my head to the side.

It rang a third time.

Johnny undid the last snap. His eyes met mine, and it was electric. He looked more animal than man, completely in control, gorgeous.

The machine clicked over.

"Mira? It's Kennie." Her voice trembled.

The moment hung suspended in the air like a glass globe. Her next words shattered it.

"Gary Wohnt has been shot."

ELEVEN

JOHNNY AND I WERE out of the house and in his truck in under five minutes. On the seventeen-mile drive to the Fergus Falls hospital, I copped to the dead body I'd skated over in the ice. I expected him to be horrified, but his predominant emotion was concern. I accepted his free hand in mine as he drove.

"Do you think the body in the ice is connected to Gary being shot?" he asked, after I assured him that I was fine, though the words felt far away when I spoke them.

"I don't see how they could be, but I guess I don't even know what shape we're going to find him in."

It was a frozen, foggy night, a sure sign that a thaw was coming our way. Johnny pushed down on the gas pedal despite the dangerous conditions, and we picked up speed. And why not? We knew where the chief of police was right now, and I had to assume all the deputies were investigating the shooting. We reached the hospital in record time. Johnny parked his truck while I charged into the ER waiting room.

Kennie was perched on the edge of a plastic chair looking like she'd just lost the title of Mrs. Minnesota. Mascara ran down her chin, and a stream of snot snaked out of her nose. I speed-walked to her.

"How is he?"

Kennie gave me the first honest glance we'd ever exchanged. "You came."

"Of course I did. As soon as you called." Three chairs over, a man threw up into a plastic bag. Across the room, a teenage boy held a bloody towel over his hand. This was a dismal place to spend a Saturday night. "What are you doing here alone?"

Her shoulders moved the tiniest bit. "Who else would come with me?"

Her comment pushed me back, like a puff of wind. Surely Kennie had friends, didn't she? But I couldn't think of one. Heck, I usually went out of my way to avoid her. The thought humbled. "Where'd it happen?"

Kennie shrugged and blew her nose into a Hello Kitty handkerchief. I felt bad for it. I imagined it had signed up for glitter and lipgloss, not copious boogers. "Just north of town. It was a routine pullover. Speeder. Gary got him on the side of the road and called in the license plate number. Ginny was working the call station. She heard the shots over the radio. When she couldn't get Gary to respond, she sent an ambulance to his location." She hiccupped.

"Is it bad?"

"I haven't seen him. They won't let me. The doctor said Gary will make it, but that's all he could tell me because I'm not family. I'm not *anyone's* family!" She blew her nose again. It came out as a sobbing honk. I reached over to the admissions desk and yanked a handful of tissues out of the communal box.

"Here." I waited while she blew her nose some more and wiped at the smudged mascara. I grabbed another fistful of clean tissues and waited until her breathing grew regular.

"They wouldn't tell you he was going to be okay if he wasn't," I said. I started to pat her back, but it felt odd, so I stopped. "It's probably just a flesh wound. And I'm sure you have family. Don't you?" I realized how very little I knew about the mayor of Battle Lake.

"Aunts and uncles sprinkled around the country, cousins ... " she trailed off.

"Parents?"

The pause made me expect the worst. "They live in Florida," she finally said.

I exhaled. "Well, that's family."

"We don't get along. And besides, I meant my own family. A husband and kids. A dog. A garden."

The man three chairs over retched into his bag. It seemed like an appropriate reaction. Still, the smell was wafting toward us, so I pulled Kennie to her feet and steered us to the other side of the waiting room. "You don't even like to garden, and you hate kids. And where did all this come from?"

She patted her platinum hair. "I don't know. Gary going into the hospital has brought me closer to my mortality, I guess. What is my legacy on this earth, Mira? What am I leaving behind so people can remember me?"

I couldn't assure her that she was going to live for a good long time, because I bet that's what the man I'd skated over last night had woken up thinking, too, right before he got iced. I scoured my brain for an answer. "I know! Last night, you told me you're a plant and pet psychologist. You're helping two of the most important things in the world. That's a wonderful legacy!"

"I suppose," she said glumly.

"Oh, I'm sure you're very good at it. I bet people will talk about it long after you're gone." Like a truly obnoxious party crasher, I thought, or a particularly rotten smell.

"Do you really mean it?"

The hope in her sad eyes squeezed at my heart. "Of course."

She sat up straight, her expression immediately cleared. "Wonderful. When do you want me to come over for your plant and pet consultation?"

My mouth dropped. Had she just played me?

"Close that piehole, Mira. You don't know what sort of germs are flying around this place." She yanked a calendar out of her mammoth fringed purse. "Tuesday evening might work for me, but my schedule is filling up quickly, so let's keep that appointment floating, shall we? In the meanwhile, what say I officially deputize you so you can go find out how Gary is. I truly am worried about him."

Many questions battled in my head. What came out was, "You can deputize someone?"

She lifted her shoulders. "Why not? I'm mayor."

"You're mayor of Battle Lake. We're in Fergus."

"Then just be a good little detective and go ask that doctor. He was the one I spoke with before."

She pushed me out of my seat and toward a white-haired man wearing scrubs. At the same moment, Johnny entered through the sliding front door, his face drawn. I motioned him toward Kennie and strode to the doctor. "Excuse me? I'm wondering how Gary Wohnt is doing."

The doctor glanced up from a chart. "Are you family?"

"I'm his sister." I firmly believed that you shouldn't overplan a lie. Rather, it's better to be ready to hop on the lie boat if it drifts your way. "Mira Wohnt."

Shoot. I'd taken it too far by adding details.

It seemed to work, though. The doctor nodded and scratched behind an ear with his pen. "He's in surgery now. The bullet went in his upper left leg and out the back. Missed the artery. Once he's sewn up, he should be fine, though he might not agree. It'll be a while until he's able to move as he'd like."

"Thank you." I swiveled to walk away. The doctor made a small coughing sound in his throat. I turned back.

"Would you like to know what room he'll be in after recovery?" He raised an eyebrow. "So you can tell the rest of your family?"

"Yes!"

He consulted his clipboard. "He's scheduled to be moved into 227, barring any unforeseen circumstances."

"Thanks again," I said, smiling. Then, it occurred to me that a grin might be unnatural for a woman whose brother has recently been shot, so I frowned.

The doctor's eyes narrowed, but he walked away without comment. I raced over to Kennie and Johnny to share the little I knew.

Kennie, for all her denial of her feelings for Gary and her scamming me in the waiting room, seemed incredibly relieved by the news. "Did he say what time Gary would be out of surgery?"

"No, but he'll be in room 227."

She patted my cheek. "Thank you, doll."

I nodded. Johnny slipped his hand into mine. I looked down at it, surprised. I'd had to deal with a lot since I'd moved to Battle Lake, and while I had wonderful friends, I'd been forced to handle most of it alone. I looked over at Johnny and recognized strength in his eyes. I squeezed his hand.

Kennie honked her nose again. "Say, did you hear? They ID'd the man in the ice. They think he's a transient. The only identification they found on him was a Chicago Public Library card. His name was Maurice Jackson."

TWELVE

I SPENT A CHASTE, troubled night curled in Johnny's arms, both of us too tired to clean up the kitchen before we tumbled into bed. It sounded like Gary was going to be okay, but Maurice most certainly was not. Mrs. Berns and I were likely two of the last people to see him alive, besides his killer. Something Kennie had said was niggling at me, too. She'd said Maurice was a transient, but I knew better. He'd been clean and focused every time he'd entered the library, not to mention a regular for a whole week. I made a mental note to call the Chicago Public Library system to see if they could tell me anything about Maurice, up to and including whether or not he'd recently checked out any books.

I must have fallen asleep near sunrise because next thing I knew, I was alone in my bed and the clock was telling me it was 7:14 AM. I sat up, trying to rub the sleep out of my eyes. I was disoriented, and at first I thought it was because Johnny was gone. Then I realized that the problem was I was sleeping on the mattress for the first time in weeks. I fought the anxiety, leaning over to sniff Johnny's empty pillow. The faint scent of his spicy shampoo was comforting. I sighed and ran my fingers through my hair. At least I meant to, but it felt like the booglies had set up camp in it for the night. Dragging myself out of bed, I made my way to the kitchen, patting Luna's happy head on the trek. Tiger Pop stretched when she saw me.

"What time did Johnny leave?"

Luna tried to beat the answer in Morse code using her tail, but alas, I was too dumb to understand. Thankfully, Johnny had left a note on the kitchen counter, which he must have very quietly cleaned while I slept:

Sorry I had to leave before you woke up. Early day at work. You looked beautiful sleeping.

I smiled and pushed a lock of my brown hair out of my eyes. The whole tangled mass moved as one. I ignored it and kept reading:

I baked these cookies last night for dessert, but we didn't have time to try them. I hope they're good. I have evening commitments all week. Can you make it to our show on Friday? Call me.

—J

I was sorely tempted to scribble little hearts on that note and hide it under my pillow. That feeling doubled when I lifted the cover next to his note and uncovered a plate mounded with peanut butter cookies, my favorite. I was trying to lose a couple pounds in my belly, so I ate three of them fast following the time-honored maxim that a cookie eaten quickly has no calories.

My next duty was to scrub out Luna and Tiger Pop's water bowls, fill them with fresh water, and pour their daily ration of food. Somehow, Luna turned her portion into a lean German Shepherd machine. Tiger Pop managed to put on weight, even though the ratio of her food to her body size was the same as Luna's. I suspected she'd figured out how to break into the cat food cupboard while I slept, or better yet open the fridge for snacks, then kick back on the couch and click on the TV to watch Animal Planet's blooper reels when I wasn't around. She was a cat, though. If she didn't want me to know, I wasn't going to know.

I scratched them both behind the ears as they ate. We weren't terribly active in the winter, which I occasionally felt bad about. Luna had her run of the acreage whenever she wanted, but I knew they both missed me when I was gone for long days.

"Maybe we could hit the sledding hill sometime this week," I suggested. Tiger Pop arched her spine when I scratched the sweet spot where her back met her tail.

Once I was satisfied both animals knew they were loved, I hopped in the shower, applying extra conditioner so I stood a chance of forcing a comb through my shoulder-blade-length brown hair afterward. I also shaved, though I had to change razors halfway through. I lotioned up afterward, rolled on some honey-flavored lip balm, tossed myself into a clean pair of blue jeans, my comfy white bra (which I had to dig out from behind the nightstand), and a rainbow t-shirt that read "Freedom to Love."

Today's plans were informal. The library was technically closed on Sundays, though I had agreed to open the space to host a birthday party for Matthew, one of my favorite story hour regulars. He turned five this week. Before the birthday party, I had a meeting scheduled with an attorney at the Litchfield Law Firm. He said he had a small investigative job that he'd like to talk about over a cup of coffee. I also needed to interview Gilbert Hullson about Jiffy, the ice-diving dog, and I wanted to stop by the nursing home to visit my friend and amateur historian Curtis Poling to ask him some questions. Dangit, I wanted to stop by the hospital in Fergus and check on Gary, as well.

Phew. I was tired just thinking about my supposed day off. I gave the animals some more love, tugged a cap over my wet hair and my down jacket over my t-shirt, and headed into the cold world.

THIRTEEN

Chuck Litchfield was in his seventies, white-haired but sharp. His son had hired me back in November to investigate an apparent hunting accident. Two corpses later, I solved the crime, but not before uncovering an ancillary drug operation very close to home on top of nearly losing my own life. The fact that Chuck was willing to hire me told me that his law office had very low standards. Fine by me.

"Ms. James! So glad you could make it."

He motioned me to sit across the booth from him at the Shoreline Café. The Shoreline was the Winchester House of Battle Lake, perpetually being added onto. It had started with a cute dining room and kitchen. Then, a cavernous dining room had been added in the back beyond the restrooms. Next, a bar and ice cream parlor were attached, and a bowling alley was added on to that. The layout felt a little jigsaw puzzled, but this was easy to forget once you dug into their fluffy omelets, or better yet, their heavenly eggs Benedict.

Chuck had chosen a booth at the bay window facing West Battle Lake, the perfect location to see who was coming and going. In the distance and to the right, I spotted the top spires of the ice castle peeking over the trees.

"Have you been waiting long?" I asked.

He pointed at a small white plate dusted with crumbs. "Long enough to polish off a piece of homemade cherry pie. My wife would kill me if she knew I was having that for breakfast."

The three cookies in my stomach nodded in sympathy. "It's Sunday," I said. "A day of rest and desserts."

He leaned forward conspiratorially. "Don't suppose I could talk you into your own piece of pie? I'd feel better if I wasn't the only one who slipped."

I took the seat across from him. My jeans were already feeling a little tourniquety around the waist. I'd figured they'd loosen as the day wore on and the fabric had a chance to stretch. It felt good to have a plan. "Sure. Caramel apple for me."

He ordered that and another piece of cherry for himself, because "a gentleman never lets a lady eat alone." I added on a cup of coffee with real cream. While we waited, he slipped into the reason he'd brought me here, Lutheran-style—which is to say, inefficiently and roundabout.

"Heard about the hoo-ha at the lake yesterday. Damn shame. Do they know who the young man you found in the ice was?"

The waitress set my coffee mug down and poured me a steaming cup. The rich smell comforted me instantly. I studied Chuck covertly as I mixed in the cream and two sugars. Previously, I'd only met him in passing when dealing with his son at the law firm. I knew he came from a farm background and was the first in his family to attend college. By all accounts, he'd worked hard for everything he had, and he was well-liked around town. Even so, there was something crafty in his eyes that put me on guard. "They think he was a transient."

Chuck rubbed his chin. "Been a lot of fly-by-nighters around Battle Lake lately, it seems. It used to be that I recognized everyone in town in the winter. Now, I can't go to Larry's without running into at least five strangers, some of whom look like they're from the rough side of the tracks. Do they think that drugs were involved?"

I sipped the coffee. The creamy, sweet liquid poured down my throat, sending shivers of satisfaction to my fingertips. "No idea." I took another sip and watched him. Would he be disappointed that I couldn't tell him more? If so, tough noogies. I wasn't on the clock. Yet.

He shrugged, glancing back toward the pie cooler. The waitress was pulling out two pies that had been baked fresh that morning, no doubt. The apple pie was unbroken, the lattice work crust on the top drizzled with thick ropes of homemade caramel. A little bit of drool ran out of my mouth, and I wiped at it, hoping he hadn't noticed.

"Well," he said, pulling his attention back to me. "It's a sad business, but not why I asked you here. What can you tell me about Eric Offerdahl?"

"Never heard of him, though I know the Offerdahl name is tied to the Prospect House."

Chuck nodded. He'd expected that. I was starting to think nothing I could say would surprise him. He'd known exactly how this interview would go before he walked in the door, and truly, it felt like a job interview. "Eric is about your age, maybe a little younger. He was a troubled kid, might still be. Troubled, that is, obviously not a kid anymore. I was hoping you could track him down."

Some stubborn streak in me refused to ask him why. "Do you have an address?"

"We think he's living within fifteen miles of Battle Lake."

"Any idea of who his friends might be?"

"He graduated high school here, but all his friends, if he had any, have moved on."

"How long do you think he's been back?"

"A month, maybe two."

A lovely wedge of warm caramel apple pie with a scoop of melting vanilla ice cream was slid in front of me. I smiled. Yesterday might have been a crap sandwich, but today was going pretty well so far. I ate my pie and pretended to contemplate everything Chuck had told me. I hoped my face was somehow radiating thoughtful intelligence because my brain was cycling over two words, again and again: *pie... amazing.* I finished the whole slice barely coming up for air, wondering if the speed-calorie conversion applied to pies as well as cookies.

"You must have been hungry," Chuck said.

I looked up to see he was only on his second bite. Second bite of his second piece, though, which did not exactly give him carte blanche to the judgment chair.

"Thank you," I said. "For the pie. It was delicious. If I take the case, how much time do I have to find Eric Offerdahl?"

"Two weeks from today."

I did the math in my head. "I could give you twenty billable hours in the next two weeks, at forty dollars an hour. I'll log all the sites I visit and leads I follow. If I don't find him, you still pay."

I'd made all this up on the spot, but he nodded as if what I was saying was reasonable.

"Deal." He held out his hand.

I shook it, trying not to notice the thick cherry ooze smeared across his teeth like blood.

———

My meeting with Gilbert Hullson had far fewer layers. In fact, I'm not even sure it had one layer. I tracked him down at the hardware store where he worked part-time. He was in the screw aisle sorting through a bin.

"Mr. Hullson?"

"None other."

He kept sorting, not bothering to glance my way. He wore flannel and, except for a spectacularly bulbous nose, looked like your average middle-aged Midwesterner.

"I'm Mira James. From the *Battle Lake Recall*? I'm here to interview you about Jiffy."

That got his attention. He immediately stood, his eyes alight. "You shoulda seen it! One minute I'm planning her funeral, and the next, she's shooting out of a fishhole like popcorn. Poor thing was wet and shivering to beat the band, but she was alive. Ooh, if she could talk, she'd have a story to tell, wouldn't she?"

"So she really went into one hole and came out the other?"

"As real as these two hands." He held his gnarled palms toward me. He was missing the ring finger on his left hand, which confused the analogy somewhat.

"Do you have witnesses?"

He flashed a sly smile. "I'm a fisherman. I can always come up with witnesses."

I felt a mirror smile tugging at my lips. The guy was an absolute weirdo, and he was beginning to grow on me. "Good enough. Don't suppose I could come by your house later tonight and snap a photo of Jiffy? To run with the article?"

He returned his attention to the screws. "She'd be pleased to meet you."

FOURTEEN

In eighth grade, our health class took a half-day trip to Paynesville Manor, the local nursing home. We were each assigned an honorary grandparent, and our job was to listen to their history and write a mini-biography from it. That's one of those exercises that must look great on paper, a bunch of teacher's chuffing each other around a table, talking about active and experiential learning. In reality, we were already struggling with acne and the unshakeable belief that human interaction was merely a set-up for humiliation à la face plants, sneeze-farts, spontaneously inappropriate confessions, and/or getting the answer wrong. To expect us to navigate an unfamiliar elderly population was pure cruelty.

Because of that experience, and because in my teens and twenties I'd been confident I'd never grow old and so why bother hanging out with those who were, I'd never entered another nursing home. Until I'd moved to Battle Lake. A series of circumstances led me to the Senior Sunset, and specifically to seek out Curtis Poling. He was believed to be in the middle stages of dementia by those who didn't know him, an incorrect assumption that he cultivated by casting off the roof of the Sunset into the dry lawn in the back whenever it was sunny and "the fish were likely to be biting." In truth, Curtis was as wily as they came, with sharp, clear blue eyes that didn't miss a thing. He'd gone from being my informant to my friend, the man I visited weekly to play cards with, laugh with, and, in the summer, get gardening tips from. He'd also introduced me to Mrs. Berns last March, though she had since moved out of the nursing home and into her own apartment, labeling her temporary residency there a "misunderstanding."

Today, as I strolled into the foyer of the Senior Sunset, I was struck by how comfortable the predominant scents of a nursing home—antiseptics, Bengay, and dusty-floral old-lady perfume—had grown to me. I signed in at the front desk and made my way to Curtis's room. I knocked at his door.

"Who is it? Is it Satan? Because I'm not ready to go just yet."

"Hey, Curtis. It's me. Mira."

"Timothy Leary? I'm too old for that psychedelic crap."

"Mira," I repeated, keeping my voice level. I smiled as a short, chunky nursing assistant walked past, wearing burgundy scrubs and a suspicious expression. "Mira James."

"Etta James? What are you doing this far north?"

I sighed. "I brought donuts."

"Door's unlocked."

I let myself in. Curtis lived in a standard room, set up much like a hospital room except for the dresser and the plants in the window. His room featured a bed and a nightstand, a TV mounted to the ceiling, an easy chair by the window and a plastic chair for guests, a closet, and a private bath. He was sitting by the window, reading H. G. Wells's *The Time Machine*. Upside down. When he was sure it was me, he flipped it right side up.

"Why do you pretend?" I asked. "All the smart nurses must know you're not crazy."

He shrugged. "I make it easy on 'em by being consistent. And the crazier I act, the more they leave me alone." He was wearing a dark blue terry cloth robe. His thin calves poked out like chopsticks. Thankfully, his bony feet were stuffed into the toasty knit mukluks I'd bought him for Christmas after I'd accidentally caught him barefoot. Old farmer's feet are the stuff of nightmares.

"Where are they?" he asked.

"What?"

"The donuts."

"I lied about those." I pulled up the plastic chair so I was sitting across from him. "What was the deal with giving me the runaround in the hall?"

"New nursing assistant. Comes up about to your shoulders, shaped more like a square than a circle?"

I nodded. "She passed by while I was trying to get in. She looked fine, maybe a little curious."

"Shows what you know. She's convinced I'm not really crazy and has made it her mission to prove it."

"Smart, too. I think I like her."

He scrunched up his lips in a pout, and for a moment, he resembled a baby more than an old man.

"Fine," I said. "I'll bring donuts next time. Promise. Do you have a few minutes right now?"

"That might be all I have. Never know when the ticker is going to punch out." He winked. "So what do you want to know?"

First I asked him about Gary's shooting. He'd heard that it'd happened, of course. You might not think someone in a nursing home would have their finger on the pulse of a town, but you'd be wrong.

He still had friends on the outside, and stories were the currency of the Sunset. The elderly traded news like gold and pearls, and it all, somehow, rolled downhill to Curtis. Unfortunately, he didn't have any more information on Gary than I did, and was in fact happy to learn that Gary's wound was not serious.

The next topic of conversation was Maurice Jackson. Curtis didn't ask me if I was okay after finding another body, and I loved him for that. He treated me like I was normal. He did say that he'd heard there were new drugs in town, and a gang on the fringes, and that he assumed they were connected.

"What do you mean, 'on the fringes'?" I asked.

"They don't live in Battle Lake, near as I can tell. In fact, I don't know why they'd even bother coming here, with our small population. But they've been showing up often enough."

"Do you think Gary's shooting is connected to the gang?"

He rubbed his chin. "I'd be surprised if it wasn't. I've lived here for ninety-three years and never has a Battle Lake police officer been shot. It'd be quite a coincidence if a gang comes to town at the same time Gary's attacked, and there's no thread between the two. What'd you think of the Prospect House?"

"I never made the press tour," I said, noting his abrupt shift in topic but not commenting. "I'm hoping for an email back scheduling a private tour."

He stared out the window. I was struck by how ocean blue his eyes were, and how similar they were to Johnny's. "She's a gorgeous old building, that Prospect House. I'm happy other people are going to get to experience her. I stole my first kiss there, did you know that? She was a girl from St. Louis, visiting for the week with her parents. They owned a mercantile back home, I believe. I courted her all of those seven days she was in town, and the night before she left, I snuck into the Prospect House and met her at the base of the grand staircase. I pecked her cheek. She giggled and ran upstairs. Never saw her again." His eyes grew misty and faraway.

I couldn't help smiling. "That's beautiful. What was her name?"

"Amelia. Prettiest girl you ever saw, except for my wife, God rest her soul."

His use of the word *girl* reminded me of the face I'd seen in the window when I'd been skating. I didn't see any reason to bring it up. In fact, the further I got from the event, the more certain I was I'd imagined it. I'd need a full night's sleep soon or I'd be completely loony. "Sorry to bring you back to earth, but I have one more question. What can you tell me about Eric Offerdahl?"

His eyes immediately focused. He began chuckling. "How much research did you do on the Prospect House?"

"I know it was built by Barnaby Offerdahl. I imagine Eric is related to him."

"Good. I was worried you were getting soft. Eric must be the, let me see now ... the great-great grand-nephew of Barnaby. There might be even one more great on there. Eric can trace his lineage straight from Barnaby's brother. He has blood from the bad side of the family."

"Meaning?"

"He's been nothing but trouble since he was born. That's true of that whole remaining Offerdahl branch. Eric's parents still own a lot of the land surrounding the Prospect House, but they had to sell off the house to pay gambling debts. I'm surprised they haven't sold the land as well, given how much that would be worth."

"Are his parents still alive?"

"His mom, no. She died a decade or so back, heart attack I think I heard. His dad is older, in his seventies, I believe, but as far as I know, still alive. They had Eric late in life. He's an only child. After he graduated high school, they moved to Phoenix or Texas. Somewhere warm."

"Any idea where Eric is now?"

"How many donuts are you planning on bringing me next visit?"

"How many do you want?"

He chuckled. "This is worth at least a half dozen Long Johns, but not with that fake chocolate in the middle. I want jelly."

"You got it."

He kept the smile on his face. "Last I heard Eric blew back into town about the same time the gang did." He raised his eyebrows to make sure I understood what he was implying. "He's living somewhere around Swederland."

Swederland was a two-bars-and-a-post-office town a five-minute drive from Battle Lake. "That's where the new brewery is, isn't it?"

"O'Callaghan's. But *that* is a whole other story, and you'd have to bring me a dozen donuts for that."

I wanted to hear more, but his eyes were drooping, and Curtis's hands had grown minutely shaky on his lap. He was tired, and he was trying to tell me gently. I stood and kissed the top of his head. He still had thick white hair, which was a point of pride with him. It smelled like Brylcreem. "That's a deal. I have to be running, though. Have an appointment and all that."

He took my hand. His was as dry as paper, but strong despite the tremor running through it. I glanced at his face, surprised by the affection.

"You are going to be okay, kid." He smiled and released my hand. "You're like a cat, curious as the day is long, and always landing on her feet."

I smiled back. "See you soon," I said. I glanced over my shoulder on the way out. His eyes were closed.

I arrived at the library with a full hour to go until the birthday party. I decorated with a roll of crepe paper and flicked on the twinkle lights, then went to my computer. Navigating into my paid database, I first ran a search on Eric Offerdahl. There was only one hit, his current address listed as north Minneapolis. I also uncovered a list of misdemeanor crimes committed by him, including vandalism, petty theft, and public intoxication. Most of his crimes took place in Minnesota with the exception of a case of trespassing in Chicago. He'd done jail time, a month here or a month there, but on paper, he appeared to be more of a directionless punk than a serial criminal.

I tracked down a single photo of him, a fuzzy shot where he had his arm wrapped around a woman's neck in a possessive hug. He had brown hair. I couldn't tell what color his eyes were, but he wore a spike through his right eyebrow. The rest of his features were bland. The woman had a beautiful, heart-shaped face accented by a lip ring and thick black liner rimming her eyes.

I clicked on the photo and was brought to the woman's Facebook page. I knew of Facebook, of course. Who didn't? I didn't have an account I posted to, though, just a skeleton page to allow me to log in and research others. What had our culture come to that people needed to advertise that they had a cold and were going to shop for cheese later that day? Made my job easier, but still.

The woman's name, according to the page, was Lil Angie, and she lived in Minneapolis. I couldn't find any other photos of Eric on her page or any more mention of him. I wrote down the URL and left Facebook, glancing at the clock. The birthday party guests would arrive soon.

I had time for a curiosity-driven search on "Maurice Jackson," so I returned to my subscription database. I received twenty hits on the name in the greater Chicago area, with phone numbers and addresses for all of them. Whether they were current or whether any of them were the iced Maurice would remain to be seen because at that moment, the first knock came at the glass front door. It was Matthew and his mom. I waved them in with one hand and clicked the Print button with the other.

Matthew's friends weren't far behind, and soon I had the library filled with giggling, Duck Duck Gray Duck–playing kids. They were extra-crazy, hiding in plain sight under chairs and telling jokes with no punch lines. It must be the weather, which one parent told me was going to reach the low thirties today.

"Above freezing?" I asked.

"I know!" she said, as surprised as I was.

Mrs. Berns, who had promised to help me with today's party, showed up as the worst was over and we were about to cut into the cake and ice cream. "Nice timing," I whispered, as she laid her coat over the front counter.

"Thank you!" she said brightly. "Is it marble cake? That's my favorite."

I glanced over at the sheet cake Matthew's mom was cutting into, slicing right into the green frosting tail of a brontosaurus. Marble cake was my favorite, too. Could I have cookies for breakfast, pie for a snack, and cake for lunch? I was excited to find out. "I don't know yet. Where were you?"

"Late night," she said. "I was playing bridge with some friends, and then I went to the Rusty Nail to sing karaoke."

I asked, despite myself. "What'd you sing?"

"'Like a Virgin,'" she said, straight-faced. "Let me help!" she ran over to where Matthew's mom was sliding the first slice of cake onto a plate. "I can be your distributor."

Matthew's mom smiled gratefully and handed the plate to Mrs. Berns, who added a big scoop of vanilla ice cream on the top and then returned to my side.

"Aren't you going to pass it out to the kids, first?"

"Charity starts at home."

I threw my hands in the air. She was being particularly difficult today. I scurried over to help with the cake, making sure all the kids and parents had what they needed, all the while wishing I'd laid plastic on the floor. It looked like I was going to have to bring in a professional to shampoo the carpet after this shindig. The thought killed my desire for cake, so I made my way back to Mrs. Berns. She was talking to a woman who'd brought her grandson to the party. The lady was showing Mrs. Berns a photo book. I assumed the pictures were of her grandson and was surprised to make my way out to the side and see they were instead of a golden retriever.

"It's my Sandy," she said in answer to my expression. "She's lived with me for two years. I don't know what I'd do without her. Dogs are the only things that love another person more than themselves."

"You've obviously never been to an Al-Anon meeting," Mrs. Berns muttered under her breath.

"Wait, you have?" I asked her.

The grandma took that moment to snap her book closed and return to the party, an annoyed expression on her face.

Mrs. Berns wiggled her eyebrows. "There's a lot you don't know about me, missy."

I was taken aback. She was absolutely right. She was so honest and forthright and I was so comfortable with her that I hadn't bothered to plumb her past. Her husband had died ten years ago, that much I knew, and she had kids who had tried to confine her in a high-security nursing home last October. I also knew that she got laid more in a bad week than I did in a good month. She'd lived in or near Battle Lake her whole life, she never let life get her down, and she preferred to wear replica six-guns holstered at her sides, though she'd given up this accessory for the winter. But did she dream of traveling the world? What had her life with her husband been like? What was her favorite drink?

"Quit looking at me like that," she said.

"Like what?"

"Like I'm a commercial for an animal shelter and your brain is running some pitiful commentary along the bottom of my screen. I just made that crack to get rid of Emma. If she'd referred to her dog as her 'child,' I woulda had to kick her, and the Al-Anon comment seemed kinder."

I cocked my head. She was sounding more like her old self. Still, something was a little off. "You sure you don't want to talk?"

"You sure you want me to tell this room full of children that when you're alone, you dream of Chief Wenonga walking his fiberglass legs over to your house and showing you his totem pole?"

"Okay," I said, turning to the children and clapping loudly, my voice dripping with false cheer. "Time to get cleaning!"

The kids groaned and fell to the ground as if their bones had turned to rubber, but we were already fifteen minutes over the scheduled time. Even if I didn't have Mrs. Berns's threat burning the tips of my ears, I wanted to make visiting hours at the hospital so I could check in with Gary. The moms glanced at their cell phones or watches and began cleaning up the party area with the precision of worker ants. If the United States could only harness the power of moms, we'd break our dependence on oil once and for all.

The library was cleared out in less than twenty minutes, and I swear it was cleaner than it had been pre-party. No thanks to Mrs. Berns, of course. She'd snuck out as soon as the picking-up began. I made a note to myself to track her down soon so I could ask her more questions about herself. At this moment, though, my priority was visiting one Gary Wohnt so I could question him about the shooting.

———

Entering the hospital empty-handed seemed in poor taste, but I didn't want to buy Gary flowers and I didn't know what kind of food he liked. Using the tried-and-true maxim, "If you bring something you like, you know at least one person will be happy," I purchased four Nut Goodies at a gas station on my way. I polished off one before I hit the parking lot, leaving three, which seemed like a better number anyhow, and here's my reasoning: if there was someone else already there, we'd each have one. If I brought in four Nut Goodies, though, it'd devolve into one of those embarrassing social situations where everyone had to pretend like they didn't want the extra one.

Gary's room was on the second floor. I made my way to the elevator, trying not to stare at the people wearing robes and pushing IVs as they shuffled down the hallway. It seems to me that if you're admitted to the hospital, you should stay in your room or go home, but what did I know?

No matter how many times I'd visited a hospital, I still couldn't get used to the sense that germs were settling on every inch of me in a light mist. I hit the "2" button in the elevator with my elbow, smiling apologetically at the man I was sharing it with.

"Germs," I said, showing him my jazz hands.

He pretended not to hear me, and so I pretended the elevator came to a screeching stop on the second floor, forcing me to rub my germy elbow against him to keep my balance.

"Sorry," I said. I'd been hanging out with Mrs. Berns far too long.

Following the signs to room 227, I stood outside the cracked door. It struck me—probably much later than it should have—that I was about to see Gary Wohnt vulnerable. In bed. Possibly wearing little more than a gown.

I took a deep breath, steeling myself, and slipped through the crack in the door.

No part of my imagination could have prepared me for what I saw.

FIFTEEN

"MIRANDA RAYN JAMES!"

Gary knew my middle name. And he was alone. The top half of his bed was raised so he could sit comfortably. One leg lay relaxed on the bed and the other was bandaged and suspended from the ceiling in some sort of sling. Both appendages were naked, but that wasn't what shocked me. It was his expression. He looked as joyful as a child who'd gotten a pony for Christmas, and he was directing all this happiness at me.

I glanced behind me. Had someone else entered, a woman with the same name as me but whom Gary actually liked?

"Come in! I was hoping you'd visit." His words were slurred and his dark hair tousled, a thick lock of it dangling over an eye. He was wearing a blue hospital gown, and I was thankful to see boxers peeking out from the bottom of it.

"Gary?"

"Have a seat!" He patted the small open spot on the single bed he was occupying. There's no way I could sit there without our hips touching. This from the man who regularly treated me like I was something he'd accidentally stepped in.

"Have you found God?" I asked.

He visibly pondered the question. While he did that, I checked the tag on his IV drip. Cephalosporin and morphine. Mystery solved.

"I have looked for God, I truly have."

The corner of my mouth tipped. I reveled in the moment. It had been a crappy couple days. Hell, it'd been a crappy decade. You can let that get you down, or you can find joy in the small moment, like this one. I actually had the upper hand over Gary.

"You are not wearing pants," I said, both to test his awareness and to divert a possible sermon.

"Pants." He pronounced the word as if he was tasting it. "Pants."

"When do you get out?"

"Groundhog's Day?" he asked, giggling. It was a deep, cheerful sound, but he covered his mouth like a schoolgirl while he did it. "But only if we have six more weeks of winter."

I pulled up a chair. Gary Wohnt, high and pantsless. This was going to be more fun than a room full of nuns with Tourette's, to borrow one of Mrs. Berns's favorite sayings. "What happened to you, anyhow? Who shot you?"

He glanced at his leg, surprised. He fought for focus, and for a moment he looked like Police Chief Wohnt. "White male, twenty-five to thirty, wearing a cap yanked down low. I pulled him over for speeding and driving without a license plate. I approached, he shot."

My heart clutched. I realized how lucky Gary was that it hadn't been worse. "What kind of car?"

He turned toward me. "Is that your business?"

Dangit! Had the morphine just worn off? I flicked the IV tube with my finger in case there was blockage. "I want to help."

"You can help by getting me some water." He pointed at the table just out of his reach.

I stood and poured him a glass. When I turned, I caught him staring at my butt as though it held the secret of the Sphinx. I cleared my throat.

"Miranda Rayn James! You came to visit me." He accepted the water, the glassy look back in his eyes. "So many dead bodies you could be finding, and instead you're here with me." He giggled again. There was something infectious about it.

"Well, I gotta keep it lively," I said, winking.

"Yes, you do." He knit his brows together. "Say, can you help me?"

"You want me to reach something else for you?"

"I want you to gather information on the guys who are bringing the drugs. The gang-bangers. Can you do that for me without getting into trouble?"

"Was Maurice a gang-banger?" I asked, pulling my chair up close.

"Dunno." He sat back. "Do you know where the remote is?"

"Gary." I put my hand on his arm. He studied it. "Was Maurice part of a gang from Chicago that is bringing drugs into this area?"

"Dunno. But I do know the gang showed up the same time as the OxyContin patches. Don't know where the base is. We just know it's near town."

"Battle Lake?"

He smiled dreamily. "Battle Lake."

"What did Maurice die of?"

"Death." His smile widened. "Have I ever told you how beautiful you are?"

My skin flushed from head to toe. I definitely had not foreseen this conversational turn.

"Kiss me. Kiss me now."

I stood so fast that I knocked over my chair. This couldn't only be the morphine talking. He must also be having an allergic reaction to the antibiotics.

"Um, I should be going."

"Pretty, pretty, pretty. I think you're as pretty as a peach." He held his finger to his mouth in a comically exaggerated "sssh." "Don't tell Kennie," he said, in a drunk man's whisper.

The fun was definitely over. This was not at all what I had planned. "How about we don't tell *anyone*? In fact, how about we forget that I even stopped by?"

I was in such a hurry to escape that I dropped a Nut Goodie. I would have gone back for it, except Gary was singing "Unforgettable." I stress ate the remaining two Goodies before I reached my car.

SIXTEEN

I'D FORGOTTEN THE MAURICE Jackson print-out at the library, so I had to stop by there on my way home. Once inside the toasty building, the encounter with Gary fading to an unpleasant memory, I decided I might as well finish my research as long as I was there. I flicked on the track of lights over the front desk, turned on the computer so I could cross-reference as needed, sharpened one of the stubby library pencils, and grabbed two manila folders. I labeled one "Operation Offerdahl" in honor of the case I was actually getting paid to research. I tossed around a couple names for the second folder before settling on "Cold Case." It was dark humor, to be sure, but the name had less to do with the way Maurice had died than the fact that I had few leads and no reason to look for more. I had no tangible stake in finding out who Maurice really was and what had happened to him, no incentive other than curiosity and a feeling like I owed him something.

Once my meager paperwork was organized, I made my first call, to a Maurice Aames Jackson at 1355 West Greenleaf Avenue in

Chicago, Illinois. There was no answer. I put a chicken scratch next to his name, shorthand for "tried once."

The next name on my list was Maurice Carver Jackson, living at 1640 North Orchard Street. He picked up on the second ring. He sounded old, and I hadn't rehearsed what I was going to say.

"Hello, sir! I'm calling from the Chicago Public Library, and someone has returned a library card with the name of Maurice Jackson. Have you by chance lost your library card?"

"Chicago Public Library?"

"Yessir."

"Then why does my caller ID say 'Battle Lake Public Library?'"

Shit. He was going to make detective before me. "All our library calls are routed through one central location."

"Izzat so? I suppose you have a bridge you want me to buy, one that just so happens to span the Dumbass River?"

I was torn between the urge to hang up and the desire to ask him if he was single so I could set him up with Mrs. Berns. "I'm sorry. I am calling from the Battle Lake Public Library. It's in Minnesota. I really did find a Chicago Public Library card with the name of Maurice Jackson on it, and I'm trying to track him down."

"It ain't mine, but can I offer you some advice?"

That's a question that rarely deserves a yes. "Sure."

"Tell the truth." Click.

He had a point. Then again, I had so few natural skills—lying being toward the top of the list—that it seemed counterintuitive to limit myself arbitrarily. I tried three more numbers. Two were home, both dead ends. It was a bit demoralizing, particularly since I didn't even know how old the library card was. Maurice Jackson could have moved out of Chicago months ago. I decided to take a break from calling numbers to do the work I was actually being paid for. Going on Curtis's tip that Eric Offerdahl had been seen around Swederland and specifically in the vicinity of the new brewery, I dialed their number.

"O'Callaghan's." The voice was female and perky.

"Hi. Is the brewery open for tours?"

"Of course! In the winter, we have tours at the top of every hour Tuesdays and Saturdays from noon to eight."

"Do I need a reservation?"

"Not this time of year."

"Sounds good. Hey," I said, hoping I sounded like I just thought of it, "is Eric Offerdahl working this Tuesday?"

"I'm sorry. We can't give out employee information."

Was it my imagination, or had her voice gone frosty? "I don't need any personal info. I'm just wondering if Eric is working there. I haven't seen him in a while. It'd be great to catch up."

"I'm afraid I can't help you with that. Is there anything else I can do for you?"

I recognized a brush-off when I heard it. "No, thank you. I appreciate your time."

"O'Callaghan's thanks you for your interest! We hope to see you soon."

That they will, I thought, as I hung up the phone. *Probably this Tuesday, in fact.* I was about to shut down the computer when the front door opened. Hadn't I locked it?

"Sorry," I said. "We're not open on Sundays."

The track of lights above me was illuminated, but I hadn't bothered to turn on the lights over the front door. The person was definitely a male, his head leaning so far down that the top of his cap was facing me.

"Sir? We're not open. You can come back tomorrow at ten."

He stepped into the light at the same time he lifted his head. It was Ray, the mewling, tweaking freak Maurice had saved me from.

SEVENTEEN

EVERY CELL IN MY body lifted its skirts and ran for high ground. I stepped back involuntarily, one hand fumbling for the phone and the other scrabbling inside my desk for something substantial to whack Ray with. Why had I left the stun gun in my car?

He kept moving toward me, and the closer he came, the clearer the tattoo on his neck grew. The barbed tail of a manta ray licked at his ear, leading to a widening of the body, most of which was tucked into the collar of his thick winter jacket. *Stingray.* I wondered if the tattoo had given him his name, or vice versa. I also wondered where he'd gotten the warm winter coat and how the helicopter I'd been stupid enough not to lock the door.

"Stop. I have a gun. And I've pushed the alarm."

"Shit, this is a library. What you got that anyone wants to steal?" He stopped, though, and glanced behind him, his hands shoved deep into his pockets.

"That's close enough. Now, you have exactly two minutes to get out of here before the cops arrive."

"Two minutes all I need."

Two minutes?!? Why couldn't I have said thirty seconds? Our eyes were locked. His pupils were far less jittery than the night we'd met. He also wasn't making that trapped baby animal noise. In fact, he appeared entirely calm. Still, when he began to draw one hand slowly out of his pocket, I instinctively raised my stapler.

He saw it and started laughing wheezily. "Stop! Don't collate me." He held up his empty hands in mock horror.

"That's a pretty odd verb choice," I said, still gripping the stapler.

He dropped his hands and shrugged. "I used to work in a copy shop. I got what, a buck thirty seconds now? Here's the deal. I heard there was a chick detective in town and that I could find her at the library. I got a letter I was supposed to hand over to the police if anything happened to Mo."

"Mo?"

"Maurice. My friend who was ganked. They found his body in the lake yesterday."

"Wait," I said, dropping the stapler by my side, "you didn't kill him?"

Ray scrunched up his face. "What's wrong with you, woman? We don't kill our own. So you want the damn letter or not?"

"I thought you were supposed to give it to the police."

"I look like I get along with the police?"

Point taken. "Say, speaking of police, I don't suppose you happened to shoot an officer of the law last night?"

His eyes narrowed dangerously. "I ask you one more time: You want the letter or not?"

I leaned over the desk and held out my hand. He pulled a crumpled sheet of paper from his coat pocket and stepped forward as if he was going to drop it into my hand. At the last second, our hands so close I could feel his body heat, he balled up the paper and tossed it over my head.

"Sorry." His eyes had gone as flat as a doll's. "It must've slipped."

He raised an eyebrow and started slowly walking backward to the door. My heart thudded a sick beat against my ribs. I held eye contact. In this brief interaction, I'd made the dangerous mistake of thinking he might be human since he'd done a favor for a friend. He was reminding me what he really was and who held the power in this room.

I let him walk out, neither of us blinking or dropping our gazes. When the door closed behind him, I snapped off the overhead lights and simultaneously flipped on the lights outside the door. The contrast made me feel a tiny bit safer. I watched him slip into a rusty white sedan. When Ray was out of sight, I darted out from behind the desk and locked the door, leaving on the outside lights. Then I scurried back to my desk and fumbled in the drawers until I located a penlight I'd received for free when I'd opened a checking account at Farmers and Merchants County Bank. I flicked it on and was pleased to see that the light was narrow but bright. I quickly located the crumpled paper and then tucked myself behind the tall counter where I could read the letter without anyone seeing me.

EIGHTEEN

I SMOOTHED THE PAPER on the carpeted floor and shone the flashlight beam into the center of it. I discovered it was a grainy photocopy of a handwritten letter:

18 January 1865

Dear Loretta:

I wish I could write with better news. In Minnesota, they do not believe the messages I bring. I do not think I can stay here. I pack my bags to return home tomorrow. Should anything happen to me, look to the tunnel of justice.

With a heart that beats only for you,
Orpheus Jackson

I flipped the letter over. It was blank. I flipped it back and reread it. The letter raised more questions than it answered. Was the date accurate, and was Maurice Jackson a descendant of Orpheus's? If so, who is the "they" and what were the "messages" referred to in the letter? And more importantly, what in the world did a hundred-and forty-year-old letter have to do with Maurice's murder? I sighed and rubbed my temples. For all I knew, Ray and Hammer had killed Maurice and dreamed up this letter based on something he'd seen at the copy shop and were using it in a ridiculous attempt to throw the police off their scent.

I wish I'd had time to read the letter before Ray left so I could question him. Then again, I was happy that he was gone. I peeked over the top of the desk and pulled the phone toward me, bringing it down to ground level. I dialed Jed's number from memory.

One ring.

Two rings.

Three rings.

Click. "Hey, you! Thanks for calling me. You know it's Jed, right? Well, I'm not here right now, so leave a message with the phone, and I'll call you back when I get home." *Beep*.

"Hey, it's Mira. Hope you're well. I'm calling to find out what you know about any recent drug or gang activity in the area." To anyone else, that message might sound a little offensive; Jed didn't operate on that level. "Give me a call back."

I hung up and considered calling Johnny to ask him to walk me to my car. If I did that, though, where would it stop? I'd never be able to go anywhere on my own again. Besides, if Ray had wanted to hurt me, he would have. No way did he buy that I had a gun or an alarm. I just had to be alert from this moment forward.

But not stupid.

I called Gilbert Hullson and told him I'd be over in ten minutes to meet Jiffy and asked him to call the police if I wasn't. I placed my skimpy research into the appropriate manila folders. Then I set the library door to lock automatically behind me and dashed to the car with such speed that my feet barely kissed the icy ground.

———

Funny. Running to my car, I'd wished for ol' Z-Force, the stun gun, more than anything in the world. Now that I'd spent thirty minutes sitting across from Gilbert, who had Jiffy perched on one meaty thigh and a fishing scrapbook on the other, I was glad I didn't have Z. I would have either zapped Gilbert to shut him up or myself to keep awake. He had struck me as odd during our first meeting in the hardware store, but I'd found myself warming to him by the end of the conversation.

Always trust your first impressions.

The tiny bungalow two miles north of town hadn't been hard to find, and the neat yard with a shoveled path leading to the house gave no indication that Gilbert was a hoarder. The sheer mountainous concentration of stuff crowding the house's interior was overwhelming. He'd carved a path inside the house mirroring the one outside, and it weaved through shoulder-high piles of food wrappers, fishing magazines, tackle, old life jackets, decoys, and more. It was as if someone had emptied a gigantic fishing boat into his house at the end of a trip, and it smelled like that trip had ended a decade or two ago.

" … and that was 1984. My 1985–90 albums are more walleye-oriented. Let me grab—"

I sat up so quickly that Jiffy erped, which is how dogs that size must bark: *Erp*. "I really appreciate your time, Mr. Hullson, but I'm afraid I can't stay. I just need a photo of Jiffy." She wagged her stumpy little tail at the mention of her name. She was a darling miniature poodle, though she had that weird eye goop that breed of dog always seemed to sport. She'd been staring at me desperately since I'd arrived, almost begging for me to take her out of this paean to accumulation, fishing, and pop cans.

"Well," Gilbert said, sensing, I imagine, that he was about to lose a 135-pound white girl, "you should at least see a picture of the hole she fell into before you go."

"Really? You're going to show me a picture of a hole?" Resignation, not surprise, colored my voice.

Jiffy *erped* again: *You have to save me, lady from the outside! This isn't my life!*

"Sher thing," Gilbert said, pulling out a thick photo album labeled *Miracle Jiffy.* He paged through it until he found what he wanted. He flipped the album so it was facing me and thrust a sausage finger at a blurry square. "See?"

I leaned forward to look at the photograph. The Naugahyde ottoman I was sitting on—the only accessible piece of furniture besides Gilbert's easy chair—squeaked as I did so. Gilbert flashed me a look, but I didn't bother making excuses. He owed me that much.

In the photo, Gilbert had placed a paperback next to the ice hole to lend perspective.

"She must have just fit in there," I said.

"Yup. She's fished with me a hundred times and never fell in. If it wasn't for those gangsters shooting up the ice, I never would have let her out of my sight. I think she was going after a fish. I almost lost her." He bundled Jiffy into his arms and hugged her. She closed her eyes and ducked her head into his arm.

My ears pricked up. "Gangsters?"

"Two of them. Couldn't get a good look at 'em because they were far away, but I could tell by their clothes that they're not from around here. Hoodies, baseball caps. No fisherman wears that. They were shooting into the air, hollering. I turned around to ask Jiffy if she thought I should call the police, but she wasn't there. I panicked. By the time she popped back out of the ice a few houses over, the kids were gone."

"What night was this?"

"Thursday night. Right before they started setting up for the festival on West Battle."

"Is that where you were? On West Battle?"

"Yup. Not far off from the ice castle."

So, two men who were "not from around here" were near where Maurice's body was found two nights before he died, and wearing clothes very similar to those Ray and Hammer were wearing that same night they attacked Mrs. Berns and me.

The letter supposedly written by Orpheus Jackson was looking fishier and fishier.

NINETEEN

MONDAY MORNING DAWNED BEFORE I did. I lay under my bed, eyes closed, wondering if I'd left the bathroom faucet on. *Drip. Drip.* Willing myself not to care, I snuggled deeper into my patchwork quilt in the dark safety. The alarm hadn't yet gone off, which meant that I had more time to sleep, though I could tell by the light filtering underneath the edges of the bed that the sun was beginning to rise.

Drip.

I sighed. The water wasn't going to let me sleep. I rolled to the edge of my bed and cracked one eye. A knurdled pair of socks and yesterday's jeans lay on the floor, inches from my face. I crawled over the fallen clothes, then like a puppet master, hauled my upper body into a sitting position. I ran my fingers through the front half of my hair, stopping when I met resistance. I'd slept terribly last night, fitful murmurs of rest pockmarked by nightmares of skating over a frozen lake, hundreds of corpses suspended in the ice, and just below that, undulating, predatory sea creatures waiting for the ice to melt enough to drop their prey.

As if that wasn't bad enough, the same nightmare featured a symphony of tiny white dogs popping out of holes that erupted like geysers. I'd tried to skate to safety, but the more I sliced at the ice, the farther away the shore moved.

Ugh. I stumbled into the bathroom and tightened both of the sink faucets. Still, I heard the drip. Next I tightened both faucets in the shower, even though the shower head was dry. The same was true of the kitchen faucet. Luna followed me to the center of the house, wagging her tail but also whining.

"What's dripping, sweetie?"

She wagged and padded to the door.

"You want to go outside?" I yanked the front door wide open, hoping the fresh air would clear my mental cobwebs. There it was—the dripping, louder than ever. It was coming from the side of the house, where all the icicles were in a mad race to see who could thaw first. The snow had the ice-sheen of water melting in on itself, and the air smelled like the color green.

"Luna! A real January thaw! I guess those farmers knew what they were talking about."

To have a smell other than ion and snow was a gift. I knew it wouldn't last—it couldn't—but in this moment, I was filled with the hope of spring. It temporarily pushed away my stress like only hopeful weather can do. "Whoo-hoo!"

Luna dashed outside and ran crazy circles over the snow drifts in the yard, picking up on my energy. I glanced over my shoulder at the wall clock hung in the living room. It was 7:12 AM. I had time to shower, drive to the Fergus hospital to show Gary the letter, and still open the library on time.

———

"Knock knock." I'd arrived empty handed. I couldn't afford to bring any more treats to people. I barely fit in my jeans as it was. All I carried with me was a fervent wish that Gary's morphine dosage had been lowered. "It's me, Mira."

I ducked my head in. Gary was in the same position as yesterday, except his leg was no longer in the air, and he was wearing a crisp navy blue Battle Lake Police t-shirt and matching sweatpants. He also wore reading glasses halfway down his nose and was holding a newspaper. He did not glance my direction.

"Gary?"

He still didn't stir. I stepped into the room. "I have something to show—"

"Halt," he commanded, still not looking at me.

I stopped. I counted to thirty. He didn't say anything. "Did they switch your meds?" I asked.

"I don't know what you're talking about."

"When I came yesterday—" This time I stopped myself with his help. Was that a blush creeping up his neck? "You remember I was here yesterday, right?"

"I was on heavy painkillers. They shouldn't have allowed anyone in." His voice was sharp.

"You were pretty fun," I said, beginning to enjoy myself. "A real laugh riot."

The blush made a full migration to his scalp. He must have just enough memory of yesterday to be embarrassed. I tamped down a smile and pitched my voice serious. "You made me deputy, Gary. You promised we could start a task force as soon as you were released from the hospital, and that we'd go on stakeouts together. You don't remember any of that?"

He turned the page on the newspaper with such force that it sounded like slap.

"Gary," I said, making my voice soft and falsely injured. "You told me you loved me."

He glanced at me, stricken. Then he caught my expression, and pure fire began to burn in his eyes. I swear I could have roasted marshmallows over it, which I normally would find funny except for the flash of unguarded emotion I'd just witnessed. It had been only an instant, but it was enough to unsettle me. Did he have feelings for me? I immediately discarded the idea as impossible. He was drawn to me like a cat to water. I must have seen something else in his expression. Indigestion?

He returned his attention to his newspaper. "Get out."

"My pleasure," I said, adopting a bravado I certainly didn't feel. Whatever emotional roller coaster he was riding made me infinitely uncomfortable. I stepped out of the room, the letter tucked safely inside my jacket. No way was I going to show it to Gary now. I stomped out of the hospital, feeling more unsettled than angry.

TWENTY

THE BOOK RETURN BIN was overflowing when I arrived at work. How it could fill up when the library was closed always amazed me. There must be some sort of traveling virus that compelled mobs of people to bring back all their books at once. Either that, or it was connected to the phases of the moon. It didn't matter because reshelving books was one of my favorite parts of the library gig. It provided for me the same satisfaction as weeding my garden in the summer, letting me sink into the meditation of putting things where they belonged, removing stuff that didn't, and generally restoring order to the universe.

My opening duties took all of twenty minutes. I unlocked the front door three minutes early and stopped by my computer to check email before the first patrons arrived. My inbox was littered with spam offering me big boobs, sexy love mustache partners, and access to Jessica Simpson's beauty secrets. If I possessed any one of those, I was sure I wouldn't need the others. I deleted the spam and was left with one legitimate message, from Carter Stone at the Prospect House:

Mira,

Sorry you missed your visit in all the commotion, but of course we understand. Stop by anytime for a private tour.

Carter

I hit Reply and wrote that I'd like to stop by after work today between five and six o'clock. Might as well get to it lickety-split. Email responded to, and since I didn't yet have clientele or any pressing work, I figured I might as well open up the Cold Case file and call the rest of the Maurice Jacksons in Chicago so I could cross another item off my to-do list. Finding someone who could tell me more about him might shed light on what he had been doing in Battle Lake, and specifically what had gotten him killed.

I made thirteen successful calls in that I reached either a Maurice Jackson or the wife or child of a Maurice Jackson, but all thirteen were dead ends, either not owning a library card or never having been to Minnesota. I left a message with the two others, one that had a male voice on the answering machine and the other with a female voice. I left my name, my home number, and said I was calling from Minnesota and looking for Maurice, and then I made a note next to both numbers so I'd know who I had left to talk to. The library was starting to pick up, so I organized my notes before going to work helping people find books, shelving returns, and generally picking up the library.

Mrs. Berns showed up around lunchtime, still seeming a bit off. She didn't want to talk about it, though, so we both kept about our business. I was trying to clean a dusty, musty corner of the textured ceiling, all the little boinkies dropping on my upturned face and shoulders, when I heard a familiar throat clearing.

"Hi, Brad," I said, not glancing down. Brad—Bad Brad, as I referred to him in my head—had been my boyfriend in Minneapolis when Sunny first asked me to house-sit. We broke up right before I moved, and ending our dating life was one of my smartest moves ever. It was a comical irony that he was now living in Battle Lake. *Good one, Fate. Maybe you could reintroduce into my life every bad choice I'd ever made on some sort of rotating schedule, starting with my seventh-grade Ogilvie home perm.*

"Hey, Mira."

I recognized the particular voice he saved for rare moments of sadness. I chose to concentrate instead on delicately wiping the ceiling boinkies, imagining them to be ancient stalagmites and my dust cloth a huge bat weaving in and out.

He sighed, a long, tortured, drawn-out sound.

I did the same. "What is it?" I finally asked, dropping my arms. My hands instantly began to tingle as the blood returned to them.

"What do you mean?"

I rolled my eyes. Bad Brad was a handsome guy, it was true, with sort of a blonde Jim Morrison thing going on. Plus, he was in a band and I'm sorry, but that counts for something. Unfortunately, he was as smart as mud and as deep as a wading pool. And right now, his mascara was smudged, make-up being his new hallmark since he'd formed his latest group, Iron Steel, tagline "twice the metal."

"You look like you've been crying."

His shoulders slumped even farther, and he made a pitiful swipe at his eye. "I think my girlfriend is cheating on me."

I snorted, but at his wounded expression turned it into a cough, which ultimately came together as some sort of donkey honk. Cuz here's the deal. Did I mention that I had actually *caught* Bad Brad cheating on me? I still wasn't sure if "caught" was the right word. I witnessed him giving skin flute lessons after a hunch had me staring down a skylight into a borrowed bedroom, but I never confronted him because I sincerely doubted he could juggle an erection and a confrontation without burning through his wiring. So I'd simply moved without telling him why.

"The vomit returns to the dog," Mrs. Berns said, walking by with a stack of books in her arms. I didn't know if she was referring to me or Bad Brad. I glared at her in case it was me.

"I'm sorry to hear that," I told Brad, mostly truthfully. It's easy to forgive an ex after you finally realize you never should have dated him in the first place.

"I was going to marry that woman," he said, his face hanging so low that he resembled a bloodhound. Opening for KISS. He was wearing a leather jacket, a scarf, and a full face of make-up, after all.

"What's her name?" I asked, unsurprised at his confession. Bad Brad's marriage proposal was a cheap dress worn by too many women. He'd proposed to me twice while we were dating, once because he felt bad for showing up late and another time because he really liked my dress.

"Samantha. She's an insurance salesman in Alexandria."

"I think you mean 'agent.'"

"No," he said. "She sells insurance. For sure. I've been to her office."

My head hurt. A home perm would actually be preferable to this conversation. Heck, I'd even wear jelly shoes and acid-washed jeans while Fate put the curlers in. "That sounds really crappy, Brad. I'm sorry for you. But I've got a lot of work to do."

"That's what I'm here about," he said, his face brightening marginally. "I want to hire you to find out what Samantha is up to."

Mrs. Berns cackled from the other side of a bookshelf. I stepped off the ladder I'd been using and stood in front of Bad Brad. I had to crane my neck to look him in the eyes. Up close, he smelled like the Calvin Klein Obsession cologne I used to buy him.

"I can't help you," I said. "It'd be a conflict of interest since we used to date." *And you're always broke, and I'd rather roller skate naked through town than dig around your personal life.*

All hope drained out of his face. My heart tugged for a moment, but I held firm. It really was the best thing for him. Plus, Mrs. Berns was now laughing so hard that I couldn't hear myself think.

Bad Brad nodded dejectedly and shambled out without another word. Mrs. Berns walked over to me and together, we watched him go.

"I'm not saying the boy's dumb," she said, "but I'd be real surprised if he could fart and chew gum at the same time."

I nodded. Truer words. "Do you think his girlfriend is cheating on him?"

"I sure would," she said. "He's got the cute, but that doesn't fill up a woman for long. Anyways, why would you care? He's getting what's coming to him."

"I suppose." I turned my full attention on her. "Hey, why do you have your coat on?"

"I'm punching out early today. I got errands."

"Like what?"

"Like none of your business."

And she left.

TWENTY-ONE

THE DRIVEWAY LEADING TO the Prospect House had been recently salted, which was good, as the unusual warm-up had slickened the roads. I'd also noticed it was making people crazy jumpy like hibernators that've been awoken prematurely. I caught two separate patrons—regulars, both of them—walking out without checking out their books first, and one couple making out behind the encyclopedias. When I dropped a heavy book to get their attention, they both jumped up and scurried away, their expressions dazed. The weather was doing something to us. I could feel it in my own blood, which seemed to be moving a little faster and hotter than usual. Too bad Johnny was out of town tonight, performing in the Cities with The Thumbs.

As I parked my car, I realized it was the only one in the Prospect House lot, which gave me the opportunity to pretend like everything I laid eyes on was mine. I climbed out of my Toyota and glanced at the rear of the stately, shabby chic mansion with its ornate woodwork and matching servants' building next door. Maybe I was just returning from a quick jaunt to Italy to check on my vineyard, or a short flight to New York to visit with my stockbroker? Maybe my housekeeper was waiting inside with dinner. Or, maybe I had slipped on yesterday's jeans this morning, the only pair that hadn't shrunk overnight, and was about to get a tour of a cool old mansion so I could write a story about it. Yeah, that version fit best.

The front of the mansion, the side facing West Battle, had an ornate oak door trimmed with hand-carved designs and a huge metal knocker hung in the center. That door, Carter had informed me, was unused because it needed too much work, which is why the path wasn't shoveled. He'd instead requested I enter through the rear, a very plain wooden door that opened just as I reached for its knob.

"Mira James, I presume? Welcome!"

Carter Stone and I had never crossed paths, which in a town the size of Battle Lake was a small miracle. I'd seen photos of him on the *After the Battle* contributors' page, but those had been black-and-white and fuzzy. In real life, he was a handsome man in his sixties with an aging Peter Fonda à la *Easy Rider* air about him. His face was defined by a bushy gray-brown mustache and smile crinkles at the edges of his brown eyes. He was wearing a Civil War–style cap, a flannel shirt tucked in dark blue jeans, and work boots.

"Thank you. And thanks for making time to see me."

"Glad to have you. Any press we can get for the Prospect House is good press."

He led me into the kitchen, which looked and smelled like any farmhouse kitchen, though larger, with a mix of antique vases and modern appliances crowding the cupboards. A moveable butcher's block stood in the center of the kitchen, loaded with memorabilia. The far wall displayed reproduction postcards of the Prospect House from the early 1900s.

"These are so pretty," I said, stepping over for a closer look. "Do you have the originals?"

"Thousands," he said. "When I bought the house, every square inch was packed."

I thought of Gilbert Hullson. "Were the owners hoarders?"

He pushed his hat back and scratched the top his head before pulling the cap back in place. "I don't think so, at least not in the traditional sense. Everything was neat and organized. It's just that the house had become so expensive to heat that they ended up using it more as a storage space than anything."

"That's terrible."

He shook his head. "Best thing that could have happened, really. I don't have all the rooms cleaned out yet, but the ones that are have given up treasures you wouldn't believe. That's why I turned this into a museum. We've got Battle Lake's history here, and a good piece of the Civil War to boot. Unfortunately," he said, chuckling, "I'm a bit house poor at the moment. I'm hoping to get the place on the Historical Registry so I can save it, but until then, I've got to keep people coming through here so I can afford to heat and update it. That's why I'm offering tours before all the rooms are done."

"How much are you charging?"

"I ask for goodwill donations."

"What? How're you going to make money that way?"

He shrugged and led me into the next room, the dining room. "Anyone who wants to should be able to check out what we have here. Like this—see this rug?"

I glanced down at the gorgeous ruby-red Persian nearly as large as the room and patterned with exquisite golds and greens. I nodded.

"I cleared off boxes and found it underneath, good as new. I had an appraiser here who said it's a hundred years old." Every room he brought me into had a similar story of some treasure discovered. My favorite was the master bedroom, where he'd found pearl and jade jewelry from the 1920s that were now lying out on a dresser.

"Can I touch them?" I asked. I was drawn to a carnelian necklace, the stone the size of an apricot pit and set in gold. The chain was cleverly crafted into an interlocking leaf pattern.

"Be my guest."

I picked up the ornate necklace. It was surprisingly heavy, the gold so bright yellow that I questioned its authenticity. I flipped it over. TIFFANY & CO. was stamped on the back of the carnelian's setting. My breath caught. "You just leave this jewelry lying out?"

"Yup."

"What if someone steals it?"

"We don't have the money for locked viewing cases yet. If I don't set them out, people won't be able to see them."

"Can I take photographs?"

With his permission, I began snapping pictures of the jewelry, hand-crafted furniture (some of it original), and delicately hand-painted wallpaper. The building and collections were amazing, stunning, and right in my backyard. I couldn't believe he let people walk through here unsupervised, for free if they couldn't afford better. Even if everyone was as honest as Carter seemed to believe, what would stop a child from slipping a shiny bauble into her pocket? That thought spurred a memory. "Can I see the attic?"

He stopped, his hand on the third-floor stairway newel. "Afraid not. It's sealed off. I just recently cleared out space in the landing that would take you there."

I called up a picture of the little girl's face as it had appeared in the attic window on Saturday while I'd been skating. I now knew definitively that it had been a sleep-deprived illusion. Yet . . .

"Any rumors of this place being haunted?" I asked. Suddenly, the stairway felt like a threat, the shadows malicious rather than quaint.

He kept walking and I followed, tamping down my fear. It wasn't easy, as I had the feeling he was deliberately avoiding answering me. We'd reached the third floor, which had an Alice-in-Wonderland feel due to the close walls and six-foot ceilings. He pushed a black button in the wall, and a string of yellow lights lit up. He pointed toward a far corner, past desks and tables and boxes and garbage bags. "That leads to the attic. As for haunted, it's an old house. There's always been rumors. Most of them center on the hanging."

I swallowed hard. "What hanging?"

"A black man hung himself on the grounds near the end of the Civil War. Didn't know if he was from the North or the South, didn't know where to send his effects. It was the landowner's daughter, an Offerdahl, who found the body. She was staring up at it, if the stories are true, and she was mute from that day forward, until she died a year later."

I felt the devil walk up my spine. "I think I've seen enough up here," I said.

"Then let's go to the basement!" His eyes danced. "That's where all the Civil War memorabilia is."

———

Two hours later, I had my head full of Civil War facts, dreams of vintage jewelry, and a nagging sense that I was missing an obvious connection. Maybe food would help. I stopped at Mrs. Berns's downtown apartment on my way home to see if she wanted to join me, but no one answered her door. I popped into the Turtle Stew to purchase tater tot hotdish with a side of green beans to go. My stomach growled as I waited. Had I eaten lunch? Could I drive and eat hotdish at the same time?

When the waitress handed me the Styrofoam square, it had a satisfying weight. I took a big sniff, enjoying the smell of crispy, salty tots layered over a creamy blend of mushroom soup and ground turkey. I may have moaned a little. I wanted to race home to eat it but decided to stop by the library to pick up a copy of *After the Battle*, so I could further research the Prospect House from the comfort of home, my animals by my side, my belly protruding as it happily digested two pounds of hotdish like a snake with a rabbit.

Unusual for me, my strategy unfolded exactly as planned. An hour later, I'd licked out the inside of the Styrofoam, settled onto the couch with Luna at my feet and Tiger Pop on my lap, and was paging through *After the Battle*, an open notepad at my side. I turned the pages slowly, sucked into the history of the town against my will. The book contained photographs of downtown Battle Lake in the 1800s looking exactly like a *Little House on the Prairie* set, and copies of newspaper articles a hundred years old with titles like "America's Answer to Humanity's Challenge." There was even a photo of Richard Nixon visiting Glendalough State Park in 1956.

I eventually made it to the page devoted to the Prospect House, which I'd read before but not with the same perspective as I had now. Unfortunately, it didn't offer any new information, so I read through the newspaper articles looking for anything related to the House. This is the first I found, a near identical recounting of the story Carter had told me:

"Young Offerdahl Girl Finds Negro Hanging in Woods"

Poor Elizabeth Offerdahl, who lost her mother the day she was born and whose father died a hero in the war, has been dealt another blow. In a gruesome discovery, she found the body of an unidentified man, believed to be a recently freed slave, hanging from an oak tree in the woods behind the Prospect House. The body was in a serious state of decay, leading authorities to believe he had been hanging there for at least two months. He was dressed in a black jersey sweater, a collared shirt, gray or brown trousers, and new black shoes. The rope he hung himself with was new and much better preserved than his clothes or flesh. He was dangling nearly three feet off the ground, and it is surprising his body was not found earlier, as it was in a well-traversed area, though it is winter.

Unless identifying information is found in the effects or someone comes forward, the hanged man's identity will probably never be known. Elizabeth is currently under the care of her uncle, Hugh Offerdahl, and his wife, Adelaide Offerdahl. She is being treated by Dr. Olson for debility.

The article was dated March 7, 1865. I read it twice and could still not process the focus on Elizabeth Offerdahl over the poor man whose life had been lost. I realized it was different times, but the reminder of just how different left me unsettled. I continued to page through the newspaper section of the book, hoping for a follow-up article. My search seemed fruitless, I thought, as I flipped one page after another and scanned the headlines. Then, I turned to the final page, and there it was: "Scarlet Fever Epidemic Claims Its First Victim: Elizabeth Offerdahl." Below that was a photo of an eight-year-old girl with haunted eyes and the exact same heart-shaped face I'd seen in the attic window of the Prospect House.

It wasn't a hallucination. She was haunting the House.

A greasy cold crawled down my spine. I suddenly had a strong urge to lock my door, even though that would be little protection against ghosts. Still. It couldn't hurt. I gently lifted Tiger Pop off of my lap and stood, glancing over my shoulder and all around.

"Hey, Luna, come to the door with me." It was all of seven feet away from where I'd been sitting on the couch, but that suddenly seemed a great distance.

She was game, though, and stood, tail wagging. I smiled. "Thanks—"

Before I got out her name, her ears flattened to her head, and she growled, a low, primal sound that scared my last wit, the one that had been holding strong. She was staring at the front door. Her scruff stood in the air, and she crouched. The room was charged with a buzzing energy. I was soul-terrified, prickles of heat and cold alternating across my skin.

Just when I thought I'd lose my mind in that humming, horrifying waiting space, a knock struck the front door like Death's knell.

TWENTY-TWO

I SQUEAKED AND DROPPED to the ground. Where that instinct came from, I didn't know. Maybe a fainting goat as a distant ancestor?

I considered my situation from the crouch on the floor. I had been standing in front of the sofa when the rap on the door came, facing the bay windows which were jungle-thick with green plants, the closest I could get to gardening in the winter. The plants and my attention on the book explained why I hadn't noticed the person walk to the door, right? For sure it wasn't because my guest was actually an invisible ghost who could reconstitute herself enough to knock when she returned to feed on living souls.

I listened to my shallow breath, the nub of the carpeting digging into my sore knee. I'm sure there was a perfectly safe, normal, live human on the other side of my door.

Still, all instincts said a dark closet was the best place to be right now.

I was in mid-scurry, pointed toward the bedroom, when the front door opened. Kennie popped her head in, her glance immediately going to me on all fours scuttling across the room.

"Yoo-hoo! You said to come in, didn't you? What're you doing down there? Did you drop something?"

Only my heart and about five pounds of chicken fat. "What are you doing here?"

Kennie cocked her head like a curious bird, an effect enhanced by the feathered Mardi Gras mask she'd pushed to the crown of her platinum hair. She was otherwise sedately dressed, for her, at least the parts of her I could see peeking inside the door. She wore a brown fur stole around her neck, matching gloves, and a black cloth coat. "I told you I was going to stop by, silly. To counsel your pets and your plants?"

Luna amped up her growl, but at a blinding smile from Kennie, she switched to a whine and hunkered down on the ground next to me. I felt bad for her. She was a smart dog, but like most canines, she didn't know she could prevent many things from happening to her. For example, me putting sunglasses over her tail and taking giggling pictures of her "gonzo face," or turning her ears inside out and telling her I could see her brains. Tiger Pop, on the other hand, took advantage of the open door to slip outside and away from Kennie.

I stood and brushed off my knees. That's when I noticed that her fur stole was wiggling. Luna observed it too, and she growled low in her throat. I put my hand out to comfort her.

"Are you *wearing* Peter?"

Kennie's face brightened, and she stepped fully into the house, closing the door behind her. She reached around her neck to pull the alert wiener dog off and into her arms. "I sure am," she said, nuzzling his pointy nose. "It's easier than carrying him when he has one of his spells. So, where should I start?"

Resistance only makes it stronger. "I don't have many plants, just these in the window," I lied. "And Luna." Tiger Pop would surely not return while Kennie was still around.

"Perfect." Kennie set Peter on the floor. He wiggled over to Luna, and they sniffed noses. Luna placed her big German Shepherd paw on Peter's side and pushed him gently to the ground. Peter stayed there, feet in the air, tongue lolling out. Luna smiled back at him, then went into the kitchen to drink some water.

Kennie ignored both animals, instead focusing on my aloes, jade tree, ferns, ivy, African violets, and ficus. She introduced herself to each one of them and gave them a chance to say a little something about themselves. At first I was sure it was one of the craziest things I'd ever seen, but then I started to feel a bit jealous. What if they liked her more than they liked me? Or worse, what if they revealed some of my secrets? Oh my god. Crazy is contagious.

"Will this take long?" I asked Kennie.

She slipped off her coat, revealing a dress constructed of green, purple, and yellow Mardi Gras beads. "Not too long, love. I have a party to go to."

"Mardi Gras isn't until February."

"Mmmhmm," she murmured, staring at a jade tree I'd grown from a clipping as if it were telling her its life story. "It's not a Mardi Gras party."

Underneath the dress, she wore fishnet stockings and four-inch black heels. I had to admit, she had killer legs. I was positive I didn't want to know any more about the party, however. I knew for a fact that Kennie did things behind closed doors that should never see the light. In fact, I'd stumbled upon a house full of such activities last May. "Are you almost done?"

She ignored me, staring fixedly at the plants as if her eyes were the sun. I began to clean my kitchen, slamming cupboards a little louder and running water a little longer than necessary. It made me itchy having Kennie in my house, and particularly watching her bestow attention to something besides herself.

"Know anything about Gary Wohnt?" I asked when I couldn't bear her silence any longer.

"He gets out of the hospital tomorrow," she said. "He'll be behind the desk for a while, but he should be fine. As far as I know, they still have no idea who shot him."

"How about the body in the ice? Do they know any more about him?"

She turned to face me. The lamplight reflected off the lip of her perched mask, giving her eyes a deep-set, glittering cast. "Maurice Jackson had two gunshot wounds in his chest, but they don't think that's what killed him. He had water in his lungs. You know what that means, right? Somebody shot him and then shoved him in the lake to drown."

TWENTY-THREE

My RESTLESS, FRETFUL, UNDER-BED sleep was fraught with nightmares of pink piñata pigs dressed in Mardi Gras streamers and strung from the ceiling, getting whacked with sticks shaped like wiener dogs. The night before, I'd ejected Kennie from the house in less than an hour, but the damage to my psyche was likely permanent.

I rolled out from under the bed and padded straight to the shower, not even bothering to brush my hair. Standing under the hot water, I focused on sending all my stress to the skin level so it could wash off like dirt. Maurice, the man who had saved me from the whangsters, had been murdered, and I hadn't been able to locate any information about him beyond the Chicago Public Library card. The next day, Police Chief Gary Wohnt had been shot in what appeared to be a routine pull-over. In his drug-induced haze, he'd called me beautiful, which was about as desirable as finding a bug crawling in your underwear.

That was followed by one of the whangsters tossing me a copy of an obscure, cryptic letter that I didn't know what to do with. On the

Operation Offerdahl side, I needed to locate Eric, who was somehow tied to the Prospect House. In addition, I still owed Ron Sims an article on the House, something was up with Mrs. Berns, and Kennie Rogers had spent the better part of an hour cooing to my plants and sending "healing chi waves" into poor Luna's brain. Did that just about cover it? Wait—almost forgot. I now slept under my bed, and I liked it. The only normal thing in my life was Johnny, and I hadn't seen him in two days. It was too much. My head was ringing.

And ringing.

It wasn't until the answering machine clicked over that I realized it was actually the phone I was hearing. *Let the machine get it.* I stretched my arms under the steaming stream of water. I had a stress knot the size of a tangerine between my shoulder blades.

I listened for the sound of a voice through the bathroom door, but none came.

Must not have been important.

The ringing began again almost immediately. I didn't want to abandon the hot shower for the brisk morning air. Didn't want to dribble all over the floor. Didn't want to face the day. This internal whining kept me through the next cycle of ringing, which ended as soon as the machine clicked on and started up the second my voice recording stopped. Whoever was calling was not going to be deterred.

Reluctantly, I turned off the water, wrapped a towel around my hair and another under my arms, and treaded softly to the kitchen, trying not to slip in my own footprints. I snatched the phone just before the machine got it.

"Hello."

Silence.

"Hello?" I strained my ears. Was that crying I heard in the background? "Hello, this is Mira James. Do you need help?"

"Naw, hold on." The female voice had a distinct twang, a cross between Southern and inner-city. "Timothy, you get your sister a bottle, you hear? I'm on the phone."

I stood, water dripping off me and pooling at my feet. I held the towel closed over my chest and balanced the phone in the nook of my shoulder so I had a free hand to crank up the thermostat. Sixty-two degrees is great when you're saving energy but brutal when you're wet and there's snow outside.

"Yeah, this Mira James?"

"Yup." I refrained from adding *still* on the end of my sentence. The baby's wail grew louder in the background.

"This is Taunita House. You called me yesterday? Left a message looking for Maurice Jackson?"

My heart picked up, and I looked around the kitchen for a pen and paper. "You're in Chicago?"

"That's where I live, but I'm actually in Minnesota now. I'm trying to track Maurice down. His kids want to see him. So do I."

I paused with my hand halfway to the notepad magnetized to the side of the fridge. I gulped, feeling like I'd just swallowed a cold rock. I had made the connection, but at what cost? Maurice had kids, at least two. And a girlfriend, who apparently had no idea he was dead. "Maurice Jackson is your boyfriend? Can you describe him?"

I heard the shrug over the phone line. "About five-ten, hundred forty-five pounds. Skinny sucker, skinnier than me. Turns twenty-three in February. Kept his hair trimmed short, earring in his left ear. Was wearing a green Land's End parka I bought him for Christmas when he left. He took off three weeks ago to look up some old relatives in

126

Minnesota, he said. He hasn't called in two days, though, and his work leave has about dried up. It's time for him to stop this nonsense and come home, but since he clearly doesn't have the sense for that, I'm coming to get him."

The rock dropped into my stomach. That described the Maurice I'd helped at the library—and whose corpse I'd skated over—to a T.

"Have you tried all his friends?"

"I have. And now I'm trying you. In your message you said you were looking for him, too. Why?"

The crying in the background had stopped. Now I heard a giggle. "How many kids do you and Maurice have?"

"Two," she said impatiently. "Timothy is three years. Alessa was born last year Christmas. Maurice said it was his present for me. I told him he better get me something that makes less noise next holiday." She laughed ruefully, then her voice grew serious. "I miss him. Have you seen him?"

I couldn't do it. I couldn't ram the truth into her ear with her kids laughing in the background. I told her the version that I could bear. "I live in Battle Lake, northwest of the Cities? Maurice came into the library where I work last week. He left his Chicago library card, and I was hoping to track him down."

"Well, that's some service," she said wryly. "If he stops by again, tell him Taunita and the babies want him to call, okay?"

"Will do," I said, feeling like a monster for not coming clean. I kept that feeling with me as I finished getting ready that morning, and it was hung so thickly over me that I almost walked out of the house without noticing my plants. Something was off with them.

It took a lot of squinting before I realized what it was: they looked healthier than they ever had.

TWENTY-FOUR

THE PARKING SPOT IMMEDIATELY in front of the Fortune Café was open, which was the first good thing that had happened since I'd woken up. I steered my Toyota snugly between a Ford and a Chevy pickup, one rusty and the other spanking new but road-splattered and sporting a Ducks Unlimited sticker in the rear window. A handful of people on the street took mincing steps as they went about their day, trying their hardest to stay upright as the two previous days' brief thaw—warmer during the day, freezing at night—had turned the sidewalks into treacherous frozen sheets. I chose to not lift my feet off the ground, instead skating over the top of the greenish-black ice.

When I pulled open the door to the Café, I was immediately awash in the warm scent of freshly ground dark roast and cinnamon scones, and the happy burble of gathering people. Buddy Holly was crooning softly in the background. I yanked off my mittens, tapped the winter off my boots, and got in line. I didn't recognize any of the half-dozen or so people sprinkled around the main room, though I spotted

Bernie Nordman, co-owner of Ace Hardware, make her way into the computer/library/board game back room with a steaming mug in one hand and what appeared to be a cherry Danish in the other. My stomach growled so loud that the woman in front of me turned and flashed a smile.

I grinned back, embarrassed. When my turn came, I knew exactly what I wanted. "Everything bagel, toasted, with Greek olive cream cheese and a slice of fresh tomato, a large green tea with honey and soy milk, and maybe a cherry Danish for later?"

"Hi to you, too," Nancy said, grinning. She owned the Café along with her partner, Sidney. Sid was not a people person by nature but was a brilliant pastry chef and kept mainly to the kitchen. Nancy was friendly and never seemed to become stressed, no matter how many people were in line. She'd helped me through a tough patch in July, and we'd been fast friends ever since. "You must be hungry."

I blushed for the second time in under four minutes. "Sorry. You seem so busy. I didn't want to waste your time with chit-chat."

"Like talk about a police chief who was shot, or a mayor with a strange new business, for example?"

I pointed my chin at the gorgeous row of plants lining her front window. "You obviously don't need Kennie's help. I've never seen your plants look better."

"Kennie *was* here," Nancy said, sounding as incredulous as I felt. "I think that's why they look so good. Maybe she finally found her thing."

I was surprised to feel another pang of jealousy. Gardening had been *my* thing. I loved digging my hands into the dirt in the summer, dropping seeds into the thick black earth, watering them, mulching them, petting the soft shoots when they first popped up. Weeding was my meditation. Come winter, I'd started a mini-greenhouse herb garden in the back bedroom, which I'd intentionally hidden from Kennie. I felt the jealousy sprout and took a deep, deliberate breath. Really, what was to be envious about? The more love the plants received, the better.

"Maybe," I said agreeably. Well, almost agreeably. Okay, I was still pissy.

Nancy continued to talk as she poured the hot water into the travel mug I'd brought and popped the two halves of my bagel into the toaster. "Know anything about Gary?"

"Kennie said he's getting out of the hospital today, but she didn't know anything about who might have shot him."

"As uptight as he can be, it'll be nice to have him back, what with all the robberies." She ducked her head into the counter fridge and came out with a tub of cream cheese.

"Robberies?" My stomach growled again. The Fortune's cream cheese was amazing, the perfect blend of creaminess accented with salty slices of green and black olives.

Nancy nodded. "Empty cabins around the lake. Whoever is doing it is taking TVs and computers, some kitchen appliances if they look valuable, I guess. They're not damaging the cabins except for the new one that went up on the north side of Silver Lake. Almost over in your neck of the woods. They trashed that one."

I knew the area well. I'd had a run-in with a scalped corpse there a few months back. The memory made me shudder.

Nancy glanced at me sympathetically, as if she were reading my mind. She slid the wax paper–wrapped bagel into a small brown bag, and stacked a cherry Danish and a lemon Danish on top of that, another thin sheet of wax paper separating the two. She winked. "For lunch."

"Thanks," I said, taking the bag and sliding her a five. The food was ridiculously inexpensive. "Wait! I almost forgot. I owe Curtis some treats. Can you make up a bag for me to take to the Sunset?"

Another five dollars later, I was out the door with two bags in one hand and my travel mug filled with steaming tea in the other. I was in the process of transferring it all to one hand so I could open the Fortune's door with the other when it swung open. In walked Mrs. Berns.

"I have had just about the most terrible day of my life," she said to me, as if she'd expected me to be standing exactly where I was.

"What happened?" I looked her up and down, checking for an injury or torn clothing.

She scowled. "Is that any of your business?"

"What? You just … forget it." I would have thrown my hands in the air if they weren't so full. Something was clearly still off with Mrs. Berns, and she was going to tell me in her own sweet time. "Are you coming to work today?"

She stretched her arms. "Doesn't sound too exciting. What else can you offer?"

I sighed. "I'm touring the new microbrewery in Swederland as soon as I close the library. It's part of a small case from Litchfield."

"Now you're cooking with Crisco! Pick me up at five o'clock."

She held the door open for me as I eased out and mostly slid to my car. I balanced the bag and the tea on the Toyota's roof and brought them in with me as soon as I had the door open. I let my car reheat while I devoured half my bagel, loving the chewiness of the fresh-baked roll, the cream cheese oozing out the sides, the sharp earthiness of the tomato the perfect foil for it all. The second half was polished off before I reached the nursing home. I ran the treats into a grateful Curtis then pulled into the library parking lot fifteen minutes early.

All in all, I'd had worse mornings. At least, I had until I saw Bad Brad standing outside the library door, hands in pockets, head hung like a dog on the way to the vet.

TWENTY-FIVE

RATHER THAN SPEAK TO Bad Brad, I acted as if he wasn't there at all. He followed me into the library like a droopy shadow and stuck close to my side as I went about my duties. It got so I almost forgot he was there, until he chose to speak.

"Have you looked at her Facebook page?"

"Whose?" Of course I knew who he was talking about.

"My girlfriend's."

"Why would I look at your girlfriend's Facebook page?"

"I thought you'd change your mind about the conflict of interest and help me out."

"Nope."

I turned on the front desk computer and stepped from behind the counter to switch on the public computers. When I returned to the front, I saw Brad was standing at my desktop, clicking away.

"What are you doing? You can't be on that."

His shoulders dropped lower, if that was possible. He pointed at the screen. "See for yourself."

I sighed. "If I look at your girlfriend's Facebook page, will you leave?"

"Yes."

I dragged my feet around the counter and stood beside him. A blue-rimmed page was pulled up on the computer. It featured a head-shot of a pretty blonde. A lake panorama was spread out behind her head. Her name, according to the page, was Samantha Lehmkuhl. "I don't see anything."

"That's the problem." He pointed to a white box under her photo that declared her birthday and that she was female. "Why doesn't it say she's in a relationship?"

I squinted at the screen. "It's supposed to say that?"

"It can, if the person chooses to make that part of their status."

Wow. I did not like this new world where there were so many more ways to be bonkers. My brain flitted through some possibilities. A person could break up with you on Facebook, and the whole world would know before you did. And after the break-up, you could return to your ex's page and check out what they were up to, maybe see if they'd moved on before you had. It was enough to make a person sick. Thank goodness I had dependable, sane, loyal Johnny. The thought of him sent a delicious wave across my nerve ends. Man, that boy was good-looking. And an amazing kisser who also smelled clean, laughed at my jokes, and cleaned up after himself. Why hadn't I immediately rescheduled our Sunday night interrupted date? I added him to my mental to-do list.

"Are you hot?" Brad asked, studying me. "Your face is all red."

I flushed deeper. Last spring, it had taken him two weeks to notice I'd moved to Battle Lake, but here he was being all Amazing Kreskin with my arousal state. "I think I'm allergic to Facebook."

He minimized the window. "Will you take the case? Please, Mira. For me. I love this woman."

I had a million retorts to that, but none I could summon in the face of his obviously heartbroken state. "Fine," I muttered.

"Thank you!" He bundled me into his arms and kissed the top of my head. "I owe you one. Whatever you need, you just tell me."

"I need you to leave so I can get some work done."

"Great! All these books make me nervous, anyhow. What if people see me in a library?"

"That will surely set their tongues a-wagging," I said dryly. "Now, be off. I'll be in touch if I find anything."

"You're a good person, Mira," he said, before the door closed pneumatically behind him.

I watched him disappear around a corner. I had zero romantic feelings for him, but maybe we could be friends. His case would have to wait, though. I pulled out my Cold Case file and retrieved the letter supposedly written by Orpheus Jackson from my pocket and smoothed it on my desk.

18 January 1865

Dear Loretta:

I wish I could write with better news. In Minnesota, they do not believe the messages I bring. I do not think I can stay here. I pack my bags to return home tomorrow. Should anything happen to me, look to the tunnel of justice.

With a heart that beats only for you,
Orpheus Jackson

I had a hunch that if Maurice hadn't been related to Orpheus, he at least believed he was. Was this somehow connected to the relatives Maurice had told Taunita he was coming to Minnesota to find? On a hunch, I strode back to the local shelf where Maurice had spent many hours the week before his death. I paged through all the references, looking for notes or dog-ears, and tipped them all sideways hoping something would fall out. Nothing.

But my Cold Case file was thin, and I sensed there was a connection—real or imagined—between Maurice and Orpheus, so I began researching Orpheus. Using the search terms *Orpheus Jackson* and *1800s*, I didn't come up with a thing. When on a hunch I threw *Barnaby Offerdahl* into the mix, though, I was brought to a full article on the Battle of Honey Hill, a Civil War battle fought in South Carolina on November 30, 1864. O. Jackson was listed as a freeman from the north serving in the 54th Massachusetts, and B. Offerdahl as a landowner in the 1st Minnesota Artillery Battery. The battle was a failed expedition under Major General John P. Hatch. The Confederates were too well-entrenched to rout, and the Union lost 89 men, with 629 wounded and 28 missing.

The date on Orpheus's letter suggested he was one of the Union survivors, but was this the battle that had killed Barnaby, and if so, what did that have to do with Orpheus, and why was he in Minnesota in 1865? Was he bearing a message from Barnaby? And what could this message possibly have to do with Maurice, nearly 150 years later? I had more questions than answers. To save myself the headache of carrying them spinning in my head, I wrote them down and shoved them into my Cold Case folder before moving on to Operation Offerdahl and the search for a *present-day* member of the family.

I returned to my database and set a wider search for Eric, looking for anyone who shared the surname. There were tens of thousands of

Offerdahls, but when I narrowed it to Minnesota, there were far fewer. When I narrowed it even further, to criminal history, I found a Gregory and Patrice Offerdahl. A quick call to Curtis verified that had been the name of Eric's parents. They were both mostly crime-free except for a line of bounced checks following them all the way to Phoenix, Arizona. My records showed Patrice had died four years earlier, and that Gregory still owned seven prime lakefront acres abutting or near the Prospect House, but little else. Gregory was seventy-eight and currently resided at 1923 Orangetree Lane, Phoenix, Arizona. I printed out the records and got to work running the library.

My morning passed in a blink. I finished four special orders, including tracking down and ordering a nonfiction book on abominable snowmen and another on tapping into your psychic ability. I watered the plants and dusted their leaves, wondering if I should have Kennie visit as a favor to a snake plant that was looking yellow and tragic around the edges. I showed an elderly man how to access the Internet and watched happily as he began researching his family tree. For lunch, I slammed both Danishes and promised myself I'd start working out just as soon as nature joined my team and melted the rest of the snow.

The afternoon was spent preparing the library's February budget, helping patrons check out books, planning activities for next week's children's hour, answering emails requesting use of the library's public meeting room, and updating the library website. By the time closing rolled around, I felt like I'd run a marathon. I did a last walkthrough of the stacks to make sure I'd shooed everyone out and no surprises had been left behind before running across town to pick up Mrs. Berns. I was hoping we could make it to O'Callaghan's for the six o'clock tour.

My car idled outside her apartment building. I honked, hoping to save myself a trip into the cold air. I fumbled with the radio knob while I waited, hoping as I always did for something more than country or Journey. I settled on "Saturday in the Park." My car was too old for a CD player, and I didn't have the heart to carry mixed tapes with me. I took what I could get.

A flash of color caught my eye, and I glanced up and to my right. Mrs. Berns was leaving the building wearing lederhosen. She was carrying her own massive beer stein. When she slipped into the car, she smelled like face powder and dish soap.

"Lederhosen?"

She held the stein in the air, a broad smile on her face. "*Prost!*"

I smiled back. I couldn't help it. She was lovely with her apricot-tinged white hair curling around her ears, penciled-in eyebrows, her watery blue eyes rimmed by uneven green eye shadow, her mouth a perfect heart of coral lipstick. The deep lines of her face were highlighted by the wide grin.

"I think they supply cups with their samples," I offered, indicating her stein.

"Pah. Probably little Dixie cups. I need a woman-sized taste to know if I'll like it or not."

We drove in companionable silence for three or four miles. At least I thought it was companionable, until Mrs. Berns punched me in the arm.

"What was that for?"

"You didn't ask me what's wrong."

"I asked you a couple days ago, and then the day after that! You nearly bit my head off."

"That's how you know I care."

I tapped my signal to turn right onto County Road 23 and rubbed my arm. "Your love kinda hurts."

"Hmph." She crossed her arms.

"All right, I'll bite. What's wrong?"

"What makes you think something is wrong?"

I groaned in frustration. "Besides you asking me to ask you just now? Well, you've been a Crabby Appleton since you made that Al-Anon crack at Matthew's birthday party, and it seems like you're avoiding me."

She didn't respond. I tossed her a tentative sideways glance and was horrified to see fat tears rolling down the canvas of her face. I pulled over immediately and pushed the button for my emergency lights. I gathered her into my arms, amazed at how fragile she felt, like a grounded sparrow.

She pushed me away almost immediately. Almost. "I'm not a big baby. You can let me go. I just had something in my eye. An onion, I think."

"I'm not going anywhere until you tell me what's up."

"Fine." She pulled a handkerchief out of her chest-freezer-sized purse and blew her nose. "My husband was a drinker. He was a good man who paid the bills and never raised his hand to me or the children, but once his work was done, he'd drink whiskey until he passed out."

Sounded familiar. I wondered why Mrs. Berns hadn't told me any of this before. She knew all about my dad.

"When he finally died ten years ago, I didn't know what to do with myself. I loved him, of course, but between taking care of him and raising my kids, I'd never had my own life. I started going to Al-Anon and went willingly into the nursing home because that's what my kids wanted. Then one day, about when you came to town, I realized it isn't what *I* wanted. I wanted to finally be my own person. So I rented an apartment and started living my life in the open. Turns out I like to dance, and sing, and kiss men half my age. Hell, I love it. I love everything about my life."

"Then what's wrong?"

She tried to set the beer stein on the dash, but it was too tall. "It's my grandkids. They're coming to visit this week."

I had met Mrs. Berns's five kids, most of whom lived within an hour or two drive and another who lived in Arizona, but never her grandkids. "Isn't that good news?"

"They haven't seen the real me. They remember me from when their grandpa was still alive, or from me visiting them. They haven't seen me in my natural habitat."

"But you don't care what anyone thinks of you!"

She laid her hands in her lap. "I guess I do. It matters to me what my grandkids think. I've decided it's easier to pretend I'm someone else for a couple days, but that decision isn't sitting well."

It took me a minute to digest this. Mrs. Berns was pure confidence, or so I'd thought. She was everything I wanted to be when I grew up. "How old are your grandkids?"

"Trevor is a year or two older than you. Michelle is twenty-seven. They live in Arizona. The last time they visited, I was in the Sunset and plenty happy to act a role for them. It's what grandparents do, so all you kids don't know we have better sex and take better drugs than you could ever dream of."

Her words carried the ring of truth. "Are they brother and sister?"

"Yup. Only one of my kids had kids, which should tell you something. They're coming because Michelle is being transferred to Fargo, and Trevor wants to help her move and visit family."

I thought back to July, when Mrs. Berns had faux-kidnapped the adult male mascot from the Chief Wenonga Days parade. She'd had her cap guns slung low at her side and he'd been dressed like a stereotypical Indian when they'd last been spotted. A friend had been about to file a missing person's report on the mascot's behalf when the two of them were discovered in a very compromising position. How had she ever kept a personality like that under wraps?

I exhaled loudly and patted her arm. "They'll love you exactly as you are, hun. In fact, I'd be pretty surprised if they didn't know more about the real you than you think."

She studied my face thoughtfully. A quiet moment stretched out between us. "You are a wise, dear friend, Mira. I don't know what I'd do without you."

I felt a tear warm my eye. "Really?"

"No. That was pure horseshit. You know what I'd do without you? I'd see fewer dead bodies, that's what. What I was doing there was a little thing called acting, and I happen to be very good at it. Now drive. I've done enough whining. It's time to soldier up and accept the inevitable."

I put the car into first gear. "You gonna show them the real Mrs. Berns?"

"I'll let you know when I decide. And if you tell anyone about my moment of weakness, I swear to God I'll tattoo a mustache on your face in your sleep."

"I love you, too," I said, smiling inside.

TWENTY-SIX

THERE WERE PLENTY OF signs pointing the way to O'Callaghan's, all of them featuring a green shamrock and the promise of "the best beer brewed in Minnesota." It was no coincidence that I thought that "best beer brewed in Minnesota" was about as significant as being the "tallest leprechaun," but that might be an unfounded stereotype.

We took what was promised to be the "final turn before O' Callaghan's" and found ourselves in the circular driveway of a farm. The grounds consisted of a cute, slanted-roof farmhouse, a red barn and two matching outbuildings, and a tow truck with the words *Tyrannosaurus Wrecks* painted on the side.

"T Wrecks? This can't be right," I said. I drove up to the house intending to turn around when I noticed the man leaning on the porch rail wearing lined Carhartt coveralls. He appeared to be staring at a lone cow in a pasture about 300 yards away.

"Is he cute?" Mrs. Bern said, squinting in his direction.

"Hard to tell from here. I'm going to ask him where the brewery is."

"I'm coming with," she said. "It's time to diversify my dating menu. Besides, remember that you're on the job. You might need backup."

I doubted it. He was maybe five-eight, a little paunchy. In his sixties, judging by the way he hunched and the bits of gray I spotted sneaking out of his John Deere cap. Mrs. Berns got jazzed about "working cases" with me when she had a chance, though, so I didn't stop her.

"Hello?" I said as we approached the porch.

He must have heard the car pull up and the doors slam shut, and he most certainly heard my greeting. He didn't turn.

"Sir? We're looking for O'Callaghan's. Are we close?"

By way of answer, he pointed at the cow. She was your standard black and white, standing in a barren snowscape broken only by a metal pole and a heated water barrel. "You see that?"

"Yes," I said, exchanging a woo-woo look with Mrs. Berns. "The cow?"

"Not just any cow. She is my nemesis. Kicks me when I try to milk her, breaks free of the fence every day and out of the barn every night no matter how often I mend both, and moos so much I want to cut my own ears off. I want to catch her to sell her, but she's too smart. See that metal pole? I coated it with salt. Figured she'd lick it and I'd get her good. But she won't lick it. She just stares at it."

Mrs. Berns walked around to the farmer's front and flicked him on the head. "That's about the batshit craziest plan I ever heard. Why don't you just corral her in the barn?"

He stepped back, surprised. "I can't. She slips away."

"You're getting what you deserve, then. Now where's the brewery?"

The front door of the farmhouse slammed open and a woman dressed in head-to-toe winter camo and holding a James-Bond-spear-gun-looking weapon tromped onto the porch. "You folks lost?"

"Yep," I said, taking an involuntary step back.

Mrs. Berns did the opposite. She leaned forward and touched the gun. "That a paintball gun?"

"Zenith Azodin," the woman said proudly.

"What're you hunting?"

"Hunters."

A crafty smile crossed Mrs. Berns's face. "Only thing legal to hunt right now is wolves."

"Exactly," the woman said. "I have no problem if someone wants to hunt for meat. If you're going to hunt for sport, though, prepare to have the tables turned." She held her weapon in the air.

"I'm in!" Mrs. Berns said.

"The more the merrier. I've got an extra gun inside. Name's Vienna, by the way."

I stared in disbelief. "You can't hunt hunters! They've got real guns."

"I wear orange," the woman said, "and I'm in a deer blind."

"That is the worst idea *ever*," I said, "and I've heard some pretty bad ideas." I looked to the farmer for support, but he had returned his full attention to the cow in the field, who was in turn staring at the salty metal pole as if it were a Gordian knot.

"I took a wrong turn and ended up in Insane City, Iowa," I said, shaking my head in disbelief. "And I thought Battle Lake could get weird."

"I thought you were looking for O'Callaghan's," Vienna said.

"I thought so, too."

"The turn is a hundred feet past our driveway. Their land abuts ours. You can't miss it, once you know where to look. Hopefully when they get the new sign up yonder, people'll stop pulling in here."

"Are you coming, Mrs. Berns?"

"Pick me up on your way back," she said, tugging on the orange vest the woman handed her. "I'm going to seize this moment."

I felt the distinct stress knot between my shoulder blades expanding as I drove away. It was grappling toward my arms, head, and lower back like an octopus after prey. Deep breathing didn't touch it. Maybe beer would. I'd gone on the wagon in October and fallen off a couple times since. I didn't want to go down the same path as my dad and had pinballed between exactly reliving his drinking habits and being completely dry. Neither seemed to work for me, and so last month I'd decided to try drinking like a normal person. This was a hard thing to gauge in a county where consuming alcohol qualified as a winter sport, but my goal was to only imbibe socially and never have more than two at a sitting. I had no interest in ever being drunk again. I'd made too many bad choices in that state.

The second road past the T Wrecks driveway led me directly to O'Callaghan's, a sprawling log lodge planted next to a factory building, both tucked behind a hill and so invisible from the road. A dozen or so vehicles peppered the parking lot in front of the lodge, and a large banner with white letters was strung over the door "Welcoming All to O'Callaghan's Microbrewery!"

Just inside the door, a woman in her early twenties with a wide smile handed me a grapefruit-sized sticker in the shape of a shamrock. "Are you here for our six o'clock tour?"

"I am." I gaped at the enormous interior. It was one big room, with tills lining the wall directly inside the door, a shopping area in the middle, a full bar in the back left, and tables in the back right. The ambience was half box store, half Irish pub.

"Wonderful! Stick the shamrock on your coat, and you can wait over by the rear door with the rest of the folks."

I followed her finger to the other side of the lodge where I counted eight people—two couples, two kids, and two college-aged men—wearing green shamrocks and standing by a metal door marked TOUR. "That's quite a few people for a Tuesday," I said.

"We've been very popular," she said, her smile widening.

Her name tag read AEDNAT. I pointed at it. "Is that Irish?"

"Yup. It's pronounced 'ey-nit.'"

"Do your parents own the brewery?"

She laughed. "I wish. We have the option of taking Irish names for our shifts."

I thought back to the woman I'd spoken with on the phone when I initially called O'Callaghan's. "Does everyone do it?"

"That's up to us," she said, "but you'll find out all about it on the tour. It looks like they're leaving, so you better skedaddle!"

She was right. A man in his late thirties dressed all in green and wearing a leprechaun's hat had appeared at the rear door. He must have said something funny because the tour group started laughing. I threaded my way through the racks of O'Callaghan's sweatshirts, mugs, bottle openers, and knick-knacks, tossed a glance at the carved-wood bar on the far side of the lodge backlit by the crackling fireplace, and tried to blend into the tour.

"Welcome!" the tour guide said. "What's your name and where are you from?"

Judging by the expectant looks I was getting, I assumed everyone had already introduced themselves. "Mira, from Battle Lake." That was the first time I'd uttered those words all in the same sentence. I was born and had grown up in Paynesville and spent most of my twenties in Minneapolis before relocated to Battle Lake. I was pleased it sounded comfortable rolling off my tongue.

I indicated his name tag. "And your name?"

He looked down. "Niall," he said. "Pronounced like the river in Egypt."

I wondered if he also went by Eric Offerdahl. The single photo I had seen had been fuzzy. Niall's hair was brown, at least what I could see of it peeking out from under his hat, but he did not have a spike through his right eyebrow and appeared about fifteen years too old. The spike could have easily been removed, however, and if he was heavy into drugs, that could have added years to his face. I vowed to get to the front of the group at some point during the tour so I could inspect him up close.

Niall led us outside. It was already dark, but the path was lit by white twinkle lights sparkling beautifully off of the iced snow. The drifts were so perfectly formed that the grounds behind the lodge looked like the top of a lemon meringue pie. It was cold, the brief thaw over, but above zero with no wind, so the short walk to the factory was pleasant. Niall was lecturing about how the O'Callaghan family—originally from Ireland but based out of Chicago in the past eighty years—had been searching the Midwest for the perfect location for their microbrewery. They had made their money in the carpet business but wanted to build something more creative and return to their family roots. When their realtor found the 100 acres just south of Swederland a little over a year ago, they realized it would be perfect. The lakes area brought in thousands of tourists every month, taxes were low, and labor would be cheap. They bought the land, began building immediately, and had begun distributing their beers and offering tours in the past few weeks.

The company grounds, he said, were made up of the lodge we had just left and the brewery we were walking toward, plus the dorms and the O'Callaghan family home on the other side of the far hill.

"Dorms?" I said, interrupting his speech.

"Yes," he said, smiling. "Room and board are part of our employment package. The dorms are like our own little village. Plus, we get health care and money for college."

I narrowed my eyes. "That sounds too good to be true."

He chuckled. "That's what I thought too, but it is true. The O' Callaghans figure if they are good to their employees, that we'll stay on and work hard. And they're right. They treat us like family."

He fell back into his spiel. Right now, O'Callaghan's was producing four different beers: a seasonal ale, their signature dark, and two lagers. The recipes were passed down from generation to generation. Apparently, the original O'Callaghan's of County Galway had been whiskey distillers and brewers. Though it was too early to tell how the O'Callaghan's beers would be received, early buzz was good, no pun intended.

Niall held open the factory door. The warm scent of yeast and something sour washed over us. I was the last to pass Niall, and I stared right into his face. I was disappointed to see no visible hole in his right eyebrow.

"Say," I said, before slipping inside, "can you tell me what time my friend Eric Offerdahl's shift starts? I was really hoping to run into him."

Niall didn't skip a beat. "Eric Offerdahl? That doesn't sound very Irish." He tipped his hat and moved to the front of the crowd. "This is the main factory." He spread his arms to indicate the Wonka-esque room filled with enormous copper vats and tubes that ran to and fro and all the way to the top of the giant, open three-story room. He walked us through the malting, milling, and mashing, passing around a test tube of hops for us to inspect. Then he explained the lautering, boiling, fermenting (which accounted for the faintly sour bread smell), conditioning, filtering, and finally, packaging. The packaging area was a separate part of the factory set up exactly like I assumed Laverne and Shirley's workplace had been arranged. The label maker was the most fascinating part to me, turning an ordinary brown bottle into a tiny, perfect, utile piece of art.

"Who designs all your labels?" I asked over the din of the operating factory.

"I do. I used to do graphic design for the carpeting company in Chicago, and now I design the labels, the marketing materials, everything." He bowed. "And lead tours, of course. At least until we expand our line. Many of the employees here multitask."

"Cool," I said, accepting the sample label Niall handed to me. It was for O'Callaghan's seasonal beer, called Ice Castle. The image on the front looked familiar. It took me a few beats to recognize that it was a cartoon version of the O'Callaghan's-sponsored ice castle on West Battle. I wondered how the bad publicity was affecting business, but it seemed rude to ask. Niall finished up the tour, fielding questions about beer flavors (they'd add more in the summer if the current stock sold well), whether they were hiring (not at this time, but applications were always welcome), and how long it took to brew a single bottle of beer from the malting stage to the bottling (twenty-two to forty days on average, depending on what type of beer it was). When all the questions had been answered, Niall asked who was ready to try some beer. Apparently, everyone but the two children had come for exactly that reason, and the group headed toward the exits en masse. I lagged behind so I could sing "Schlemiel, schlimazel, hasenpfeffer incorporated" under my breath and snatch another label from the on-deck machine feed, this one far more interesting to me.

The colors had initially attracted me—deep blues and purples with a flash of silver—but it was the name that hitched my breath: Sutler's Civil War Ale. I thought immediately of the Prospect House, and Orpheus Jackson. The label's spidery font was old-fashioned, and the words were undercut by the sharp edge of a bayonet. The overall effect was a peculiar cross between edgy and quaint, but somehow it worked. On impulse, I stuffed the label into my coat pocket and caught up with the rest of the tour. I passed a door I hadn't noticed before and tried the handle on impulse. Locked. The room must contain fragile materials, or be where they hid the garbage.

The cold outside was bracing after the steamy closeness of the brew factory. A soft winter breeze had picked up, sending tiny eddies of snowdust over the frosted drifts and making the twinkle lights glitter magically. The tour group was nearly inside the building when I caught up with them. Niall was holding the door. He tapped my shoulder lightly as I passed by him.

"Did you get lost?" His smile seemed genuine, but his eyes carried an emotion I couldn't read, more than a question but not quite a warning.

"Sorry," I said. It wasn't really an answer, but I'd discovered the word was a ticket out of most minor social infractions. I plucked my two beer coupons from his outstretched hand and made my way through the main lodge and into the bar in the rear. Although the lodge itself was one open room, the bar had been cleverly designed with open sides and its own faux-cobblestone roof to make it seem like a separate, authentic Irish pub within the larger space. My tour group had already bellied up to the buttery wood counter and were enjoying their first taste of beer. The kids were sucking down root beers.

I considered whether I should imbibe. I absolutely loved beer, but I didn't know if this counted as a social situation. Plus, I didn't want to get schlitzy before I drove. A couple sips couldn't hurt though, right? In fact, I was almost obligated as part of my research. I slid the blue coupon to the bartender when he strolled to my end of the bar. He was in his forties, too old to be Eric, and his name tag read TURLOUGH.

"A sample of the Civil War Ale, please."

He shot me a quizzical glance. "Excuse me?"

I almost pulled out the label. "Sutler's Civil War Ale. I saw the labels in the factory."

He smiled and handed me a menu. "I'm afraid that one will never see the light of day. Something in the recipe was off. Here's a list of what we do offer."

Peculiar. You'd think they'd test the recipe before bothering to print out labels. I studied the menu. "I'll try the chocolate stout, please." Beer that tastes like chocolate? Hi, really good idea.

He opened the tap into a miniature mug that I assumed they used only for tastings. The beer pulled out deep and creamy with a gorgeous head. When he set it in front of me, the smell hit me first: bitter, dark, and rich. I closed my eyes and inhaled. When I opened them, he was still standing there with his hands on his hips, watching me like a proud parent.

"The chocolate stout is my favorite," he said.

I smiled and held the glass to my lips, smelling it through my open mouth before tipping back the glass and letting it wash in. The flavor was transcendent, dark chocolate notes on my tongue, a light carbonation on the sides of my mouth, and a deeper, wiser flavor in the back of my throat. I swallowed and moaned. "Amazing," I sighed.

He nodded in satisfaction. "You can see why we guard the recipes so carefully."

"Where can I buy some?" I swiveled in my stool. I hadn't noticed beer for sale amidst all the other O'Callaghan's merchandise.

He began wiping mugs, keeping one eye on his other customers. "Minnesota law. Breweries can't sell their bottled beer on site."

"What?" I drew the chocolate stout closer to me. This might be all I got for a while.

He shrugged. "Something about distribution lobbyists needing their cut, I think. You can buy it in the area liquor stores, but we can't sell you anything but growlers, and we don't have the space or license for that. Only samples."

A more ridiculous law I had yet to hear, but the delicious headiness of the beer might have been fueling my righteousness. Everyone should be able to drink this nectar wherever they wanted. It was filling my empty stomach with a nice bubbly bliss. Actually, I decided on the spot that it was dark and thick enough to count as a meal. I finished all four ounces and handed him the mug.

"What would you like to try next? Our pale ale is very popular."

I shook my head. "No more for me, thanks. I have to drive." I started to walk away and then turned back. "Oh, hey, I almost forgot. Can you give this to Eric Offerdahl for me?" I held out the first item I pulled out of my pocket, a Turtle Stew receipt for the hotdish I'd ordered the other night.

Turlough smiled amiably and reached for it. He almost had his hands on the paper before his face tightened. He withdrew his fist and shot a glance toward Niall, who was talking to Aednat at the front door. Niall wasn't looking, and Turlough turned his back to me to help another customer.

That was all right. I'd gotten what I came for.

TWENTY-SEVEN

I SAT IN MY idling car outside the T Wrecks farmhouse and honked my horn. I wasn't sure if Mrs. Berns would be back from her expedition or not, but I hoped so. I was relieved when she popped her head out, waved at me to hang tight, disappeared back inside the house, then ran to the car five minutes later with her arms full of books.

"Holy moley," she said, hopping in next to me. "What a busy afternoon!"

"What's that smell?" I sniffed around her hair. The odor reminded me of woodsmoke, but sweeter.

She shrugged. "I'm an old lady. It could be any number of things. Check this out." She held up the top book on a stack of seven. It's ragged cover proclaimed *Yoga Spirit!* in a 1970s psychedelic font. "I'm gonna be a hippie!"

"You're only a few decades late for that train." I took another whiff. "That's it! You smell like pot. Were you *smoking*?"

"I'm too old to start smoking anything. I have plans for these lungs. Bob and Vienna may have been partaking, though."

"What kind of name is Vienna for a person, anyhow?"

"I had the same question. Her dad's name was Vince and her mom's name was Alenna, so they named her Vienna."

"Does Austria know?"

"Why are you so crabby? Aren't you happy that I have a new friend?"

I found myself pouting as I drove onto the icy blacktop. I performed a body scan and realized that I was tense all over. First it was Kennie with the greener thumb, and now it was Mrs. Berns making a new friend. But of course I wanted her to have as many people in her life as possible. I tried to turn my attitude around. "Sorry."

"You should be. That late husband of mine who was a drinker? He was a jealous one, too. Kept a tight rein on me, as if I went anywhere besides home and the grocery store. I vowed never to let anyone possess me again."

"You sound like a heroine of a romance novel."

"But you get my point."

I sighed. "I said I was sorry."

"It's all right."

One of the many admirable things about Mrs. Berns is that if she accepted your apology, she meant it. I knew we wouldn't be speaking of this again.

"Now listen," she continued. "Vienna is amazing. She's sixty-nine and has the body of a fifty-year-old. She says it's because of yoga and how she eats. She teaches classes and everything, and does most of the cooking for the kids who stay on at the brewery. I'm going to turn back the clock!" She pumped a tiny bird fist into the air, her smile lighting up her face in the dark of the car.

"Too late," I said fondly. I let her ramble on about all the ideas Vienna had given her and all the life changes she was going to make. In the back of my mind, though, I realized I was missing Johnny terribly, and maybe that's why I was being so possessive of Mrs. Berns and my plants. It had been three days since I'd seen him, and that was too long. Rather than get grabby about things that weren't mine, I should appreciate what I had.

The owners of Bonnie & Clyde's in Clitherall let Johnny's band use the back half of their bar as practice space on Tuesdays. It was a slow night so no one minded if the music was a little rough. I could drop Mrs. Berns off, go watch Johnny practice, and maybe even see if Bonnie & Clyde's was carrying O'Callaghan's chocolate stout. Then, after Johnny was done working, he and I could slip back to his house and finish what we'd started the other night. The thought of it revved up my blood and sent it to all sorts of delicious places.

"What?" I asked, becoming aware that Mrs. Berns was quietly watching me.

"Have you heard a word I said?"

"Several."

"You know how some people have faces like statues?" she asked.

"Yes."

"You're not one of them. Say hi to Johnny for me. And drop me off at the Rusty Nail. They've added karaoke on Tuesdays, and I have a hankering to sing 'If I Could Turn Back Time.'"

She didn't wait to get out of the car to start practicing. I promised her I'd drop the borrowed books off at her apartment, and I did just that before heading east to Clitherall, another two-bars-and-a-church town four miles up the road from Battle Lake. Bonnie & Clyde's was situated directly across the street from the Sportsman's Bar. They were both decent dives to hang in, but Bonnie & Clyde's had the bands and the feel. When I parked out front, I heard the jukebox playing "Crazy Train." Johnny's band must be taking a practice break.

I left my car and glanced up at the crossed rifles on the Bonnie & Clyde's sign, suddenly feeling self-conscious. I wasn't wearing any make-up, which wasn't unusual, but I also hadn't combed my hair since this morning and was wearing everyday clothes. Plus, a string of sleepless nights had left dark bags under my eyes. Johnny would be with his friends and there would most certainly be a cadre of lady fans of all ages. He had his very own groupies, even on practice nights.

I jogged back to the car, dragged a brush through my hair, and coated my lips with honey-flavored lip balm. That was the best I could do, though I decided to enter through the back so everyone wouldn't stare as I entered. I made my way to the rear, passing the white equipment van used by The Thumbs. I heard some soft talk and giggling near Bonnie & Clyde's back door and almost turned around to enter through the front. Instead, I peeked around the corner to make sure I wouldn't be interrupting anything uncomfortable.

I blinked for several seconds and still couldn't make sense of what I saw: Johnny, his arms wrapped around a stunning blonde.

TWENTY-EIGHT

No matter how much I stared, it just didn't make sense. When my eyes began to fog, I realized it was tears and yanked myself back. Luckily, Johnny hadn't spotted me. His attention was completely focused on the blonde. I speed-walked back to my car, my head down, my legs numb. I started the engine automatically and pointed the Toyota toward anywhere but here, taking the sharp corner known as the Clitherall Carwash so quickly that I started fishtailing.

Breathe, I told myself. I pulled my car back into a straight line and began rationalizing. It was bound to happen. Johnny was gorgeous, smart, funny, kind, and in a band. How had I ever thought he'd want more than a fling? When I'd finally slept with him in December, I knew I'd put it off for so long because I was afraid this is exactly what would happen. I slammed my palm into my steering wheel. How could I have been so stupid?

We hadn't said we would be exclusive, though. Had we? I kept driving, but it was hard with the tears streaming down my face. I'd be okay. For sure I would. I'd survived worse. I should have known better than to get my hopes up in the first place, though. I was punching way above my weight class with Johnny.

I found myself standing outside the Battle Lake Municipal Liquor store. The mirror of the glass door reflected a red, puffy face, a runny nose, tears glistening off my cheeks. I rubbed a mittened hand over my face and entered. I passed the display of O'Callaghan's and went straight for the vodka. I kept my head down as I paid, not wanting to see the pity in the cashier's eyes.

I knew I wasn't bringing this bottle home.

For a crazy moment, I considered driving to Kennie's house, but then it hit me. I knew exactly where I was going to sleep tonight.

TWENTY-NINE

"Hey baby, you want waffles?"

Whose voice was that? I opened my eyes and saw only blackness. I was blind! It was exactly what I deserved. I shifted my head slightly. My brain had a distinct lag behind my skull, and it hammered against its cage when it finally caught up. I groaned, but I realized that I had been face down. With my head now to the side, at least I could see.

"Cuz if you do, you'll need to go out and grab some waffle mix. Oh, and syrup. Butter, too, if they have it. Man, waffles sound good. And bacon."

Sweet Jesus, was that Bad Brad's voice? I groaned again, this time sounding like a wounded whale. I could not begin to imagine the half-life on a mess-up like this. I slowly pulled myself into a sitting position and cracked my eyes wider. I was on his couch. Daylight was slicing through his dusty blinds like blades of fire. I rubbed at my face, feeling the imprint of his cheap stinky couch from forehead to chin. Maybe we could just pour syrup on my face. I sucked in a breath and let my hand fall lower, to where my clothes should be—*dear god, please let me still be wearing clothes.*

Shirt, check. Bra, check. Underwear, never wore 'em. Pants, check. I almost cried in relief.

"Hey, did you sleep in those clothes? Weirdo. Right before I crashed last night, I told you to make yourself comfortable, and you told me to make myself invisible. Ha! I forgot how much fun you are when you've been drinking."

I focused on Brad, who appeared to be wearing only tighty-had-once-been-whities. I held up my hand to shield my sight, and he slapped a cup of coffee into it.

"Here you go. It's instant, but you have got to need this. Man, I didn't know you could sing."

Sing? My fifth-grade choir teacher had taken me aside after the first day of class and quietly asked me if I wouldn't mind lip-syncing. I hadn't warbled in public since. I took a tentative sniff of the coffee. It smelled like ashtrays and butt. Again, exactly what I deserved. I sipped it in penance.

"Good thing I had my recording equipment here. It's still okay if I use it as a backing track for Iron Steel's punk cover of 'The Gambler,' right? 'You gotta know when to hold 'em!'" He screeched like a cat while air guitaring.

"Brad." It came out as a whisper so as not to unbalance the delicate gyroscope of my spinning brain. "Brad." A little louder this time, but still not loud enough to break through. "Brad!"

"You don't need to yell, baby."

"Did we do anything last night?"

"Yeah, totally. We recorded those tracks and played quarters and talked philosophy of life. Oh, we played hide and seek, but you kept trying to, you know, conceal yourself under the kitchen sink, except you didn't fit."

That explained the egg-sized lump on my head. I hoped. "No, I mean, did we...make out?" The sip of coffee I'd swallowed threatened to return to its cup.

"Naw, man, don't be stupid. I'm with Samantha and you're with Johnny. That's what you kept telling me, anyhow, though I'm still confused about the part where you're going to let him have multiple wives if that's what he needs?"

My pain dropped from my head and rose from my stomach, landing squarely in my heart. Johnny was seeing another woman. That's why I'd come here in the first place. Scratch that. I'd come to Brad's because I was weak and scared. Thank god the dumb monkey had been his best self last night. Maybe dating him wasn't the worst mistake I'd ever made. Top five, no question, but no longer dead first. "I have to go."

"Bathroom's right over there."

"I mean I have to leave for work." I tried standing and only swayed a bit. "What time is it?"

"Quarter to ten."

Crap! The library was supposed to open in fifteen minutes. I didn't have time to run home and shower, or even change. I wobbled to his bathroom and made do with scrubbing my face with Ivory soap and water, using my pointer finger with some toothpaste on it as a toothbrush, and slapping on a layer of Brad's industrial deodorant. It would have to suffice.

I yanked on my shoes and snatched my jacket, cursing the nausea that threatened with each fast movement. I paused on the way out. Brad was sitting on the couch, earphones in his ears and a distant smile on his face as he bopped along to a silent beat. I motioned for him to remove an ear bud.

"Thanks," I said.

"What for?" he asked, his voice far too loud.

"For being a friend."

He waved and tucked the earbud back in his ear. I scurried out to my cold car and started it up, feeling somewhat refreshed by the frigid air. She turned over on the first try and was purring within seconds. I brushed a light snowfall off the windows with the wipers. It was one of those blinding days where the sun has no barrier between itself and new snow, turning the landscape into a shimmering diamond mine. I was not in the proper state to appreciate the visual splendor and slipped the car into first gear, leaving before it warmed up.

Thankfully, Brad's apartment was on the other end of town and so I arrived only seven minutes after the library's scheduled opening. My heart sank when I spotted Mrs. Berns waiting outside the door along with two patrons.

I turned off the car and jogged to the door, key already out. "Sorry," I said, deliberately avoiding eye contact with Mrs. Berns. "Car trouble."

"Sorry to hear it," Mrs. Berns said, leaning into me. "Say, is that a new perfume you're wearing? It smells like stupid and guilty."

I swallowed hard and hurried into the library, flicking on the lights and turning up the heat on my way to the front computer. To my chagrin, Mrs. Berns followed so closely that she tripped me near the main desk. I caught my balance but not without knocking my elbow on the corner of a table.

"Ouch," I said, rubbing it but still not looking at her.

"You look like a puppy that got caught peeing on the rug. Out with it."

I pulled my eyes to hers. Her arms were crossed and she was tapping a foot. The determined look in her eyes told me there was no way through this but straight. My confession spilled out in one long, rushed sentence. "I surprised Johnny at practice last night but he was with another woman so he didn't see me but I saw him and I was so angry that I bought a bottle of vodka and went to Bad Brad's but nothing happened and I regret it so I don't need to feel any worse."

Getting it out felt a little bit better, right up until Mrs. Berns swatted me on the side of my head.

"Why in the world would you go to Brad?"

She'd hit me right on the goose egg I'd hatched trying to sneak into Brad's cupboards. I rubbed at the double-sore spot.

"Johnny is cheating on me."

"How do you know?"

"I told you. I saw him hugging another woman. And they were all whispery, like they knew each other naked."

"I give a grand total of zero shits about that. You don't know anything for a fact, and rather than find out the truth, you chose to spend the evening with a man who, if he were any more stupid, would need to be watered twice a week. Can you explain that?"

I felt tears pushing up. I was about to apologize when Mrs. Berns gathered me into her arms, just as I had done for her yesterday. She was four inches shorter than me, but somehow, she made me feel safe.

"Look," she said while she was patting my head, "you have to make yourself vulnerable in love. There's no other way to do it. Maybe Johnny stepped out, maybe he didn't. Either way, you're going to be okay. But you need to find out the truth, and you need to be able to stand by your choices, even the ones you make when you're down."

I nodded, my chin bobbing on her shoulder. "What will I do if Johnny doesn't want to be with me?"

"You'll feel like shit for a while, and then you'll get better. But don't borrow trouble. Focus on what you know, which is nothing."

I sniffled. "You're right."

"Of course I am, dummy," she said gently. "Now go blow your nose. My jacket is made out of polyester, not vinyl."

She let me go, and I looked straight at her for the first time that morning. "Did you get your hair done?"

"Yup. Me and Vienna met at the hairstylist's this AM and got perms. We're going to shop later and maybe catch a movie. She's the most fun I've had without liquor or a man for a long time."

I quelled the now-familiar surge of jealousy. One problem at a time, thank you very much.

"Oh, don't look at me like that. You're fun, too. You're just familiar. Vienna is new. Plus, she's got kids and grandkids, so she understands what I'm going through. It's exactly what I need to pull me out of my funk." She glanced at the wall clock. "I better get going. I have some grocery shopping to do before this afternoon. I just stopped by to tell you I can cover lunch if you have anything you need to do."

"Thank you." My head was throbbing, and I still felt like a hung over, cheated-on lump, but at least I had Mrs. Berns. She left me to get my face in order and run the library. I had to rush the opening duties as much as my battered brain allowed. I was almost on track when Jed walked through the door. I didn't recognize him at first because he had the fur-lined hood of his parka up. The gigantic jacket came nearly to his knees.

When he slipped off his hood, he was half wide smile, half curly crazy hair. "Mira Bo Beera! I'm returning your call."

I tried to smile back, but it hurt to move my face. "What call?"

"You rang me up Sunday," he said, pulling off his massive mittens on his way to the front desk. "You wanted to know about new drugs in the area."

Mrs. Craigmile, a retired second-grade teacher and library regular, was twirling the mystery rack near the front of the library but paused mid-rotation to shoot him and then me a shocked look.

"For the article I'm writing," I said in an exaggerated voice, staring directly at Mrs. Craigmile. She quickly withdrew her eyes, but I could tell by the way her head was cocked that she was still listening.

"Whatever," Jed said, shrugging amiably. "Sorry I didn't get back to you sooner. I've been doing a lot of work on the ice castle for O' Callaghan's."

"They're still opening it? I thought they were closing down all those lake attractions since the body was found."

He reached for the box of tissues I had on the front counter and blew his nose before arcing the crumpled ball into a nearby garbage. "They shut it all down for the Winter Festival, sure, and had me dismantle the Darwin's Dunk. No one wants any part of that. They're still opening up the ice castle, though. Something to do with a new beer they're unveiling."

"Wasn't the ice castle already good to go?"

"For outside viewing, yeah, but they want to expand on it and make it so people can go inside. I'm working with a crew. I don't know what it's going to look like when it's done, but it's going to be pretty cool. There are even ice sculptures around it now."

I wondered how this was the first I'd heard of it. "I'm glad you're finding work." I lowered my voice. "Have you heard of any new drug activity around here?"

Jed leaned in with a stage whisper loud enough to be heard in the rear of the library. "I have."

I waited. He waited.

"And?" I finally asked.

"They're new to town, some sort of gang out of Chicago. Guess it was getting too hot for them there. I got high with a couple of them at a party on New Year's. They started out nice, a little edgy. Cool tattoos, all of 'em. They didn't want to stop at pot, though, and so I left. Haven't seen much of them since, but I know they're selling. OxyContin, mostly."

That fit with what Gary had told me, back in the moment when he'd been high enough to like me. "Do they show any signs of leaving?"

He held up his palms. "No idea."

"You know anything about Eric Offerdahl?"

"The Dahlster." He nodded agreeably. "Yeah. He graduated about the same time I did. I heard he's been back in town a month plus but is laying low at the brewery."

"A month plus. Is that about how long the gang has been around?"

He put a finger to his chin. "About. Might be coincidence, though."

"Maybe," I said, pulling the Operation Offerdahl folder out from under the counter. My experience was that coincidences were rare. "I really appreciate your help."

"Anything for you," he said, the sweet smile back on his face. "How's Johnny?"

I cracked the lead of my pencil on the notebook. "Good. You seen him lately?"

"Nope. Seems like he's practicing all the time. The Thumbs are playing Friday. Are you going? We could catch it together."

"Maybe," I said, brushing the lead off the paper. "Can I get back to you on that?"

"Sure!" He grabbed his mittens off the counter. "Anything else you need to know?"

"I'm good for now." My head hurt too much to nod. I wanted to eat a pie-sized ibuprofen.

"Then I better get back to work." He shoved his hands in his mittens, pulled up his hood, and headed back into the cold morning.

THIRTY

CHUCK LITCHFIELD'S OFFICE ASSISTANT rang me through immediately. Chuck picked up on the second ring.

"Hello?"

"Hi, Mr. Litchfield." For some reason, his first name felt too uncomfortable. "It's Mira James. I'm calling about the Eric Offerdahl investigation." It wasn't really an investigation. In fact, that's exactly why I was calling. The hangover was riding me like a troll, and sure, that was my fault, but I found myself unwilling to give up Eric Offerdahl until I knew why Chuck Litchfield wanted to find him. Or, maybe I just wanted to pick a fight.

"Mira! Did you find my boy?"

I paused. Had this descended to the realm of soap operas? "Eric Offerdahl is your son?"

He laughed. "No. It was a figure of speech."

Hmm. An odd one for anyone but Thurston Howell III. "I haven't turned up anything yet," I lied, "but I'm following some leads. I'd like more information before I proceed. Specifically, why do you want to locate Eric Offerdahl?"

"I'm sorry. My client has asked me not to reveal that, as I mentioned. You can locate him without that information, am I correct?"

This guy had a knack for rubbing me the wrong way. I ignored his question. "If you can't tell me that, can you tell me why you believe he's back in Battle Lake?"

"Rumors."

I wasn't in the mood. "You've got nothing?"

He laughed again, but it sounded tight. "Not anything that you couldn't find out on your own. That's why I hired you."

I decided right then and there that I'd investigate Chuck Litchfield—and specifically why he was after Eric Offerdahl—before I told him that I'd likely located Eric. I didn't have a solid reason for my evasiveness, just a sense that I didn't want to show my hand yet, even if Litchfield was paying for the cards. I thanked him for his time and promised him a full report within seventy-two hours. I hung up the phone and sketched a couple angry faces in my notebook. Nobody likes being in the dark, but I had a special intolerance to secrets, always had. Maybe it was due to growing up in a house that held a lot of them. In any case, I craved answers like a fish desired water.

I glanced at the clock. Noon. If Mrs. Berns showed up over my lunch hour as promised, I could jog to the police station and find out if there was any new information on the local gang activity, Gary's shooting, or Maurice's murder. Noon became twelve thirty, though, which quickly turned into one o'clock. When my stomach's growl drew annoyed glances from patrons, I headed to the break room and rummaged through the miniature refrigerator. I found a tub of roasted red pepper hummus that was good for another two days, and in the cupboard, a bag of only slightly stale spelt pretzels. I carried them to the counter and snacked while emailing overdue book notices. An automated system would be nice, but so would a lot of things that cost money.

It was two o'clock before Mrs. Berns finally sashayed in, looking relaxed and smelling like sweet smoke and delicious food.

"Where have you been?" I asked.

She held up her white bag. "I got takeout from the Turtle Stew so I could eat while I watched the place for you, just like I said."

"It's two oh five!"

She dropped the bag on the counter so her hands were free to slip out of her winter jacket. "Take it or leave it."

"You smell like pot again," I said suspiciously.

"Vienna showed up early to take me to a meditation class. Very relaxing. We listened to a Deepak Oprah tape and quieted our minds."

"Chopra?"

She glanced at my tub of hummus and shrugged. "Sure, I'll try anything once."

"No, his name is ... forget it." I lifted the lid and slid it over to her along with what was left of the pretzels.

"Is there any meat in this?" she said, sniffing the hummus.

"Why do you care?"

"I'm a vegetarian now. Vienna said avoiding animal flesh is an important component of being healthy and whole."

I raised my eyebrows but didn't comment, even though it was killing me. Mrs. Berns was the most carnivorous person I'd ever met. She swore it's what fed her sex drive. "The hummus is vegetarian."

"Great." She grabbed a pretzel, scooped a mound of hummus, and popped the whole works into her mouth. I watched her chew, a faint smile on her face. The smile turned into a grimace and she snatched the pretzel bag, spitting out the mouthful into it with all the subtlety of a hand grenade.

"What the hell was in that?" She scraped her tongue with her nails. "Who eats pumice anyways?"

"It's *hummus*. Garbanzo beans and tahini."

"Speak English," she said, dipping into her own white bag and coming out with a wax paper–wrapped sandwich. "Good thing I brought my own food."

I watched her unwrap it. "Is that a BLT?"

She took a big bite. "Mmm hmmm," she said, wiping at the mayonnaise on the corners of her mouth.

"Isn't there meat in that?"

She swallowed. "Nope, just lettuce, tomato, and bacon. Did I tell you that the meditation class was held at a cool new workout center near Vienna's house? They have a pool, workout rooms, dorms. There's even a grope room."

I thought of the distinct marijuana smell that accompanied her after her visits with Vienna. "You mean 'grow' room?" I'd had a recent experience with those last November, when I'd uncovered a healthy pot industry in the area.

"If you say so."

That would seem incongruent with a fitness center. "Did you actually see the room?"

"No, Vienna only mentioned it in passing while she was toking on a spliff. Said it's hidden, and I better not tell anyone."

Interesting, yes. Related to Eric Offerdahl? No idea. "How long can you stay?"

"I got an hour, then Vienna is coming back."

"You don't let her drive when she's smoking, do you?"

"Don't be ridiculous. I do the driving."

That would be less ridiculous if Mrs. Berns possessed a valid driver's license, but that was a point I'd never been able to make with her. "All right. I'll be back in an hour."

I retrieved my coat from the rack and left the library, trying not to jostle my tender head and hoping that Gary Wohnt wouldn't be at the police station when I arrived.

THIRTY-ONE

AND IF LUCK WERE pennies, I couldn't afford a gumball. Gary glanced up from his desk as I walked in before immediately returning his attention to an open file on his desk.

"You're out of the hospital," I said, surprisappointed.

It didn't even garner me an eyebrow raise.

"Those crutches yours?" They were leaning against the edge of his metal desk. I reached out to touch one, but he snatched them away, stacking them against the wall behind him.

I took the seat across from him and watched him work, or at least pretend to work. It must be hard to concentrate with me staring at him. His face pointed down at his papers, I had front row seats to the top of his head. He wasn't going to go bald anytime soon. I kept up the staring silence for all of four minutes before cracking. "I know about cabins in the area being robbed, and I think I know who's doing it."

He sighed but did not speak.

"I also know about Eric Offerdahl."

This earned a glance. He lifted his head slowly and appraised me with his black eyes. "*What* do you know about Eric Offerdahl?"

Good question, one I didn't yet have an answer to. "Stuff," I said cleverly. "I also know Maurice was not a transient. He has family in Chicago. A girlfriend and two kids."

"Interesting." He leaned back. I could tell he did it too fast given his recent injury, because his face paled before he regained his composure. His leg must be killing him. I was sure he wasn't supposed to be back at work this soon after the shooting.

"Yes," I agreed. "Interesting. Now why don't you tell me what you know?"

He raised an eyebrow. "Not how this works."

I thought of the letter Ray had given me. "I might have more to tell you, if you trade information of your own."

"Might, or do?"

Deputy Victor walked in, bringing a gust of cold air and the smell of drugstore cologne with him. We nodded at each other, and then he disappeared into the back room of the station.

I ran my finger along the edge of his desk. "Depends."

When I pulled my eyes back to his, he was staring at me with such intensity that it felt like an X-ray. I held his gaze, though it was one of the more difficult things I'd done that week. I could feel the flush creeping up from my neck.

"Do you know anything about OxyContin?" he asked.

"Prescription pain reliever, widely abused. Is that what the gang is dealing in?"

"How about fentanyl patches?" he asked, ignoring my question.

"Never heard of 'em."

"It's a pain reliever, a hundred times more potent than morphine." Was that a blush at the mention of the drug that had made him over-reveal? "It's highly addictive, dangerous, and popular. Doctors prescribe it in pill, sucker, or patch, but the patch is the most popular back alley form."

"Sucker? Like, candy that kills pain?" And I thought frozen Nut Goodies were awesome. Neither of my reactions—admiration and envy—seemed appropriate, so I continued. "And you're seeing Oxy-Contin and fentanyl patches turning up around here?"

"Look it up. You're the reporter."

I noticed he didn't call me a detective. "Why would you only tell me part of the story?"

He ran his fingers through his hair. He wore a fat silver ring on his right hand, and it caught the light. "The question is, why would I tell you any of it? The answer: because this is dangerous. It's not kids snitching their parents' liquor or selling pot. This is big-city drug running, and I want you out of my way."

The words weren't new—he'd warned me away from cases many times before—but the growl in his voice was.

"I have no interest in infiltrating gangs or uncovering drug operations," I said truthfully.

He scowled. I could tell he didn't believe me.

"Look, I just want to know what happened to Maurice. I found him, you know? I want to put that to rest. Also, Litchfield hired me to locate Eric Offerdahl. The sooner you help me with those two, the sooner I get out of your way."

"You've told me everything?"

"Yes." I really had. Except for the letter. I shoved my hand into my pocket, and my fingers curled around the edges of Orpheus's missive. I hadn't come in expecting to show it to him, but maybe he could help with that, too. Or maybe it would help him. This sharing was unlike me, but it felt good to not have to do this one alone.

His voice cut into my thoughts. "Good. Thank you. I don't want to see you again. Ever, if you can swing it, but if not, certainly not before this case is over. If we cross paths, consider yourself arrested."

"For what?" I sputtered, my hand shooting out of my pocket, empty.

"Don't give me a reason to decide." He held me in his stare, his eyes sharp.

"Screw you," I said, suddenly so angry that I wished I could start fires with my brain.

He raised one eyebrow mildly, which is the last view I had of him before spinning on my heel and storming out.

THIRTY-TWO

THE SOFT SHUFFLE OF the library faded into the background as I typed my article in hopes of distracting myself from the boiling anger at Gary's harsh words.

"Battle Lake's Prospect House
and Civil War Museum Opens to the Public"

The grand old Prospect House has opened her doors for the first time since it ceased being a hotel in 1924. The House is a Battle Lake original, an 18-room Georgian mansion built in 1860 by Barnaby Offerdahl, a railroad man and Battle Lake transplant. When Offerdahl didn't return from the Civil War, the house was willed to his daughter and then his brother. It left Offerdahl hands in an 1882 sale when James Allison "Cap" Colehour purchased it, turning it into a seasonal resort in 1886. The Prospect Inn was the first and largest resort operating in the area for the 38 years it was open. With a prime location near the railroad, it became a popular travel destination for people from all over the Midwest, famous for its clean rooms and excellent meals.

The Inn reverted to a private home in the early 1920s and was completely remodeled in 1929. In a rare stroke of luck, the house's furnishings have not been changed since. Carter Stone, a local historian, bought the mansion minus most of the land at auction last March. With the help of a dedicated group of volunteers, Stone has spent hundreds of hours searching through piles of treasure inside the house. They've uncovered most of the original furnishings, intact clothing and jewelry collections dating as far back as Barnaby Offerdahl's time, and an extensive collection of Civil War artifacts. According to Stone, "I found a chest filled with nearly 200 Civil War letters. I found the sleeves to Barnaby Offerdahl's original uniform with a bullet hole in each one from the first and second time he'd been shot during the Civil War. I found a fife, buttons from a uniform, a cartridge box, a tent, a cap box, a powder flask, a bullet mold, two diaries, typhoid serum, Lincoln-Johnson campaign poster, belts and buckles, a flag and battlefield souvenirs. There are many pieces of this large historical puzzle still yet to be found."

Eager to share their historically exciting finds with the world, Stone and his helpers have opened the House and Museum to the public even though only approximately half of its treasure has been cataloged. The Prospect House and Civil War Museum is truly a jewel in Battle Lake's crown. You can tour the House and Museum during their open hours and find out more by visiting their website at www.prospecthousemuseum.org.

I hit Send. Ron would proofread the article and make any necessary changes. I glanced at the wall clock. Twenty minutes to close. I spent that time searching for any online records pertaining to Charles or Chuck Litchfield. I discovered where he'd been born, how much money he made in an average year (significantly more than a part-time librarian/reporter/detective), his home and cabin addresses, two speeding tickets, both paid, and that's it. I shooed out the last two library visitors and headed home.

———

My answering machine was doing its job when I walked into my living room, shaking off the cold.

"Hey, it's Johnny."

My heart soared, then plummeted. He didn't know I'd witnessed him embracing the blonde last night. He also didn't know I'd spent the evening at Brad's.

"I have a surprise for you. Call me back. Miss you."

I felt like I was gargling my heart. It was a vile cocktail of sadness and guilt. I could address part of that by putting distance between Brad and me. Maybe I really should find out what was up with his girlfriend so I could file him away as "in a committed relationship." The sadness I didn't know what to do with.

Luna nuzzled my hand, and I dropped so our eyes were level. She licked my nose. Jed had installed the pet door while I was away over Christmas—his holiday gift to me, he'd said—and so I knew the animals had been able to come and go as they pleased, but I felt bad that I hadn't gotten them any fresh water this morning. One more chit to add to the guilt pile.

"How've you been, girl? Me, I've been pretty crappy, and that's at least half my own fault." She licked my ear this time. I strolled over to check her and Tiger Pop's food and water. I was rinsing out their stainless steel bowls when a knock came at the door. Luna didn't growl, which meant it was either someone she recognized or someone who was safe. For a moment, I hoped it was Johnny. It was not possible, given that he'd just called, but in that weak moment I yearned to make up with him.

I went to the door and pulled it open. It for sure wasn't Johnny.

THIRTY-THREE

"Can we come in? It's cold out here."

"Taunita?" I guessed. The woman was African American, early twenties, balancing a baby on one hip and holding the hand of another child, both kids so thoroughly wrapped in snowsuits, scarves, hats, and mittens that they had to tip back the top half of their body to see me in the yellow glare of the yardlight. Their names were Timothy and Alessa, if I remembered correctly from our single phone call.

"Yeah. Your dog friendly?"

I glanced down at Luna. She was trying to play it cool, sitting next to me on her haunches, but her tail was wagging against my ankle. She loved kids.

"Yep," I said, stepping aside to let them in.

"Puppy!" the little boy said when his mom led him into the house. I loved the way kids said that word. It was all wrapped in love and intense surprise, like they hadn't known until that moment how awesome the world could be. "Puppy!" he repeated.

His mom set the baby on the couch. The little child's snowsuit was so thick that she could only lay immobile like an insulated taco. Taunita talked while she unzipped and unraveled both children. "I know about Maurice," she said, "so you can stop looking so worried. I don't expect you to tell me anything new."

She'd just met me, and she already knew my worried look? Mrs. Berns must be right about my poker face. "I'm sorry. How'd you find out?"

"Hammer." She laid the snowsuits on top of each other then stacked the mittens, hats, and scarves next to them. Free of his bindings, Timothy ran over to Luna and hugged her like a champion. He was wearing one of those little matching button-down flannel shirt and elastic-waisted corduroy sets that squeezes my heart. With his curly chocolate-brown hair and wide eyes, he was a perfect, three-year-old doll. Alessa sat on the couch where Taunita had propped her, watching me with serious owl eyes. Her nose was exactly as big as a button, and her curls stood up around her head, recovering from the static shock of her hat being pulled off. I remember Taunita mentioning on the phone that Alessa had just turned a year old.

"He's not good for a lot, but Hammer at least had the decency to tell me about Maurice being gone," she continued. "He also said you're a detective. That right?"

Timothy was trying to crawl on Luna's back and ride her like a pony. She kept wriggling away and then finally rolled on her back. He trailed his fingers through her tummy hair and giggled. Tiger Pop still hadn't shown her face. Historically, she liked kids only a little more than she liked baths.

"No," I said truthfully. "I'm in training, but I've got another five thousand or so hours until I'm official in Minnesota. Is that why you came here? To see if I could find out who—" I glanced at Timothy. I didn't know if he was old enough to understand that his dad was dead. "Who's responsible for what happened?"

"Oh, I *know* who's responsible. Somebody who was buying, or somebody who was selling. That's how that works. Maurice tried to get out of that life and was almost there. That's why he came to Minnesota, you know? He was gonna look into an inheritance. He must've been offered some side work while he was here, big enough to call Hammer and Ray out with him, and he was stupid enough to take it. Last mistake he'll ever make." Her words were fierce, but tears sparkled in her eyes. Her face was swollen, as if she'd been spending a lot of time crying.

"How long were you two together?" I asked.

"Five years. We met in community college. I was going for computer programming and he was gonna be a mechanic, and then I got pregnant."

I nodded. I was frankly at a loss. Timothy had moved on from Luna and was pulling my CDs off the rack and stacking them like blocks. Alessa hadn't pulled her solemn eyes off me. "Can I get you anything to drink?"

"You can heat this bottle up," Taunita said, digging through a diaper bag. "And you can find Orpheus Jackson for me."

THIRTY-FOUR

THE LETTER. IT WAS hidden in the pocket of my winter coat. "If it's the same Orpheus I'm thinking of, he's pretty dead."

The hint of a smile touched her cheeks. "He is. He was Maurice's great-great-great-grandpa. When Mo's mom passed two months ago, he discovered the letters from Orpheus. He read them all at least three times, like they were a real page-turner. Maurice thought he had some land due him around here, land that was stolen from Orpheus. I don't have much else right now, and I'm asking you to help me find out if my kids at least got this."

I made my way to the microwave, unscrewed the nipple, and popped in the bottle, my brain working furiously, adding up what I knew. The letter Ray had tossed at me was real, or at least a copy of an authentic letter, written by Maurice's great-great-great-grandfather to his wife. In the letter in my possession, Orpheus had written, *they do not believe the messages I bring*. I didn't know where the letter had been mailed to or from, but I did know that Orpheus had served in the Civil War with Barnaby Offerdahl.

"Twenty seconds should be good," she said.

I nodded and jabbed the buttons. Timothy had followed me and was eyeing the bag of dill pickle potato chips on the counter. I'd eaten half the bag a few nights ago, and if I finished the rest, I might need to ask Timothy if his elastic-waisted cords came in larger sizes. "Can he have potato chips?"

"Sure," Taunita said, not looking up from her diaper changing.

I handed Timothy the bag.

"Thank you," he said, only it sounded like *tank-oo* because he was tiny and precious.

"You're welcome." I retrieved the bottle from the microwave, wound the top back on, shook it holding my finger over the hole in the nipple, tested it on my wrist, then handed it to Taunita.

"You have kids?" she asked.

"God no. Did a lot of babysitting growing up, though. Did Maurice mention where he thought this land was?"

"Battle Lake." She pointed out the window and made an encompassing gesture. "Here. He thought it might be around where his grandma used to own a cabin, but he found out she just rented it. Guess her grandparents took her there when she was little, too."

"Anything more specific than that?"

She shrugged, cradling Alessa as she fed her. "He said the letters didn't say much, almost like Orpheus was afraid someone else was going to read them."

"Don't suppose you brought the letters with?"

"Don't suppose I did. It wouldn't make any difference, anyways. I read 'em all myself. They don't say anything."

"Except that Orpheus was owed land in Battle Lake."

"Didn't even mention that. That's just the return address that was on the letters, and then there was some family legend that they was all supposed to be rich once they got their hands on this land."

"That's not a lot to go on,"

"I know." Alessa's eyes were growing droopy as she drank, and Timothy was sitting cross-legged near my feet, trying to feed Luna potato chips. "His funeral is gonna be here," she said softly. A tear coasted down her cheek and dropped onto Alessa's forehead. The girl's eyes popped open, then grew heavy-lidded again.

"In Battle Lake?"

"He doesn't have any family left, except us. Might as well be here."

I had a thought. *After the Battle* lay open on the coffee table in front of her. "Grab me that?"

She reached over, expertly balancing Alessa, and handed me the book. I walked to my coat and pulled out Orpheus's letter, smoothing it on the counter. Then I paged through the book until I located the article on the man found hung in the woods. Orpheus had written his letter January 18, 1865. The unidentified body had been discovered March 7 of the same year with the note that it had been hanging for at least two months. Was the hanged man Orpheus, and if so, why had he hung himself? I had some more questions to ask Carter Stone, it appeared.

"I'll see what information I can uncover," I said, "but this is a long shot."

"Thank you," she said simply.

"Where will you be staying so I can tell you if I find anything?"

She kept her eyes on Alessa. Timothy took that moment to wipe his greasy fingers on my pants leg. An awareness began to dawn on me. "You don't have anywhere to stay."

"We're quiet," she said. "And clean. I can help you out around here. Your plants look good, but you've got some cobwebs in the corners that might need a jackhammer to get them down."

I looked where she was pointing. How long had those been there? More importantly, how could I possibly live with a stranger and her two little kids? Luna whined, drawing my attention. She waited until our eyes were locked and then licked salty, giggly, boogery Timothy. *I want to keep him*, the gesture said.

I sighed so deeply that I swear the cobwebs that had just been pointed out to me moved. "Fine. You can have the guest room. But I'm not used to living with people. Especially little people."

Taunita smiled at me, the first unguarded expression I'd seen on her since she arrived. It was gorgeous, happy, grateful. Luna and I lugged in her suitcases and a box of toys out of the back of her Honda Civic and set them up in the spare bedroom. I inflated an air mattress for her and Timothy to share and together, she and I put together the travel playpen for Alessa. By the time we had the room comfortable, both kids were asleep, their faces vulnerable and perfect.

———

For the second time in four days, I was awoken by the sharp trill of the phone in the kitchen, this time in the middle of the night. My immediate reaction was chilly fear. It was appropriate.

"Mira?"

"Gary?" Even in my dream-fuzzed state, I recognized the deep, measured tone of the police chief. My next words came out like a plea. "It's one in the morning." *Please don't tell me anyone I love is hurt.*

"I'm sorry." He hesitated before continuing. Gary never hesitates.

"Who is it?"

"Curtis Poling has been attacked. He's in the Fergus Falls hospital. He's in rough shape."

I sat up in bed, my heart pounding a sick beat. "What? What happened?"

"You should get there soon. Do you need me to drive you?"

"No," I said reflexively. I rested the phone in its cradle and looked around my bedroom like it was the first time I'd seen it.

"You okay?"

I started. I'd forgotten that Taunita and her kids were here. She stood on the edge of the kitchen, appearing ghostly in a white nightgown.

"No," I said.

She nodded. She was used to things not being okay. "You need to go somewhere?"

I stood and began pulling on clothes. "Yeah. The hospital."

She disappeared and returned with my coat and boots. "I'll watch your animals. You call back here if you need anything."

THIRTY-FIVE

CURTIS POLING HAD BEEN out for a midnight walk, a habit of his that he refused to give up when he entered the nursing home. I'd caught him at it late one August night when I was one of the last customers to leave the Rusty Nail. I'd at first thought real dementia had kicked in. He'd convinced me he was out for pleasure and that he did it every night. He said he never walked far, but that he had to get out because the only time he could think was when the world was quiet. He'd managed to sneak out all those evenings without alerting the nursing home attendants, so who was I to deny him his simple pleasure?

This particular night, however, he'd been attacked behind the Apothecary. It was only good luck that Theadora had found him when she came to check on the alarm that had gone off.

"I thought he was a pile of rags." She kept twisting the tissue in her hands. "When I saw it was a person, I couldn't remember the phone number for the ambulance at first. Is that the stupidest thing you ever heard? I couldn't think of three simple numbers."

I kept my arm around her. "But you did remember them."

She nodded. "I was afraid to touch him. He looked so fragile, as if he'd been dropped from the sky. I didn't even recognize it was Curtis right away, there was so much blood. And someone had stolen his coat. Who does that?"

I had a good idea exactly who had done that. I felt as if my insides had been scoured by metal, like somehow I should have done more to stop Ray and Hammer. Maybe then Curtis wouldn't be in surgery, which is all the doctor could tell us. And when I say us, I mean me and a significant portion of Battle Lake. Familiar, tired faces had begun shuffling in, people who'd been reached by the phone tree and told that one of their own was hurting. We milled in the waiting room like zombies, our numbers growing, everyone afraid to speak too loudly, possibly afraid of waking one another and realizing this wasn't just a bad dream.

Theadora had stood by Curtis until the ambulance arrived, covering him with her own coat despite the plummeting temperatures, telling him it was going to be okay, crying. She told me she hadn't seen anyone else in the alley, just all that blood in the snow like someone had spilled a pitcher of cherry Kool-Aid.

"Weren't you concerned whoever did this to him would come back?"

Theadora blinked. I could tell it hadn't occurred to her to worry about anything but Curtis. In that moment, I loved her more than my own heart. I asked her if she needed anything. When she shook her head, I went in search of coffee. I took the corner toward the cafeteria when a familiar voice caught my ear. I tipped back and saw that Chuck Litchfield had joined the Battle Lake contingent. Behind him was Johnny, bedsheet creases still in his face. I kept walking, like the coward I am. I didn't have it in me to deal with either of them tonight.

———

I hid out in the cafeteria for an hour, peeking occasionally into the waiting room. The hospital staff eventually had to ask most of the locals to leave, saying they didn't have room for all of us, and besides, there was nothing we could do here. Once Johnny and Chuck were gone, I returned to the waiting room to beg to be allowed to stay. I would have hidden behind a plant or stolen some scrubs and tried to blend in if they'd said no.

Both Theadora and I were allowed to stick around by dint of our closeness to Curtis—Theadora in finding him, and me in being his closest friend outside of the nursing home. Mrs. Berns was a near second, but she let me stay rather than fight it out. She and Kennie both gave me a hug before leaving, and I promised to spread word as soon as we had news.

———

A little after eight o'clock in the morning, a nurse with kind eyes touched my shoulder and asked if I was here for Curtis Poling. That "yes" was one of the most difficult words I'd ever uttered. She must have seen the fear in my eyes because she immediately shook her head and told me that Curtis was out of surgery. He was in rough shape and couldn't have visitors for at least another day, maybe longer, but it looked like he was going to pull through. The tears gushed out of my eyes. I gently shook Theadora, who had fallen asleep on my shoulder. After I shared the good news with her, I used the hospital phone to dial Kennie.

After the information tree had been started, I was at a loss. The nurse had gently informed us that there was no reason to stay. I was too wired to go home or to work. I returned to the phone and called Mrs. Berns.

"I heard," she said by way of hello.

"Hi."

"My phone has been ringing off the hook. Are you still at the hospital?"

"Yep. They think he's going to be okay."

"That cat's had more than his share of lives." She coughed on the other end of the phone.

"Are you crying?"

"Are you stupiding?"

"It's okay. I know how much Curtis means to all of us."

I heard snuffling on the other end of the line, then nose-blowing. "What was that old fart doing walking behind the drugstore at midnight, anyways?"

I had that same question. Not why he was out walking, but why he was walking in an alley. "Theadora said the silent alarm was triggered, but that the police haven't yet found any evidence of a break-in." I thought of what Gary had told me about the booming pharmaceutical market in the region. "Maybe Curtis interrupted them in progress?"

"Like we did in the alley behind the post office the other night?"

"My thoughts exactly."

"Is Curtis talking yet?"

"No. The nurse said he might not even be able to have visitors for days."

"Well, I'll watch the library for you."

"What for?"

"So you can track down who hurt our man and give them a can of hell back."

THIRTY-SIX

I WAS CONFIDENT THAT my two alley-rats, Stingray and Hammer-head, had beaten up Curtis. I also had a hunch that Gary knew the same thing and was on their trail. I intended to help him in any way I could, without him knowing and without me risking my neck. It would be a delicate dance. I gassed up the Toyota, pur-chased a granola bar and a Styrofoam cup of coffee that tasted like burnt feet, and got to work, disregarding the sleep-deprived foggi-ness of my brain and the gravelly feel inside my eyelids.

My first stop was Silver Lake, and specifically the new cabin that had gone up on the north side last fall. It was a gorgeous, log A-frame on a pretty little wooded plot. I sometimes drove the long way home from work and so had witnessed the construction pro-cess, the cabin going up like a grand Lincoln Log project. I was al-most surprised when they didn't top it off with a plastic green roof and a little cavalry man to watch over the shores of the lake.

Nancy had mentioned that cabins all around the lakes had been broken into, but that this one had been trashed. It made sense that the gang was using them as a place to squat. Most lake cabins were empty in the winter. Free rent for thieves. That's when it occurred to me that I didn't know how many were in this gang. Gary had made it seem like a lot, but Taunita had made it sound like there were only a handful.

Taunita. I'd need to call her as soon as I reached a phone so I could update her on Curtis. I hoped she and the kids weren't trashing the house. I also wondered when I was going to break down and buy a cellphone. Most everyone I knew owned one, but I wasn't ready to be constantly available. Plus, they were expensive. Times like these, though, it seemed stupid not to have one.

I was thankful the weather was good. Cold, but clear, with only a light dusting of snow the night before. The January thaw had lasted all of two days, but it seemed to have brought a pile of trouble with it. The poplars and oaks lining the shores of Silver Lake were frosted with a bright white hoar. Most of the cabins dotting the shoreline appeared empty, except for one with smoke trailing up from the chimney. I wrote down the address and kept driving. It seemed unlikely that gang members would call attention to themselves by starting a fire, but what did I know from gangs? I kept driving until I hit the log cabin. It was placed far enough back from the road so that I had to pull into the recently plowed driveway for a full view of it, but I didn't need to drive far to spot the damage. The windows facing me had been boarded over, and I had to believe that the gorgeous bay window facing the lake was in the same condition.

I didn't spot any tracks. I stepped out of the car to be sure—fresh snowfall can play tricks on the eyes—but it was clear no one had been here at least since the previous night's light snowfall. The perpetrators, police, and probably owner had come and gone already. The only one left to visit was the insurance company.

I didn't actually want to locate Hammer and Ray. I just wanted to find where they were and pass that information onto Gary. My only other lead was the microbrewery, and that was a long shot at best. It relied on me being sure Eric was there—which I pretty much was—and that he was tied to the gang activity, even distantly. It was a strong possibility given his connections to Chicago and crime, not to mention the fact that he'd shown up in town the same time as the Sea Monsters Gang. Still, even if those two hunches were solid, I'd needed to coax the honorary Irish staff into giving him up, which is where my plan fell apart.

Maybe it was the giddiness of sleep deprivation that made me forge ahead despite all the long shots. Oh well. I'd worry about that when I got there.

THIRTY-SEVEN

THE FRESH SNOW GAVE the countryside a fluffy feel, like a loaf of bread just pulled out of the oven. I wasn't in the mood to enjoy it, though. I cruised past Vienna's house, noting that the T Wrecks tow truck was gone. New snow usually means new accidents, even during daylight hours. Something about the flakes messes with people's driving skills.

I'd concocted a plan during the drive. It was brief. I was confident Eric was working and possibly living at the brewery. I also knew that nobody would tell me exactly where to find him. I would chance peeking my head into the main lodge. If I spotted no one with an eyebrow piercing, I'd feign being lost and leave, my next stop the dorms/ fitness center Mrs. Berns had told me about. I hoped that no one at the lodge would recognize me as that nosy woman from the tour and spread the word.

I pulled into the lodge, noting there were no cars in front. I checked the front door. Locked. Well, that took care of that. I jogged over to the actual brewery and stepped in. The scent of sour mash washed over me. Two workers glanced up, startled. Neither of them had eyebrow piercings, and neither looked happy to see me.

"Sorry, are there tours today?"

"Not till the weekend." The man set down his clipboard and began to walk toward me.

"Thanks, I'll check back!" I smiled and let the door swing shut, hurrying to my car. He stood in the square of the door, watching me pull away. I veered off the main driveway, cruised a half a mile, and found myself in front of a building even larger than the main lodge, though without the charm. It looked like a small apartment complex, boxy, newish, with six large windows spaced evenly apart on both floors. I assumed they placed it out of view from the main building because it lacked the visual appeal.

I parked between a Toyota Prius and a Chevy Cavalier and walked in like I owned the place. I was surprised at how modern the interior was, though I shouldn't have been. I could see and smell the chlorine tang of the indoor pool, a glass wall separating me from the water and the couple splashing in it. An unstaffed desk was to my left and behind it were two doors, one marked "Women's Locker Room" and the other "Men's Locker Room." To my right was a hallway, which I assumed led to the kitchen, other workout rooms, and the "grope room." There also must be stairs somewhere that led to the second floor apartments. It was a fantastic setup for a mini-community, and I wondered if they would consider hiring me. Probably not. I had a tendency to burn bridges in situations like this.

"Can I help you?"

"Yes, I'm interested in—"

I turned toward the voice and found myself face to face with Eric Offerdahl.

THIRTY-EIGHT

THE PHOTO HAD BEEN fuzzy, but there was no mistaking the metal stake piercing his eyebrow. The brown hair and eyes matched, as well. He was my guy. I held out my hand.

"Betty Fishbacher."

He lifted an eyebrow. He smelled like cigarettes and stale whiskey and had the sallow skin of someone who didn't spend a lot of time above ground. "Eric."

I nodded, as if this was all normal. I was about to ask him about a job here when he scratched at his arm, revealing the bottom half of what appeared to be an electric eel tattoo, complete with lightning bolts of electricity zapping out of it. I thought immediately of Ray's manta tattoo and Hammer's shark ink. *Sea Monster*. Operation Offerdahl and Cold Case had just merged into one.

While my brain was processing all this, my body went a different direction and punched Eric in the chest. I didn't think about it, I didn't plan it, it didn't even occur to me that I was doing it until I saw him stumble, hand to his chest.

"What the hell was that?"

I glanced at my throbbing hand. *That* was accumulated stress, fear, and anger held in too long. I'd never punched anyone before, at least not like that. His chest had felt solid, and then it had given like wet paper when my force had overridden his, just like they'd taught us in the self-defense class I'd taken last month. "You're in the gang from Chicago."

He pulled his sleeve down. "Who the hell are you?"

I couldn't remember the fake name I gave him. My adrenaline, out of nowhere, was gushing like a waterfall. "I'm the friend of the old man you shits beat up last night. I'm the person who knows you all drowned Maurice alive and left his two little kids without a dad." I felt dizzy and realized I hadn't been breathing.

To my surprise, Eric laughed. "Hell, woman, we ain't that. We're just a bunch of dumb punks who like to pretend we're in a gang. We wouldn't hurt anyone. We might smoke a little dope, sure, but that's it. Mostly, I'm clean. I've got this job, right?" He held up his hands and indicated the rec room.

His confidence and unexpected honesty unbalanced me more. "You're friends with Hammerhead and Stingray?"

"Sure."

"The three of you didn't try to break into the Battle Lake Apothecary last night and then beat up an old man when he caught you?"

"No." He shook his head. "That sounds pretty harsh."

For a split-second, quicker than a blink, his front dropped and I saw his real self. If I hadn't been giving him my full attention, I would have missed it. Behind his friendly smile and easy half-truths, rage boiled like acid. The glimpse was gone, as fast as it had come, replaced by an open smile. Still, that peek was enough to chill me and bring me down from my adrenaline. I suddenly felt shaky and tired, and scared. But I wasn't going to make the same mistake he had, so I kept my angry face on.

"Yeah, pretty harsh. What about Maurice?"

Eric nodded, leaned back on the counter, shoved his hands deep in his pockets, studied his shoes like they held all the answers. "Real sad. We're hoping the police find out what went on there." He pulled his eyes back up to me, a new light in them. "Hey, are you the detective Stingray gave the letter to? Man, I told him he shouldn't have done that. He said you were a hot ride, though, looked a little like that actress in *The Texas Chainsaw Massacre*, the newer version, not the original. What was her name?"

I didn't answer.

"I didn't like the remake, but she was hot. Man. So maybe Stingray went in for that?" He chuckled, and then the chuckle turned to laughter. "What the hell did you tell me your name was? Fishbacher?"

I glanced at the pool. The couple was getting out, disappearing through the same door. Had they seen me hit Eric? Unlikely, or they would have come out already. I listened for other sounds in the building. I didn't want to be alone with Eric.

He pulled a lollipop out of his back pocket, a red one, and peeled off the plastic. He kept smiling as he sucked, still leaning against the front counter as if he possessed all the time and glory in the world. "I was at work here when Mo got offed, you can ask around. I heard he was a snitch who got what was coming to him, but I don't believe it. Sure, he might have gotten hung up in a real gang, but I think I would have known. He was a good guy, a good guy with weird ideas, but man, he didn't deserve to die. You know about Taunita? And the babies? Hammer said he called them, let them know about Mo."

I didn't like him being in charge of the conversation. "What do you know about Chuck Litchfield?"

He pushed himself off the counter, his mask falling again. He quickly adjusted. "He's a bad-ass. I'd watch out for him."

I couldn't tolerate his slimy presence for another second. He was a liar, and worse, he was cruel. It was written in the way he carried himself, the tightness in his shoulders, how his eyes always searched for an angle. He was disgusting. I turned without another word, every bit of me listening for him to follow.

"You didn't apologize for hitting me. You sorry, baby?"

I kept walking.

———

I dropped a quarter into the first payphone I found, at the Underwood Quik Stop, and dialed the Battle Lake Police Station. Victor answered. I told him that I'd located Eric Offerdahl, that he had a sea creature tattoo, and that he was likely gnawing on a fentanyl sucker while we were talking. I reported what Mrs. Berns had said about a possible grow room in the brewery dorm, as well, and asked him to pass all the information on to Chief Wohnt immediately.

Next, I called Chuck Litchfield and told him I'd located the sorry piece of shit otherwise known as Eric Offerdahl at the microbrewery dorms and that I'd send him a final itemized bill for my services before the end of the week.

Unburdened of that information and my responsibility to my client, I returned to the hospital to check on Curtis. After much rerouting and waiting, I discovered that he was in stable condition but could not yet receive visitors. Despite this, I recognized Bernie from the hardware store, Sid from the café, and Theadora from the Apothecary in the waiting room, just in case Curtis woke up and they'd be allowed to visit him. I also recognized the owner of the Shoreline, whose first job had been working as Curtis's farmhand, the nurse from the Senior Sunset who Curtis mentioned occasionally snuck him airplane-bottle-sized liquors, and the pastor from Curtis's church.

"About time you arrived."

I swiveled to find Mrs. Berns and Vienna wearing matching, swishy track suits and fanny packs. Vienna's hair appeared freshly permed, just like Mrs. Berns's, and her pursed lips and stocky build gave her the look of a low-rent Martha Stewart.

"What are you both doing here?" I asked, the emphasis on *both*.

"Stopped by to check on Curtis while we were in town buying party supplies."

Vienna stepped back and abruptly began fanning herself, glancing at Mrs. Berns with an annoyed look on her face. "Baked beans say what? You nearly uncurled my hair with that one."

Mrs. Berns shrugged. "It's your fault I'm eating so many vegetables. I feel like a parade horse. So, are you gonna invite Mira to the party?"

Vienna pulled her hand from her nose. I smelled the same odor she did and thought she was overreacting. Or maybe I'd spent too much time with my pets and my elderly friends.

"We're having a party at my house tomorrow," Vienna said. "You're invited."

She didn't seem happy about inviting me, like her mom had told her she needed to pick me for the team. Was she feeling as possessive of Mrs. Berns as I was? A few more of Mrs. Berns's gas attacks, and she'd likely be cured of that. "I don't think I'm swimsuit ready. Besides, I was just at the fitness center, and you may want to lay low in your neighborhood for a bit."

Vienna drew herself up to her full, impressive height, her eyebrows beetling. "What do you mean?"

Not for the first time, I wondered what Mrs. Berns saw in her. She was a little stodgy, despite her hunter-hunting and her yoga and her faux-hippie lifestyle, and she didn't seem to have much for humor. Plus, Mrs. Berns hated to eat healthy. "I mean the police believe there might be some drug activity at the fitness center and maybe the brewery." I left myself out as the informant in that situation. "I don't suppose you'd know anything about that?"

"I don't draw conclusions, I draw connections."

I looked at Mrs. Berns, my eyebrows raised. *Do you see what sort of person you're hanging out with?* they said.

She raised one eyebrow of her own, it's meaning clear: *Don't judge or I'll give you a snake bite that'll make you wish you could smell my fart again for relief from the misery.*

I kept a scowl aimed at Mrs. Berns but spoke to Vienna. "The police know about the grow room at the fitness center."

Vienna crossed her arms, looking from me to Mrs. Berns and back to me again. "How do *you* know about it?"

I shrugged. "There's a gang member working there. He isn't very tight with the secrets. What I want to know, do the owners of the brewery know he might be using it as a front for drug-running?"

She laughed at me, exactly as Eric had laughed when he realized I'd given him Betty Fishbacher as an alias. "You were talking to Eric, weren't you? The young man with the piercing above his eye? He's a liar, and a troublemaker, too, if you ask me. I just do the cooking, though, and teach some classes, so it's none of my business who they hire. But no, I can assure you that O'Callaghan's is a legitimate brewery run by decent people. Eric is a bad apple they think they can reform."

"What about the grow room?"

"It's not even at the fitness center. It's just a nickname for an old cabin behind it in the woods where the kids hang after their shifts. They like that it feels secret. I can't guarantee they're not smoking any pot there, but they're certainly no front for a drug cartel." She wiped at her eyes, giggles still bubbling out.

My cheeks were hot. Getting laughed at publicly twice in one day was no treat, but what was eating me was that her story matched Eric's. Could it be that he was just an aimless doper, and that the hard drugs were coming from somewhere else? But no, Jed had told me the sea monster gang had the hard stuff, and I trusted him. That meant that either Eric had pulled the wool over Vienna's eyes, or she was in on it, too. I was weighing whether to punch her in the chest or check her purse for drugs when I entertained a thought, one I should have invited a lot earlier.

"Hey, who's watching the library?"

Mrs. Berns pretended to have a great deal of interest in the plant behind her.

"Mrs. Berns?"

She put her hands on her hips. "Fine. I left the library because I wanted to go out with Vienna. Who reads on Thursdays, anyhow?"

"You just closed it down?"

"No, I didn't *just* close it down." She rolled her eyes. "I got all the people out first."

My jaw dropped. My head was getting ready to pop when a nurse came over to me, a tentative smile on his face.

"Are you Mira James?" He glanced over his shoulder. "Marne at information told me."

"Yes." My heart drop-clutched.

"I have good news! Curtis woke up for a few minutes."

I grabbed his arm. "Is he awake now?"

"I'm afraid not. He asked about you, and someone named Mrs. Berns, and said something about a tattoo and a hurt baby animal? And then he was out again."

THIRTY-NINE

I HUNG AT THE hospital until they chased me out well past visiting hours. Curtis didn't wake up again, but the nurse on staff assured me that it was an excellent sign that he had spoken. Driving home, I couldn't remember the last time I ate. Was it yesterday? I realized I was so hungry that my stomach was cramping. I pulled into the Sunmart Foods parking lot and dipped into the deli to buy some spicy buffalo wings. I ended up leaving with the wings, a grapefruit soda, mashed potatoes with gravy, green beans, and a small bag of salt and vinegar potato chips. When I pulled into my driveway, 97 percent of the food was in my tummy and only 3 percent on the front of my coat and in my lap.

"Where have you been all day?"

Taunita was seated on the couch, Timothy tucked under her arm and Alessa in her lap, reading an *Olivia* picture book to both of them. I glanced at the clock. It was 6:28 PM.

"My friend's in the hospital. He was in critical condition, but it looks like he's through the worst of it." Away from the hospital and anyone who really knew me, I began to melt. The tears came first, followed by the kind of crying that made it hard to breathe.

It was embarrassing to be so emotional in front of a near stranger, but she pulled me over to the couch. I'd been doing too much of this crying thing lately. When my sobs had subsided to whimpering, I wiped at my eyes and saw that Timothy had put his soft blankie across my lap and gone to play with Luna. Alessa was on the other side of her mom, still watching me with her serious eyes, her thumb stuck in her mouth.

"Sorry," I said, pulling away and going for a tissue.

Taunita watched me. "We all need a good cry sometimes. What put your friend in the hospital?"

I told her, starting with who Curtis was and what he meant to me, how he'd become a close friend and honorary grandpa to me. He was my guy. I counted on him. I needed him. "I guess he woke up for a short bit this afternoon," I finished. "He asked for me, and another friend, and said the guy who attacked him had a tattoo and made a sound like a hurt baby animal."

"Aw shit." Taunita stood and began pacing. "Ray beat up an old man? Outside a drugstore? Shit," she repeated.

Timothy's eyes grew wide. I expected we would hear him trying out that word very shortly.

"Sounds like," I said. "I don't know anyone else with a stingray tattoo. I told the police what Curtis said before I came here."

"But your friend isn't awake yet?"

"He wasn't when I left. He won't be talking to anyone before tomorrow at the earliest."

She glanced at her jacket. "You mind watching the kids while I go out for a while? I gotta get out of the house."

Timothy was brushing Luna with a hairbrush that looked suspiciously like my own. Also, a distinct smell had begun to emanate from Alessa's quadrant of the room, and it wasn't chocolate.

"How long will you be gone?"

"Not too long. I need air."

"Fine." The woman had just watched me break down. What else could I say?

Ten minutes later, on her way out the door, she hit me with another zinger. "Oh, and a really hot guy stopped by looking for you. Almost gave me a taste for blondes, except he looked so sad. Said his name was Johnny?"

———

"Peeza."

"Your mom said you already ate." Alessa hadn't warmed to me yet, but neither was she crying. It had been just the three of us for nearly an hour. For most of that time, Timothy had alternated between saying "ship" (thank goodness he couldn't say his "t"s well) and "peeza." I'd spent a lot of those minutes trying not to think about Johnny. I knew I should call him, but not now. I was busy. I'd think about it tomorrow.

"Peeza."

Had to give the kid points for consistency. "I have string cheese. Do you want some of that?"

"Peeza."

My shoulders slumped. Pizza delivery, like high-speed internet, had not yet come to rural Minnesota. A gas station in Battle Lake offered in-town pizza delivery. I lived three and a half miles outside of town.

"I'll try." I grabbed the phone. After two minutes of negotiation and "turn left at the Johnson farm" type directions, the delivery man agreed he'd bring pizza right to my door for an extra $5 delivery charge. I took it as a victory. Thirty minutes later, Timothy and I were enjoying second supper, and Alessa had allowed me to hold her, though she craned her neck like an owlet so she could watch me while I did so.

"Does your sister ever smile?"

"Dinah-sore!" Timothy dropped his pizza slice, arched his fingers into claws, drew back his lips, and growled.

I was getting ready to check his temperature when I felt the chuckle in my arms. Alessa was laughing at her brother, a deep Buddha giggle that rocked her whole body. It was contagious, calling up bubbling giggles from inside me. The more Alessa and I laughed, the more faces Timothy made, from monkey to giraffe to "monter-bot-a-rawr."

"Hey," I said spontaneously. "Do you guys want to go sledding?"

Timothy stopped in mid-mouse and pointed at the window. "Dark. Dark out der."

It was indeed night, but a gorgeous full moon glittered on the snow like an invitation.

"Moonlight sledding! It'll be fun." I cleaned up the pizza, wrote Taunita a note explaining where we were, changed Alessa's diaper for the second time that night, and piled both kids into their winter gear. Twenty minutes later, I'd hauled Sunny's sleds out of a nearby shed and pulled the kids to the top of the sledding hill by the house. Luna was at our side, barking her excitement. The three of us slid down dozens of times, snow shushing up at us and the moon smiling down. I was amazed and grateful that Taunita trusted me with such incredible, valuable, creatures. They giggled. They begged for more. Boogers ran down both their faces like open faucets, and still they didn't want to stop sledding. I thought of Maurice, and all that he would miss, and

I kept on sledding with them until we were all soaked and Alessa's eyes were heavy despite the smile on her face. I situated them both in the sled, Timothy holding his sister, and pulled them gently back.

They were both asleep by the time we reached the house, their cheeks impossibly rosy and vulnerable, their mouths both perfect little hearts. I carried them softly inside, wiped their noses, undressed and changed them, and tucked them into bed without waking them. I fell asleep on the couch so I'd be nearby if they needed me. Before I drifted off, I had a realization. The night I'd gotten the call about Curtis, I'd been sleeping on my mattress rather than under it. That meant tonight was the second night in a row that I'd slept above ground.

Something about having the kids around made me feel stronger.

FORTY

I woke to the sound of someone shuffling in my kitchen. I sat up, rubbing the sleep out of my eyes. The sun had not risen, but the murky lavender of the sky suggested it was near the horizon.

"Taunita?

"Ssh, now. The babies are still sleeping."

I smelled oatmeal and coffee and heard her humming. "Where were you?"

"Stopping a cycle." The humming continued. "Feeding justice. You must have wore out T and Alessa. They never sleep in this late."

I pulled myself off the couch and poked my head into their room. Both were still conked out, Timothy sleeping with his arms sprawled and Alessa curled around a blanket. They looked like cozy, chubby angels. Returning to the kitchen, I accepted the cup of coffee Taunita handed me.

"I took them sledding. They're pretty sweet kids."

"Sledding? At night?"

"The moon was full." I sipped at the coffee. It was bitter and delicious. I could get used to these roommates. "What do you mean you fed justice?"

"Not worth talking about. Can I borrow some money?"

I almost asked her what for, but it didn't matter. I have a rule that I'll lend anyone money once with no expectations of return. That way, I'm never let down, only pleasantly surprised. I grabbed my wallet off the counter. I had three twenties. I handed two to Taunita. "Do you know Eric Offerdahl?"

She shoved the money in her back jeans pocket. "I know the name. He's a drug punk. Maurice met him through a friend in Chicago."

"He's from this area originally and is back here now, working at a brewery."

She snorted. "From what Maurice told me, if Eric is working a legit job, it's just a front to sell drugs. Mo said Offerdahl has bad bones."

Her mention of Chicago earlier stirred a thought. "Have you ever heard of O'Callaghan's? They had a carpet empire in the Chicago area, and now they own the microbrewery where Eric works. I'm wondering if the whole business is a front for drug-dealing."

She shook her head. "Nah. Never heard of them. But if they owned an 'empire,' it makes no sense for them to mess with drugs. And why out here, in the middle of nowhere? It's probably just two-bit Eric doing his business out the side."

"Was Maurice dealing?"

She poured the oatmeal into a bowl. It smelled like apples and cinnamon. She must have brought it with her. Conflicting emotions chased each other across her face. She took her time answering.

"He said he wasn't," she said softly. "He said he was just here following up on those letters. But then he got himself killed, so I don't know. You're gonna look into what happened to him, aren't you? You said you would."

"Mama?"

We both turned. A tousle-headed Timothy stood in the doorway, his blankie in one hand and a love-worn teddy bear in the other. I wanted to hug him close, but he was looking at me shyly, as if he was embarrassed at how well we'd gotten along yesterday.

Taunita grabbed him and held him close. "Hey, baby. I heard you went sledding!"

He ducked his head into the crook of her neck. "Hungry."

She began feeding him oatmeal. I was deliberately ignoring her question. I didn't want to tell her no, but Maurice's death was in police hands now, and with the drugs and recent violence, they certainly weren't going to care about some old letter and a drafty story about a stolen inheritance.

I took advantage of her attention being distracted and slipped to the phone to call the hospital. No change in Curtis's condition, for better or worse. I ducked into the shower and got myself cleaned and prepped for work. When I returned to the living room, Alessa was awake, too, and eating her share of oatmeal with her mom's help. She put her arms up to me immediately when she saw me, and I felt like I'd just won the Boston Marathon.

I snuggled her, taking over the oatmeal feeding and managing to keep us both pretty clean.

"I'll keep my ear to the ground," I finally said. "But nothing's changed. I still can't promise anything."

Taunita smiled and nodded. She'd been waiting patiently for my answer.

"I've got to go to work at the library, and then maybe run some errands after. I don't know when I'll be home."

"All right," Taunita said.

All I could think of to help was to stop by the Prospect House before work in the hopes of talking with Carter Stone. I'd ask him what, if anything, he knew about Orpheus Jackson. It was the safest way I could think of tracking down information for Taunita.

It was a beautiful day, icy but clear, the sun sparkling off the driveway with the strength of a klieg light. The air looked and smelled beautifully clean, purified in the bitter cold. I put the temperature at five below zero, but it was only a guess. I scraped all six windows as the Toyota warmed up, or at least became less frigid. The seat was still rock-cold when I slid into it, hunched forward so I could see through the defrosted circles immediately at the base of the windshield. By the time I reached the end of Sunny's long driveway, I didn't need to hunch. The lower third of the windshield was clear. By the time I was at the Prospect House, the car was warm. Oh well.

It was eight o'clock, well before regular tour hours. I decided to walk right into the kitchen rather than knock. I surprised Carter pouring a mug of coffee, his Civil War–style cap askew on his head.

"Good morning!" His voice was surprised, and he glanced over my shoulder. I followed his gaze and spotted someone disappearing down the stairs that led to the section of the House devoted to the Civil War.

"My wife," he said, by way of explanation. "Going to do some more cataloging. Were we expecting you?"

"Sorry, no. I was hoping you could answer a few questions for me before I go to work. About Orpheus Jackson?"

He leaned into the fridge, grabbed a jug of whole milk, and poured a healthy dose into his coffee. "Who?"

"Orpheus Jackson. He was in the Battle of Honey Hill with—"

"Barnaby Offerdahl," he finished for me. "Barnaby served in the 1st Artillery. I believe the Union lost nearly a hundred men in that battle. Barnaby was one of 'em. I do recall the name Orpheus, but it's more an old legend than anything. A story really."

"Do you mind telling it?"

He shrugged, taking a deep pull from his coffee cup. "From what I recall, Barnaby didn't mention Orpheus in any of the letters to his brother that I came across, but that's no surprise. Barnaby didn't trust any of his own family beyond his daughter. What I heard, I heard through the hundred-and-twenty-year-old grapevine, so I wouldn't call any of it reliable. But there was a story that Barnaby became close friends with a free black man during the war. It was a bit of a scandal around here, in those times, because Barnaby spread the word that he was bringing the man back with him to live in Battle Lake."

"But he never did bring an army buddy home with him?"

"Not that I know of. Barnaby only came back to Battle Lake once after he started serving, shortly after the first time he was shot, but he was back in the field again soon after."

"But the free black man did come here."

He set his coffee cup on the counter and topped it off. "How do you mean?"

"The hanged man."

"Ah." Carter rubbed his mustache. "That is true."

My heartbeat started humming. I smelled a mystery here, a 120-year-old one. "I don't suppose that hanged man could have been Orpheus, returning with a message for the Offerdahls?"

"Never occurred to me, but unlikely. Why would he have traveled all this way with a message, just to hang himself?"

Excellent question, *if* he actually hung himself. And if what Taunita had said about the return address on the letters Maurice had found was true, I knew for a fact that Orpheus had spent time in Battle Lake. "I wish we knew if the hanged man had any clues on him."

Carter took a big slurp of his coffee. "That I *can* help with. I found a wooden box of his effects near the attic."

"What? How do you know they belonged to the hanged man?"

He tapped his head. "I'm a bit of a historian. Well, more than a bit. Plus, the box was labeled 'hanged man,' with the date of March 1865 on the box, same month as the body was found." He winked at me. "We're cross-checking all boxes with the newspaper articles we have so we can find out what was what. We have quite a database going."

"What was in the box?" I couldn't contain my excitement. "Anything that would identify him?"

"All I remember is the musket. I keep that on display downstairs."

"Can I see it?" The words of Orpheus's letter were spiraling in my head: *Should anything happen to me, look to the tunnel of justice.* The tunnel of justice! What else could that refer to but the barrel of his musket? For the first time in my life, a mystery was falling into place immediately. I imagined discovering a note from Orpheus tucked in the barrel of the gun, yellowed with age but bearing a map to Civil War treasure he'd buried. Taunita and the babies would be rich. I followed Carter into the basement, fighting every instinct in me to nudge him in the back, forcing him to move faster.

"Libby?"

His wife glanced up from the far side of the room, where she was holding an ornate old handgun in one hand and typing on a laptop with the other. "Yes, love?"

"You remember the hanged man box?"

She turned to face us full on, setting down the handgun. Her face was pleasantly lined, her fading blonde hair curling at shoulder level. "Of course. It's a gruesome story."

"What else was in the box?"

She returned to her laptop, typing in a quick flurry of letters. "Musket 25A, a Bible, a wooden fife, and two quarters, two nickels, and a penny."

"He had money in his pockets?" My heart dropped. So he hadn't been robbed, which suggested that he also hadn't been murdered, his treasure map taken, and then his body moved to make it look like a suicide.

"Sixty-one cents."

"Here's the musket," Carter said, drawing my attention to a nearby table.

He placed the gun into my hands. It was heavy, maybe seven pounds, the dark brown wood worn so smooth that it felt satiny. The trigger was plated silver, as was the hammer. A metal strip rested on the top and the bottom of the long barrel, three equal-spaced silver bands circling the length of it.

"That's a Springfield rifle musket, a single-shot muzzle-loader. You see the hammer?"

I nodded, touching the cool silver with my thumb.

"A percussion cap. It fired a .58-caliber Minie ball. One of the most accurate rifles of its time."

"And it was found next to the hanged man's body?" I couldn't shake the disappointment. If Orpheus had been murdered as I believed, surely his gun would have been taken.

"As far as we know. We just have the wooden box. This gun definitely would've been used in the Civil War, so the date on the box is accurate."

I turned the gun around. "No chance this could still fire?"

"None. I cleaned all the guns myself, made them safe for handling."

"I've always wanted to look down the barrel of a musket." It was a weird thing to say, but less odd than just doing it, I figured.

"Knock yourself out."

I could feel Libby staring at me from across the room. I kept my attention on the hole, angling it toward the light, still nervous about looking down the barrel of a gun despite Carter's assurance. I didn't see anything and so angled it farther, and there it was—a shadow within a shadow. There was something curled inside the barrel. I sucked in my breath.

"Well, that's one dream realized," I said, handing the gun back to Carter. I couldn't very well dig out whatever was in there right in front him. I liked him, but the residue of sleepless nights had me paranoid, and I didn't know whose team he was on.

"All right," he said, chuckling.

I appreciated that he didn't question weirdness. Too bad I had already made up my mind to break into the Prospect House that night and steal the gun. "Thanks for your time. I better be running," I said, making for the stairs. I walked past a gorgeous corn plant. "Beautiful plant!" I called over my shoulder.

"Thanks," Libby said.

I thought I also heard her say, "Kennie takes care of them," but I chose to block that out.

———

The rich, dark smell of fresh-roasted coffee washed over me, trailed closely by the homey scent of fresh-baked rolls. I would need to cut back on my eating, or at least start eating healthy, but I would think about that next week. Today, I wanted nothing more than a soy latte sweetened with fresh honey and sprinkled with cinnamon powder and a side of Sid's homemade chocolate chip–pecan banana bread. I swallowed the excess saliva pooling in my mouth and made my way to the front.

The door opened behind me, letting in a gust of icy air, but I was staring at the glass display case like one of Pavlov's dogs. I *could* have a fresh-fried glazed donut instead. Or—ohmygod, a new tray had just been slid into the display case—I could eat one of Sid's famous skollebollers, a Norwegian cardamom-scented, vanilla custard-filled, coconut-dusted bun. They were so fresh that their warmth steamed the glass. I moaned.

"We have to stop meeting like this."

I swiveled. Mrs. Berns was stepping from foot to foot.

"Do you have to pee?"

"Nope." She tugged off her hat. "Just cold. Whatcha gonna have?"

I glanced back at the case. Could I declare an emergency and budge everyone? "Skolleboller."

"Good choice."

"Why aren't you with your new friend?"

She pulled off her mittens, breathing into her fingers. "I missed you."

I felt my eyes light up. "Really?"

"No!" She punched my arm. "Ha. You're so gullible. No, I decided there's only room for one gutsy old dame in a gang, and so I dumped her. She was too bossy, anyhow. Speaking of, what's on our agenda for tonight?"

I was ashamed at how happy I was that she and Vienna had broken up. I'd get the details later. For now, I just wanted to enjoy the moment. "Quiet night."

"Hairy liar."

"What?"

"I thought we were stating an adjective and then a pertinent noun. Along those lines, I am calling you a hairy liar. Not only did I see you pull out of the Prospect House on my way back from the Shoreline, but I also see your eyes are a lighter brown than usual. That means you're excited about something."

Hmm. Maybe she was better at this detective thing than I thought. "I have to run an errand tonight for a friend."

She raised her eyebrows.

I glanced around. Ah, what the heck. There's nothing as fun as a secret shared. I leaned in and whispered into her ear. "Break into the Prospect House."

She gave a rebel yell. "I'm in!"

"I don't need a sidekick."

She snorted. "And I don't need oxygen. Besides, too late. We're already this generation's Bogey and Bacall. Or at least, Bonnie and Clyde."

"I'll think about it."

"I'll save you the time. I'm going with."

"Mira, Mrs. Berns! How're you two doing?"

We were finally at the front of the line, distracting me from my conversation with Mrs. Berns. "Hi, Nancy! I need two skollebollers, stat. And a soy café miel."

"Not until you give me some news." She lodged her hands into her hips.

I realized I'd been neglecting her and Sid. Usually, I stopped in at least once a week during slow times so I could visit them. Sid didn't talk much, but she let you know she appreciated you being around in small ways, like baking skollebollers. Lately, I'd been doing little more than grabbing a meal here or there and leaving. "Sorry I haven't stayed around to chat much lately. A lot going on."

She raised her eyebrows, waiting for me to tell her more. I didn't mention Taunita and the kids because that would bring up too many questions, and there was a noisy line forming behind me. Instead, I gave her a thirty-second synopsis on Curtis's condition, told her I was researching more deeply into the Prospect House, and updated her on the library business.

"You forgot to mention your Nut Goodie recipe in the paper," Sid said, coming out to put her arm around Nancy. "That was a winner."

"Did you actually make it?"

Sid winked. "Come over later when we're not busy, and I'll let you taste." She disappeared into the back. Nancy began making my order, talking over her shoulder as she did so, filling me in on small-town news. It was comforting.

She had my food and drink ready in a blink. She nodded across the busy main room of the coffee shop while she leafed my change out of the till. "And that's Bad Brad's new girlfriend over there. She's met him here for coffee twice this week."

I followed her gaze. All twelve tables were packed, and three women and two men lined the counter facing the main window. "Which one is dating Brad?"

"The one eating a banana."

Mrs. Berns scrunched her eyes in the direction of the window. "Who eats a banana in public?"

I homed in on the banana-eater. I was thirty and knew Brad was at least two years older than me. Samantha the insurance agent, however, appeared to be twenty-four, maybe twenty-five, with curly blonde hair, wide hips, and sensible shoes. She kept glancing at the front door between her bites of fruit. The seat next to her was empty.

"Brad's worried she's cheating on him. Asked me to look into it," I said to nobody in particular.

"Now's your chance," Mrs. Berns said, wiggling her eyebrows at me. She pushed me out of the way so the people behind us could order. "You're sharing one of those skollebollers with me, right?"

She kept pushing me toward the woman. I had no choices but to speak or look like a stalker.

"Samantha?"

She glanced at me, confusion in her eyes. They were slightly wide-set and a gorgeous deep green. "Yes?"

I held out my hand. "You don't know me. I'm a friend of Ba— er, Brad's."

"Did he tell you to tell me he was going to be late?"

"I haven't seen him," I answered honestly. "He's mentioned you quite a bit lately, though."

She reached for her coffee cup. "All good, I hope."

Something about her face made me want to tell the truth. "He thinks you're cheating on him."

She did a spit take with her coffee. "Me? Cheating? Why?"

I felt a nudge from behind. "No good reason, really. He said you didn't post your relationship status on Facebook, and that you don't seem eager to commit." I felt stupid saying this out loud, so I stopped.

"You said you're friends with Brad."

I nodded.

"Then you know what he's like. Look, I love him, though I haven't told him and I won't. He's a big child. We're having fun now, but he's not husband material, you know?"

It occurred to me that Samantha was around 90 percent smarter than I'd been at her age, or even than I was a year ago, when I'd been dating Brad myself.

Mrs. Berns peeked around my side. "Mrs. Berns," she said, extending her hand. "Pleased to meet you. Pleased to meet anyone with a head on their shoulders, really. Now, let's be honest. You're only with him because he's good in bed, right?"

"I wish," Samantha said.

I could vouch for that, as well. Brad subscribed to the McDonald's model of sex: quick and unvaried. "So no cheating?" I asked.

"I don't cheat," she said simply. "If I want someone else, then it's time to stop dating the person I'm dating."

I was beginning to think I needed this woman as a friend. Or a life coach. "Thanks," I said. "I'll tell Brad to stop worrying."

"How about I tell him myself?"

I smiled. "An even better plan."

I let Mrs. Berns guide me out the door, where she pinched one of my skollebollers. We parted ways, her promising to meet me at the end of my library shift. I told her I'd believe it when I saw it. I drove the mile to the library, sipping my creamy, cinnamony coffee as I steered through the quaint streets of downtown Battle Lake. Except for the crazy spate of crimes that seemed all connected to me, it was a wonderful place to live, I mused. I held that thought as I unlocked the library, fired up the computers, and nibbled my cardamom-scented skolleboller, promising myself that I'd learn how to bake them at home so I could eat them in herds.

The library crowd was steady, and the day passed in a pleasant drift of helping people find books, cleaning up the library's computer files, and walking the shelves. I skipped lunch out of deference to my shrinking pants and instead used the time to type a report on Eric Offerdahl. I no longer cared why Litchfield wanted to find him, or for that matter, about Eric Offerdahl at all. I was washing my hands of the whole deal. Tonight, I would treasure hunt for Taunita. The police could worry about the baddies.

By the time Mrs. Berns showed up at the end of my shift, I was actually happy to see her. Frankly, breaking into huge, haunted mansions at night is a lonely business. Plus, she offered to spring for dinner at the Turtle Stew beforehand. I drove, and we were seated in a booth near the front windows. We both knew what we wanted, and the food arrived quickly.

"What exactly is the plan?" She grabbed the pepper from my hand to douse her plate of gravy-covered mashed potatoes and meat loaf.

I snatched it back to finish peppering my French fries. "We find an unlocked window, sneak in, grab the gun, fish out whatever is in the barrel, and sneak out. No harm, no foul."

"Your plan rests on an unlocked window? In January?"

"You have a better idea?"

"Since you ask ... "

"What?"

"You promise you're not going to ditch me after I share my secret?"

I stole a forkful of mashed potatoes off her plate. Yum. Homemade. "We're already committed."

"My friend Ida is a volunteer at the Prospect House. She said they keep a spare key above the inner doorjamb of the garden shed."

"You are worth your weight in gold."

"Tell me something I don't know."

FORTY-ONE

THE GRAVID MOON LENT a soft glow to the night. All the lights were off in the Prospect House, but there was still traffic passing by on 78. Even worse, we could hear people playing a pick-up game of hockey near the ice castle on the lake. We had left the Toyota parked in the alley behind the Turtle Stew and walked the mile to the House, ducking into the sparse woods circling it when we were certain no one was looking. We'd crunched through the calf-high snow, and slipped into the shed. The key was not exactly where Mrs. Berns had said it would be, but with her on my shoulders, fumbling around in the dark interior of the shed, we finally located it. Actually, it found us, first plunking onto my head and then hitting the ground.

"Got it!" Mrs. Berns claimed triumphantly when it hit the ground.

I helped her down, rubbing at the spot where the key had hit. My noggin was taking a beating lately.

She scooped up the key, and we turned to consider the house. It seemed to be staring right back at us.

"Eerie, isn't it?" Mrs. Berns asked. "Those two windows up there look like eyes, and the back door is right between and below them, like a mouth."

I recalled the little girl's face in the attic window last Saturday, the heart-shaped face I had filed away as Elizabeth Offerdahl's ghost. Or my imagination. I punched Mrs. Berns lightly on the arm. "Shut up. I'm already scared enough."

"Better git your big girl pants on, because we're doing this." Unexpectedly, she took off across the driveway separating the shed from the Prospect House, slamming her back against the wood siding when she reached the house. I was surprised she hadn't attempted a full-body roll on the way over. I wanted to make fun of her, but even more than that, I didn't want to get caught. I copied her moves.

"Suave," she said as we stood with our backs against the house, glancing to the right and left for any sign of movement. Only she pronounced it to rhyme with *wave* because that's how cool we were.

Instead of responding, I crouched, staying low to the ground until I reached the door. The key fit in the lock like a hot knife in butter, and we were standing inside the kitchen in seconds. We caught our breath and let our eyes adjust to the light. I was aware of the clutter, and the shadow-smell of coffee brewed several hours earlier. The silence in the house was so intense that it almost became a sound itself. I'd snooped around and broken into four, maybe five places in the past eight months, all in the name of solving a mystery, but it never felt comfortable. The hyperawareness of knowing you were in a place you weren't supposed to be looking for stuff that people didn't want you to find was both exhilarating and terrifying. It gave me an intense urge to pee or giggle.

I clicked on the flashlight and directed the narrow beam to the stairs leading to the basement. "The Civil War stuff is down there."

"You first."

I tiptoed to the top of the stairs and shone the flashlight down the steps. The dusty yellow light landed in a lonely circle at the bottom, something about it suggesting ghost fingers and lurking zombies, waiting for someone stupid enough to enter.

"Tell me about your husband," I whispered. I needed something to distract me.

"What?"

"You heard me." I took the first step. Little warning feelers shot like electric bolts down my legs and arms.

"What do you want to know?"

"Did you love him?" I took the second step. Mrs. Berns was so near that I could feel her breath on my neck.

"Sure. Didn't matter back then, though. He put food on the table. He paid the bills. He didn't hit me. But he didn't live life, he worked it. And he drank too much."

"Your whole marriage?" We were now in the middle of the stairs, halfway between escape and the dungeon. The air felt heavier in front of us.

"You know how when a tree has a good year, lots of water and sunlight, and you can see huge growth when you look at its rings? It's the opposite with people. We grow more in our bad years. I grew a lot married to Harold."

Harold. Harold Berns. I took another step. Fear crawled across my skin like newly hatched spiders. Any number of horrors awaited us below, among the dusty relics of long-dead soldiers. Maybe, just maybe, something that would also help Taunita was down there, too. "Do you miss him?"

"I paid my dues. That was the past. Now, I live in the moment. It's the only way to be." She coughed, and I jumped.

"Do you hear that?" I asked.

"What?"

I stopped. Behind her cough, I thought I'd heard a moan. It must have been the wind, yet I couldn't stop the chilly sweat gathering at the base of my spine. We were now at the bottom of the stairs, large tables standing sentry on each side of the landing. It felt like we were being watched by a hundred leering eyes. I risked panning the room with a flashlight so we could get our bearings. It lit across uniforms in glass, bayonets, guns, and—

Could it be?

I brought the light back to what had grabbed my attention, my heartbeat thick and terrified.

It was.

On the far side of the room, a little girl, staring solemnly at Mrs. Berns and me.

I screamed and dropped the flashlight.

FORTY-TWO

"Wʜᴀᴛ?"

"I saw a face! We're not alone." I fought the urge to charge back up the stairs only because Mrs. Berns was blocking my exit. I snatched the flashlight from the floor, brandishing it like a weapon. That's when I noticed the face was also pointing a flashlight back at me.

It was a mirror.

"Holy crap," I said, gathering my heart from my throat. "I thought it was a ghost. It's just my reflection."

Mrs. Berns cackled and took the flashlight from me. "I don't think you are equipped to handle this dangerous tool. Now where's the damn gun? This place gives me the willies."

We held hands and shuffled over to the table where Carter had shown me the musket. I was relieved to discover it lying exactly where he'd set it down. I glanced over my shoulder, still nervous about the mirror, but the space behind us was a dull blank surface.

"Shine the light in its barrel."

Mrs. Berns complied. "I see it! It looks like rolled-up paper."

"Grab me that poker," I said, pointing at a thin metal pole behind her. With its cool metal in my hand, I began fishing inside the barrel of the gun, but my efforts just pushed the paper farther away from us. This wasn't going to work. "Dangit. We have to take this gun apart."

"Don't look at me. I fire 'em, I don't build 'em."

I held the butt with my left hand and cradled the barrel in the nook of my right arm. "Well then, it looks like it's coming with us. We'll find someone who knows guns, have them help us remove the paper without hurting it, and return it before Carter even knows it's missing." That's what I hoped, anyhow.

Rather than question my illegal and ethically murky executive decision, Mrs. Berns led the way toward the stairs, flashing the light in a steady stream. I kept my eyes trained away from the mirror, and we moved as a single shuffling beast. We were nearly to the base of the stairs when something caught her eye. She stepped over to a table to the left of the stairwell.

"Look at these!" She took her mittens off and set them on a nearby counter.

"Keep your mittens on! We don't want to leave fingerprints."

She snorted. "This is Otter Tail County, not the Big Apple. Besides, there's got to be a million fingerprints around here." She held up a brilliant blue teardrop necklace. The direct beam of the flashlight made it sparkle like a thousand sapphires.

"Do you think it's real?"

I couldn't take my eyes off of it. The main teardrop was the size of a dime, and the chain of the necklace was dripping with pearl-sized blue beads. "Probably crystal," I said, hypnotized. "I wonder what it's doing in the basement with the Civil War stuff?

A scraping sound drew our attention, a low, quiet noise on the floor above. It was short, happening so quickly that it might not have happened at all.

"Did you hear that?" I whispered hoarsely.

Mrs. Berns placed the necklace back on the table, clicked off the flashlight, and grabbed my elbow. "Sounded like a one-legged, worm-eyed pirate come to steal our souls."

If my hands were free, I would have hit her. "Let's get out of here."

I didn't need to tell her twice. We speed-shuffled toward where we thought the steps were, and took them quickly, moving toward the lighter patch of darkness that outlined the ground floor landing above. Even our hair was on high alert, quivering, as we strained to hear any more sounds. We tried to be as quiet as we could, but fear made us clumsy. Mrs. Berns dropped the flashlight, and then I bumped the gun against the wall trying to help her find it. Finally, though, we reached the top of the stairs. We didn't dare turn the flashlight back on. We'd already made enough noise.

Despite our bumbling, we made it to the back door and locked it behind us, breathing in deep, fresh gulps of winter air. I let my heartbeat slow to a steady pace, infinitely grateful to be out of the house and to have the musket in hand. I tiptoed across the packed snow to return the key to its hidey spot, Mrs. Berns right behind me.

"I didn't know Carter had dolls in his collection," Mrs. Berns said, breaking the silence marked only by our feet crunching in the snow. My ears were attuned to the potential sound of cars passing.

We reached the shed. "I don't think he does." I grunted as I reached up to tuck the key.

She hitched her thumb toward the house. "Didn't you see that girl doll on the island in the middle of the kitchen on our way out? Looked like she was floating in the moonlight. Creepy. Why people want big old dolls is beyond me."

My blood froze. "There was no doll on the island when we went in."

We swiveled our heads to stare at each other, our faces a perfect replica of fear. When our eyes locked, we squealed and ran, not slowing until we reached my car.

FORTY-THREE

BEFORE WE PARTED WAYS, Mrs. Berns reminded me that Johnny's band was playing that night. I knew she wanted to ask if I'd spoken with him since I'd spent the night at Bad Brad's, but she was friend enough not to plant a direct question on me. I told her I'd think about Johnny tomorrow. In the meantime, I needed to get this gun to the one person on the outside who could help me dismantle it without destroying it: Curtis Poling. He was still in the hospital, though. I would visit him first thing in the morning, hoping for his sake and mine that he was awake.

Taunita and the babies were up when I returned home, so I kept the gun stowed in my car. I didn't want to raise her hopes unnecessarily, so I didn't tell her about our Prospect House break-in. Instead, we chatted about the day while I helped her to bathe Timothy and Alessa. The three of them had checked out the address where Maurice had stayed with his grandma in the summers of his youth. Their retreat had been on Silver Lake, though whatever modest structure had originally been there had since been replaced by a modern A-frame.

When I asked, she allowed that it was odd that his family of limited means would vacation on a lake so far from home, friends, and family. She said Maurice had never questioned it as a kid but as he got older, wondered about the connection between Orpheus and the area.

It was about the time she put Alessa and Timothy to bed that I noticed my house was spotless. Even the plant leaves had been dusted. The air smelled fresh and lemony, and the countertops gleamed. Taunita had been busy. I wanted to thank Taunita, but the door to the spare bedroom was already closed. I crashed shortly afterward, the post-adrenaline let-down hitting me like a cement truck. My plan was to get up at seven so I could make the hospital's eight o'clock visiting hour.

I slept on my mattress.

―――

Ron Sims, editor and owner of the *Battle Lake Recall*, beat my alarm clock the next morning. "James."

He'd never been what you'd call loquacious. His wife was the voice of the operation, both their marriage and the *Recall* offices. They were a decent enough couple except that if you caught them in a room together, they'd inevitably start making out like two walruses with a limited mating season and only one chance to save the species. It meant a lot of people didn't visit the *Recall* offices, myself included, unless absolutely necessary.

I scratched absently at my arm, standing in the middle of my kitchen and squinting against the promise of sunlight filtering through my blinds. I wondered if I should take the phone off the hook so I could finally land a decent night's sleep. That, or put a line in my bedroom. "Morning, Ron. What's the news today?"

"Need someone to cover last night's break-in at the Prospect House. You in?"

I perked up like a gopher, the punch of his words knocking the air and sleep out of me. "Whoof." I actually said that, out loud. It was all I could manage.

"James?"

I sucked in a bit of air. Ron knew the Prospect House had been tossed last night, which meant the police knew. "Yeah. Someone broke into the Prospect House?" My voice squeaked.

"Someone who was not very smart."

Crap. Was he giving me a chance to confess?

"They left their mittens behind," he continued.

The vision was so clear I could have stepped into it. The flashlight catching the glint of the graceful blue teardrop necklace, Mrs. Berns pausing to remove her mittens and never putting them back on.

"What'd they take?"

He grunted. "Impossible to know. It'd be like stealing from a church garage sale. Carter called it in this morning. Said last night he thought he heard noises coming from the house—he and Libby live in the carriage house on the next lot—and he went to check. Found the house sealed tight, everything normal except for the mittens in the basement that hadn't been there when he'd locked up earlier. Plus, footprints leading into the woods."

For the love of Betsy. Had he also spotted the little pee trails we'd probably left after the ghost scared us out of there? And since when was everyone a detective? Whatever happened to people minding their own business? I was going to jail.

"James?"

"Yeah, I'll cover it. I need to run to Fergus to check on Curtis this morning, but I can stop at the House over my lunch break." *If I'm not incarcerated.*

"Probably just kids being kids. I'll expect news by the end of the day." Click.

It was now that much more urgent that I reach Curtis to see what was inside the gun barrel. If I returned it before Carter noticed that it was missing, I stood a chance of keeping me and Mrs. Berns out of the pokey. I speed-showered, told a sleepy Taunita that I'd be back that night, and was almost out the door before I realized I couldn't exactly tote a Civil War musket into a hospital without drawing some unwanted attention. I hurried back to my bedroom closet but couldn't find anything large enough. I ducked into Sunny's office, where she had piled most of her belongings before leaving for Alaska, and dug through boxes until I uncovered an old hockey stick duffel bag. Perfect. Maybe today wasn't going to be so bad after all. Maybe everything would fall into place.

Maybe pigs were right now flying through a frozen-over hell.

FORTY-FOUR

"Curtis Poling." It was the third time I'd said the name, but still the flustered woman at the information counter couldn't seem to locate him. The heavy black hockey stick duffel lay on the floor next to me like a neon sign.

"Is that with a C or a P?"

"Is what with a C or a P?"

"His name."

I wanted to tap on her head to see if her melon was ripe. "First or last name?"

"Last name," she said, as if it were obvious.

"It starts with a P. P-O-L—"

A deep voice behind me interrupted my recitation. "He's in stable condition. Woke up last night, ate solid food. Still can't have visitors."

I turned so slowly that I could hear my neck creak. No way Gary Wohnt was standing behind me, right? Stolen Civil War musket in a hockey stick bag much?

"Gary! How're you feeling?"

He was not in uniform. Instead, he was wearing denim jeans that fit him like a friend, a crisp blue oxford, and a green and gold patterned tie. He was leaning heavily on a cane, but somehow it made him look even more capable.

He aimed one pointed glance at the duffel bag.

I in turn stared at his cane, my eyebrow raised. It was meaningless, but he didn't know that.

"What's in the bag?"

Maybe he did know that.

"Curtis's favorite hockey stick. I knew he'd want it." Because what old guy doesn't want a piece of wood when they're recovering from a beating? "You said he's alert?"

Gary let the silence fill the air between us. It did exactly that, sniffing around our heads, and it judged me lacking, and then it started pointing at me as if I were guilty. So I killed it. "I'm really worried about Curtis. Can you please tell me more?" I didn't have to fake the pleading in my voice.

It did the trick. "He's going to be okay."

"Did he say anything more beyond the tattoo and the animal noise comment?"

Gary's eyes narrowed. "What else do you know?"

"That's it. I promise." I raised my hand in what I assumed was Girl Scout's honor. There's nothing like squatting on a bag of lies to make you righteous about a single truth. "The nurse told me the other night that Curtis had asked about Mrs. Berns and me, and that he'd mentioned the tattoo and the same noise I'd heard when Mrs. Berns and I were harassed in the alley. I told Victor when I called the station the other day."

Gary only nodded.

"Are you questioning anyone in Curtis's attack?"

"What do you think?"

I thought it was time to beat cheeks. "I've got to get to work, that's what. If you're not going to tell me anything, I'll be on my way."

He stooped as if to help me hoist the duffel, but his cane drew him up short. I lifted the bag myself, trying to flex my muscles only as much as would be required of a hockey stick.

"That looks heavy," he said suspiciously.

"Back in the day, they built their sticks to last." I didn't look back as I scurried out the sliding doors, but I could feel his eyes boring into me. I'd have to return tomorrow with the gun and hope to high heaven I didn't run into Gary again. For the moment, though, all I wanted was to put as much distance between the stolen item I was carrying and the Battle Lake Chief of Police as I could. The icy cold scratched at my cheeks.

"Hey. Betty Fishbacher."

I turned toward the hoarse voice, resisting the urge to clutch the gun like the weapon it was. "Eric Offerdahl."

He had been standing behind a pylon but revealed himself when I passed. A lit cigarette dangled from his lip in a deliberate attempt at coolness. He kept running his hands through his hair and then patting his pockets like he was looking for his wallet. His eyes jittered, and his mask was gone, open anger laid across his face for all the world to see.

"How's your friend?" he asked.

"You mean the Battle Lake Chief of Police whom you shot last week?" It was a blind stab. I knew he was talking about Curtis. The hit scored, though, and his face twisted even more darkly.

"Hmm. So you did shoot the chief. Why?"

He flicked his cigarette at me. I let it bounce off my shoulder. Gary was just inside the hospital doors, talking to the underskilled woman behind the information desk. I could yell for help, and he'd come. I ground out Eric's cigarette with the toe of my winter boot.

"I didn't shoot anyone," he snarled. "I'm here to tell you that Ray was arrested. Tell Taunita to watch her back, 'cause snitches get stitches."

He stared me down, shoving his hands into his pockets. My first instinct was to punch him in his throat, but then I thought of Timothy and Alessa. I did not want Eric any madder at us than he appeared. When Taunita had said she fed the justice machine, did she mean putting Ray in jail?

"What's he in jail for?"

"Taunita knows."

The automatic doors of the hospital slid open. A nurse wearing a winter coat pushed a man in a wheelchair forward. A van pulled up at the end of the sidewalk. When I looked back to Eric, he'd vanished. I realized it didn't matter why he was threatening Taunita. He knew she was staying with me, and that meant she and the babies were in danger.

FORTY-FIVE

Sid and Nancy were happy to put up Taunita, Timothy, and Alessa in the spare apartment above the coffee shop. Taunita said it wasn't necessary, that she could handle a dumb drug punk like Eric just fine, but I reminded her that the kids couldn't. Once they were settled, I used Sid and Nancy's home phone to call the hospital. They patched me through to Curtis, who sounded weak but like himself.

"What were you doing scrapping in alleys anyhow?" I asked him, my eyes clouding with tears. I couldn't believe I finally got to hear his voice.

He coughed. "Gary told me to tell you not to mess with them. They're rough people."

I knew he had been beaten up badly, but that didn't sound at all like something Curtis would say. "Is Gary there right now?"

"I told him you were smart enough to keep yourself safe."

Gary must be in the room with him, or Curtis would have answered me directly. "Don't let Gary know what we're talking about, but do you know anything about Civil War guns?"

"Of course I like honey buns. I used to collect them."

I could hear his wink through the line, and it felt like a weight being lifted. They could beat up Curtis, but they could never diminish his humor or wits. "I have one I need you to look at. It might have something to do with all of this, though I have no idea what."

"Bring 'em by," he said. "I'm sick of this hospital food. Now, I've got some people who want to talk to me. You won't want to bring those buns until tomorrow because I'll have a lot of company today."

Message received. "Love you, Curtis."

"That's about right," he said gruffly before hanging up.

I rubbed the back of my hand against my wet eyes. Curtis was going to be okay. Now, I had to make sure the same could be said about me. Next stop, the Prospect House to discover what they knew about the break-in—and the idiots who had conducted it.

FORTY-SIX

TURNS OUT, CARTER DIDN'T know much, but he did know that the hanged man's gun was missing. I had no choice but to play dumb as he showed me digital photographs of the footprints in the woods. He said the police had confiscated the mittens. The whole time we spoke, I could feel the gun burning a hole in the back seat of my car like only guilt and fear can do. At the end of the interview, I returned to run the library, type up the Eric Offerdahl report for Chuck Litchfield, and write a very brief article about the break-in.

After the library closed, there was nothing to do but go home and wait. Curtis had warned me not to bring the gun to him until tomorrow. My head was too busy to deal with Johnny or Mrs. Berns. I considered sketching what I knew, but it was so little. Hard drugs had infiltrated Battle Lake about the same time Eric Offerdahl had arrived. Maurice, Ray, and Hammer followed shortly after, possibly to help Eric distribute the drugs. However, Maurice had told Taunita he'd come for a different reason—to claim his inheritance. If that was true, if there was an inheritance, the proof had fallen into my lap through a convoluted web of history. An inheritance wouldn't erase any illegal activities Maurice had engaged in, but it might help out Taunita and the kids. Also, Eric had most certainly shot Gary, which made me believe he'd shot and killed Maurice as well. He was a loose cannon who was now gunning for Taunita because she'd turned in one of his lieutenants for beating up Curtis.

It was danger and confusion, all tied in a bundle and set on fire. All I knew for sure was that I missed having the kids around. One of Alessa's blankets had been left behind, a blue cotton square as soft as duck down. I smelled it. Sweet, clean baby. I couldn't even clean house to pass the time because Taunita had scoured everything, even alphabetizing my seven spices. I finally read until I fell asleep.

Under my bed.

———

The next morning, I was up with the dawn, filled with a rare sense of purpose despite my shame at returning to my nest under the mattress. I was going to check on Taunita and the kids, then bring the gun to Curtis for help dismantling it. We'd find Orpheus's final letter, which would lead us to the inheritance. I'd give it to Taunita, and I'd wash my hands of the entire ordeal.

I was outside the coffee shop by 6:02 AM. It was already open. I walked in. Nancy smiled up at me, her eyes tired but bright.

"No skolleboller today, but I've got coffee brewing."

"Can I just buy some Long Johns? I'm going to visit Curtis in the hospital."

She began packing them immediately. "Tell him these are on us."

"Will do. Don't suppose Taunita is up?"

"Wouldn't know. She and the kids left with a friend last night."

A cold ball of lead dropped into my stomach. "What?"

"Some old friend, he said. Looked like a punk with that barbell through his eyebrow, but who am I to judge?"

"She took the babies, too? They all left without a fight?"

"As far as I could tell. Taunita said she'd call you to let you know where she's at. Everything okay?"

I ran all the way to the police station. My chest ached, my lungs like two frozen balloons when I finally reached it. I pulled the door open. Gary started to stand when he saw me, but his injury brought him up short. The bags under his eyes and the way his mouth was drawn suggested he had worked through the night.

"Taunita. The babies. Eric Offerdahl has them!"

I spilled the story of Taunita's relationship to Maurice, and how she had narced on Stingray and maybe the whole gang and now Eric had taken her and her kids.

"They left without a fight?" Gary's eyebrows were arched so close together they were almost touching.

"That's what Nancy said." I wasn't going to cry in front of him.

"Then there's not much we can do." He turned from me.

"Offerdahl is crazy! I think he's the one who shot you."

He shook his head. "I'll look into it. That's all I can promise."

Gary wrote down a description of Taunita and the kids and sent me on my way. Outside the police station, the cold air cut at my ice-burned lungs. I had no idea where to go. I certainly wasn't going to drive home and wait. I could go to the microbrewery and search for Eric, but there was no way he'd hide out there with two little kids and a woman. I didn't know where else to dig, so I decided to look online.

I took off on foot, the brisk air cauterizing my nostrils.

I was unlocking the library door when I felt the hand at my throat.

I whipped around to face a very angry-looking Eric Offerdahl, his pupils the size of pinpricks.

FORTY-SEVEN

"I WILL SAY THIS once." His voice was low, dangerous, metal scraping against pavement. "I have Taunita and the kids. I will trade them for the gun."

"What gun?" I wasn't playing stupid. I really *was* stupid. He couldn't possibly be talking about the Civil War musket, which only me, Curtis, and Mrs. Berns knew about. What other gun was there?

"I know about Maurice's letters. I know the crazy shit thought he had an inheritance coming to him. I can't take a chance that he might be right. When I heard the stolen gun called in on the police radio, I thought immediately of that damn 'tunnel of justice.' I figure you were thinking the same thing, after Taunita told me she'd asked you to look into the whole shitpile when she come to ask Ray to turn himself in." He laughed, and it was a black sound. "Like Ray would be dumb enough to do that. But Taunita didn't even give him a chance, did she? She went straight to the police."

"What?" I felt like the world had flipped me upside down and was going through my pockets for change.

His shifty eyes landed on me. "Where exactly do you think this inheritance was gonna come from? Everyone in my family knows the story that a crazy black man showed up pretending to be a good friend of old Barnaby, claiming he had property rights if anything were to happen to Barnaby's daughter. But Barnaby's daughter didn't live and the man disappeared, and so it all went to my great-great-great-grandpa. Not much of it left, but enough, and my dad isn't going to live much longer."

It was falling into place, but into weird place. "You're not here to deal drugs?"

He laughed. "What is this, a Bond movie? You don't need to know why I'm here. Suffice to say that it's a happy coincidence that I first met Maurice Jackson a decade ago, when he was here visiting his grandma, and that we stayed in touch. And it's an even happier one that he spilled to me about the inheritance he thought he had comin'. How could he know it was tied to the Prospect House? Only people born and raised in Battle Lake know those stories. Crazy world, isn't it? But I need that gun, now, just in case there's something to it all."

"It's at home."

"Then you better get it. You think you can find the cabin on Silver Lake, Fire Number 23470?"

I nodded.

"Good. I'll meet you there in thirty minutes. You better have the gun and no one else. You show up alone, you hand me the gun, and I hand you Taunita and the snot babies. You tell anyone what you're up to, and the world has three less mouths to feed. And I'm watching you. Understand?"

I nodded again, tongue-tied.

FORTY-EIGHT

I RACED BACK TO my car outside the Fortune, pushing my sore lungs to take in more air. I didn't see anyone watching me, yet I felt a million eyes crawling across my back as the morning dawned. Plus, Eric's uncanny ability to anticipate where I was going to be made me feel as vulnerable as a cow in a slaughter chute. I reached my car and let myself in, trying to think things through as I drove. Thank goodness I'd walked to the library, or Eric would have spotted the gun in my back seat. My best bet was to drive home exactly as I'd promised him I would, charge inside, and call Gary immediately. Only in movies are people stupid enough to arrive at an isolated location alone for a trade. Who was I, Chuck Norris?

I raced home and ran to the house. Luna and Tiger Pop were both outside, appearing miffed. One glance at them and I knew what I'd find on the other side of the door: destruction.

All of Taunita's cleaning was buried under ripped-up cushions and torn-open cupboards. Potato Buds and canned goods were strewn across the floor, furniture tipped over, everything in my bedroom closet thrown onto my bed. I ran from room to room, my breath jagged, but in every space, the story was the same.

Eric had already visited, and he'd left no corner intact.

That meant he knew I'd lied to him about the gun being here. My heart dipped. I hurried to the phone, fear crawling like cold-footed beetles across my skin.

"Calling someone?"

I turned. I hadn't bothered to close the door behind me. Eric stood there, Timothy on his hip. He must have followed me, and I'd been too frantic inside the house to hear his car.

"Mee-wa!" Timothy held his arms out to me. Dried tears caked his face, and he was sniffling.

I ran forward, but Eric swiveled so his body was between me and Timothy. Luna stood just behind them both, her hackles raised and a low growl in her throat. She was confused. She liked Timothy but knew something wasn't right here.

"Thought I'd give you time to call the police, did you? What do you think this is, the movies?"

I would have laughed at the irony if I wasn't so scared. A fresh tear rolled through the crust on Timothy's face, and he was trembling like a kitten, despite the winter jacket he wore. "The gun is in the back seat of my car."

"Get it."

I hurried past him, trying not to look at Timothy. He was leaning away from Eric like he wanted to push off him but was too terrified to do so. I returned in seconds hauling the black hockey duffel. Eric closed the house door behind me, trapping the animals outside.

"Open it."

I followed his orders, pulling out the long gun.

"Is there something inside of it?"

"I can't tell," I said. "It looks like."

"Get it out."

"I *can't*. If I could, I would have already. It's shoved too far in there."

"Then smash it."

"I'm not strong enough." I didn't know if this was true or not. "Let me hold Timothy, and you can smash it."

Eric considered his options, and then tossed Timothy at me. I caught him just before he hit the floor. He clung to me like a baby monkey, trying to crawl inside my coat. I hugged him tight and whispered soothing words, all of them lies.

Eric picked the gun off the floor and glanced down the barrel, presumably spotting the same shadow of paper that I had. He raised the gun above his head and smashed it into the doorway. The crash was deafening. Luna began barking. Eric swung at the door repeatedly until the barrel separated from the stock. He laughed in triumph when he ripped them apart, revealing a scroll of fragile yellow paper.

He yanked it out and unrolled it, his hands shaking. His eyes moved as he read. He smiled. At least I thought he did.

It took me a moment to realize it was a grimace of fury. "It's a goddamned letter from Orpheus to his wife. It says to look into the tunnel of justice, that she'll find their due in there, just like the other letter."

He moved his glance to me, his eyes bright and dangerous. "You have five seconds to figure out what that tunnel of justice is." He ripped Timothy out of my arms, dangling the boy by an arm. Timothy screamed and tried to kick at him with his tiny legs, but Eric didn't flinch. I hated him with a rage I'd never felt toward anyone before. I lunged forward, but Eric balled his hand into a fist and held it over Timothy, his threat clear.

I stopped, the rage burning through me with a white heat. I breathed deeply, forcing my mind to clear, thinking as I spoke. I needed to stall until I could think of a way out of this. "How do I know what the tunnel is? It might not even exist at all. Or it might be a place they traveled through, or a..."

My breath caught in my throat. I could read Libby's inventory of belongings left with the hanged man as if the words were floating in the air. *Musket 25A, a Bible, a wooden fife, and two quarters, two nickels, and a penny.* The tunnel of justice wasn't the gun, it was the fife—a battle instrument used to signal victory.

"What is it?" Eric was eyeing me suspiciously, ignoring the squirming, sobbing child reaching out desperately for me.

"If I tell you, you'll let Taunita and both kids go?"

"What do I want them for? I just need whatever Orpheus thought he had that would give him what's mine."

I didn't trust Eric, but what choice did I have? "I think it's the fife. Orpheus was the hanged man they found by the Prospect House in 1865. The hanged man came back from the war with a fife, and I think that's what he meant when he referred to the tunnel of justice."

Whether it would have anything in it, or whether it was what Eric and I were looking for, remained to be seen.

"Take me to it."

FORTY-NINE

WHICH IS HOW TIMOTHY, Eric, and I found ourselves in the kitchen of the Prospect House, talking to Carter Stone. Eric had warned me that I better keep quiet and make sure the same was true of Timothy, or we'd never see Taunita and Alessa again.

"Tell me again why you want to see the wooden chest?" Carter directed the question at me, but he was eyeing Eric.

"We think there might be something inside it to help with the ... story I'm writing," I said. I was sweating desperation. Eric had let me hold Timothy to quiet him down, but I was hyper-aware of the Offerdahl heir's hair-trigger penchant for violence.

Carter shrugged. "It's still up by the attic. Let me tell Libby what we're up to." He disappeared downstairs and returned moments later, not making eye contact with any of us. Had he felt the terror oozing out my pores? Could he see how frightened Timothy was? Had he told Libby to call the police? I prayed to every god I didn't believe in.

"Follow me."

Eric signaled for me to trail immediately behind Carter. The hair on the back of my neck prickled and every animal instinct in me yelled not to let Eric stand at my vulnerable back, but without knowing where he had Taunita and Alessa or what sort of shape they were in, I had no choice.

As we took the first flight of stairs, Eric was too amped up to make appropriate conversation but tried nonetheless. "Must be nice to live in a house like this. You get to live here?"

Carter glanced over his shoulder, his hand on the stair railing. The Prospect House was closed for business today so the police could continue to gather evidence on the break-in. We were the only ones inside, besides Libby. "My wife and I live next door, in the carriage house."

"This used to be my family's place. I'm an Offerdahl." There was an uncomfortable note of possessiveness in his voice, like he was daring Carter to contradict him.

"You don't say."

We climbed the second set of stairs, this one steeper than the first. I wanted to run, to inform Carter what was going on, to believe that help was on its way, but I kept myself calm through force of will. My hope was that we would find exactly what Eric was looking for and there would be no violence. We ascended the final full set of stairs, the narrow ones. We had to duck to reach the third-floor landing.

"They must not have had many fat people around when they built this house," Eric remarked with a snigger.

"Over there," Carter said, pointing across the room. We stood in the only clear area on the landing. Around us was the chaos of uncataloged items that I remembered from my first visit here—cardboard boxes with scribbled labels, stacks of musty-smelling clothing, old toys, moldering newspapers. "We have a record of what's inside, but we don't know where to put it yet."

On the edge of the chaos rested a plain wooden box, so old the wood had gone gray. "Hanged Man" was written on the side of it, along with the date of March 1865. A stack of newspapers towered behind it, nearly reaching the ceiling. Behind that was one last tiny set of stairs that Carter had informed me led to the attic the first time I visited.

Eric strode to the box and kneeled. He undid the brass latches on the front and lifted the lid, pawing through the contents. Carter, Timothy, and I were all watching as Eric stood and turned, the wooden fife in his hand. It was nearly as long as his forearm, carved out of a blonde-gray wood, crudely formed but lasting all these years. Eric peered through one end as if it were a telescope. A triumphant smile slid across his face like oil.

"I see it." He dug his finger in. The sound of dry paper riffled through the air.

Behind Eric, the door to the attic, the unreachable door, began to slowly, deliberately creak open. My heart jumped into my throat. Eric, oblivious, continued to dig inside the fife. I held my breath, terrified of what would reveal itself on the other side of that door. A zombie ghost in ragged tatters, coming to reclaim his inheritance? A floating girl corpse with maggots for eyes? How bad could one day get?

But then the door was fully open, dusty sunlight trailing in. There was nothing on the other side.

"Got it!" Eric said triumphantly, holding a yellowed scroll in his hand. He was framed by mountains of papers, and above and behind, the attic door.

"Hi," Timothy said, his tiny voice reverent.

I glanced at him, confused. He was talking to the open attic door.

"Hi!" he said again, with more force.

My heart stopped. I didn't see what he was seeing. The doorway was empty. But I did witness the musty tower of newspapers behind Eric slowly rock, as if pushed by an invisible wind. Reflexively, I opened my mouth to issue a warning, but I wasn't quick enough.

The enormous pile of aged papers fell on Eric.

He dropped the fife and the paper. Both fell at my feet.

I grabbed the scroll and Carter snatched the instrument before giving a floundering Eric a firm push back into the chaos of papers. He speedily herded Timothy and me down the stairs. He shoved us into a bedroom off the base of the stairs at the second floor and locked the door behind us. He ran to the phone mounted on the far wall.

"I'm calling the police. You can explain what's going on when we have handcuffs on that waste of air."

I set Timothy on the bed, pushing aside the gorgeous, yellowed lace dresses that were draped across it. He didn't want to let me go, but I couldn't trust the lock. I leaned into the heavy oak of the dresser to the left of the door, hoping to push it over and seal the entrance. I was grunting and straining when I heard Eric's footsteps hammer down the stairs toward us. He tried the doorknob, cursed, and kept running.

We weren't in the clear as long as Eric had Taunita and Alessa. I ran to the window. The moment Eric's car sped away, I ran down the stairs. Libby was there, wondering what was going on. I handed her Timothy, told her and Carter where I was going, and begged them to call the police.

I had no illusions that I could fight Eric, especially not if he had Hammer with him. I needed to stall for time, though, and I would do that by putting myself in their path. They could be hiding out in one of the cabins, but the police had been watching those carefully since the string of break-ins. They also could be in the rec house of the brewery, though that was next to impossible as no way would Taunita have let Eric take Timothy without a fight, and the noise of that would have alerted the brewery staff.

That left only the old cabin behind the dormitory, the one Vienna called the grow room.

I drove like lightning, the roads so icy that the front of my car was not always in agreement with the back as to what direction we were going. I roared past Vienna's, past the dorm, and found the little road behind it leading to the cabin. When I spotted Eric's car there, the relief washed over me like warm water, quickly followed by fear. I had no plan, only a conviction that I couldn't leave Taunita and Alessa alone with Eric.

I squealed to a stop, tried to breathe around my pained heartbeat, and stepped out of my car.

What Vienna had referred to as the grow room was a one-room cabin tucked deep into the woods. Puffs of woodsmoke curled asthmatically out of the chimney. Naked oak branches scraped against the snow-buried roof, and the whole unpainted structure leaned a little to the right. Two murky windows stared at me from each side of the door.

Eric was inside.

With luck, Taunita and Alessa were as well, and alive.

I felt a muddy mix of helplessness, fear, and anger. Inexplicably, horribly, the image of the Candy Cane Killer rose into my mind, paralyzing me where I stood. A wave of nausea so strong it felt like vertigo washed over me. I didn't know if I could override my self-preservation instinct and force myself to enter the cabin. How could I?

But then, I heard a baby cry from inside.

Hot tears clouded my eyes, and I sprinted forward, charging into the cabin, hoping that my directions to Carter and Libby had been clear enough, and that the police were on their way.

FIFTY

My breath was a full second behind me, slamming into my back as my eyes frantically tried to take in everything. The dirty windows gave the inside of the cabin a smudgy, underwater feel. The single room was bare of all furniture except a pile of wood and a pot-bellied stove that turned the space into a sauna and a rickety table surrounded by four mismatched chairs. Hammerhead was sitting in one chair, Vienna in another.

Niall, my brewery tour guide, was seated in a third. Eric was standing behind them, had probably been pacing before I rushed the scene. Taunita was tied in a bundle on the floor in the far corner, unmoving, her face turned away from me, her hands limp. Alessa was next to her, sucking on a pacifier, a bottle filled with what looked like cola leaning against her chunky little thigh. She had one possessive little hand on her mom. Her eyes appeared swollen, and I could smell her dirty diaper from across the room.

Everyone but Taunita looked up when I flew in, their faces a palette of anger and surprise. Vienna moved immediately to the door and slammed it shut behind me and leaned against it, her arms crossed.

"You're in on this?"

She ignored me.

"Who are you?" Niall asked, standing. He was wearing a wife beater, which revealed a deep purple octopus tattoo curling down his right arm.

Eric was breathing heavily, clenching and unclenching his fists. He must have barely beaten me here. The air was still charged with whatever heated argument they'd been having when I barged in.

"That's the detective I was telling you about. She's got the fife."

Niall shook his head. "You've messed it all up, the whole thing, for a *fife*?!"

"Not just a fife." Eric tugged on the barbell above his eye. "It's my family legacy."

Niall smacked Eric alongside the head with enough force that he almost fell into the stove. On the ground, Taunita's form shifted, making me realize I'd been holding my breath. *She was alive.* Relief washed over me, making me weak.

"Now what?" Niall asked. "You think about that?"

Eric held his hand over his bleeding nose. His eyes glowed like dynamite fuses. "Now I go back for the fife. I still have one of the kids."

"Except now both of these women have seen me. Dammit, I knew you weren't worth it, Offerdahl."

"Who told you about this cheap land?" he whined. "Who connected you with all the buyers?"

Was Niall an O'Callaghan, or just someone who had the ear of an O'Callaghan and used his access to convince them to open a brewery here? I inched closer to Alessa, who was still in her footie pajamas. The diaper smell intensified. Poor baby probably hadn't been changed since they'd been abducted. I didn't have a plan, exactly, except to comfort Alessa and her mom until the police got here. I prayed Taunita was conscious, though I wasn't hopeful.

"You. Brownie. You look familiar."

I stopped in my tracks. "You led a brewery tour that I was on. Is your real name Niall?"

"Bill." He continued as if we were on a first date. "I'm the graphic designer for O'Callaghan's. Maybe I mentioned that in the tour? I did the same job for their carpet company, and it was my idea that they start this brewery. As you just heard, Eric helped us to find the cheap land. Would have been a great gig with a little drug running on the side to keep things interesting, except this shit got greedy."

He lunged at Eric again, and Eric tripped over himself trying to get away. It worried me, to see how scared Eric was of Bill. Hammer-head watched it all impassively. Vienna was fidgeting at the doorway, shifting from foot to foot.

"It's my inheritance!" Eric said.

"Doesn't sound like it," Bill said, matter-of-factly. "And you're the reason I now have to kill all three of these people. Or, I should say, why *you* have to kill them. If you hope to walk again, that is. We've got too much money riding on this. Those drugs don't grow on trees, you know? There's investors I got to pay off. Hammer, you guarantee he does what he's supposed to do. Chop the bodies up for all I care, just don't leave a mess here."

He grabbed a black ski jacket off a chair and strode toward the door, his cold authority chilling me. "Oh, and her, too." He tossed a glance at Vienna.

"What? I didn't do anything wrong."

"Except tell people about this place. You had one job, and that was as lookout, not hostess. You messed up a good thing, sweetheart."

She opened and closed her mouth like a landed fish.

"Don't look so stupid," Bill said, brushing past her. "Eric said he saw you showing some old lady around. Had to be how Brownie here found us, right?"

He glanced at me. My poker face must have given me away. "That's what I thought." He slipped out the door, slamming it behind him.

I started talking fast, the sweat running down my spine. "You're not guilty of anything right now, Eric. You kill us, though, and you're a murderer."

He looked at me blearily. "Shit, I'm already a murderer. It should have ended at Maurice, then that damn backwoods sheriff almost catches me with a trunk of Oxy. Plus, now I got this little kidnapping. What's four more bodies?" He reached into his waistband and pulled out a gun, a sleek black semiautomatic, glittering and efficient. "If I don't do it, I can't live nowhere no how. Bill has eyes everywhere. You watch the door for me, Hammer."

The giant was emotionless. He strode to the door, pushing Vienna toward the table. She was as pale as winter, her eyes wide circles of shock.

My voice was hoarse. I felt like I was choking on words, not sure which to choose, knowing that four lives rested on me picking correctly. "Kidnapping carries a whole lot shorter sentence than murder."

"I don't plan to be caught for either."

"I don't believe you can shoot us in cold blood."

He snorted, aiming the gun at me sideways, gangster-style.

"Dang, Eel," Hammer growled, his first words since I'd charged into the cabin. "Bill said not here. Then we just got a mess to clean up. Go do it out back in the woods."

I was wondering if this is what Orpheus's last moments had been like, fumbled between inept crooks who were trying to steal what was rightfully his. As long as we were talking, though, we weren't dying. I twisted the skin under my arm to give me something to focus on other than the panic. "Let me get Taunita up. I'll carry the baby. We can walk to the woods. It'll be quicker."

I hurried to Taunita's side before he could argue. I was grateful to find that she was not only conscious, but had no visible wounds other than deep bruising over her right cheek and a black eye. I didn't know how much longer we had, but her being unharmed increased our odds of survival from zero to around a tenth of a percent.

"Keep her hands tied," Eric warned.

I unknotted the rope around her ankles and helped her to her feet. Her eyes were grateful but bruised. "The police have Timothy," I whispered. "He's safe."

A sob escaped her, and she fell into me.

"Hurry up!" Eric pushed us with the butt of his gun.

I made sure Taunita could stand before I scooped up Alessa. She felt soggy and light, her tiny body hot and wiggly in my arms. "Hey, sweetheart," I said. It was all I had. I opened my jacket and zipped her inside, where she squirmed and whimpered and stank, only her head visible through the neck of my coat.

I gently held Taunita's elbow to steady her. "I'll lead the way," I told Eric.

My words sounded brave, but I felt like I was walking above myself, looking down to see our sad little trio marching to our death. I kissed the top of Alessa's head and held her tight, the honey scent of her baby shampoo thick in my nostrils, laced with the sour reek of urine.

Taunita leaned into me. Alessa's grubby little fists bunched up my shirt.

We stepped into the glare of the sunlight, the brightness blinding after the murk of the cabin.

Something even brighter than the diamond glint of the sun caught my eye, and then again, from a different angle, followed by a third glare from a new angle. I had only one second to guess what it was. I pushed Taunita down, curled Alessa into my arms, and fell over them both.

The raging thunder of a gunfight rained over our heads like judgment.

FIFTY-ONE

"I KNEW SHE WAS no good," Mrs. Berns stage whispered. She was wearing her cap guns, had in fact told me she hadn't taken them off except to sleep since her grandkids had arrived two days ago, coincidentally the same day I'd charged into the grow room. Apparently, they appreciated Mrs. Berns exactly as she was.

"You knew no such thing," I argued. Because of her grandkids' arrival, we hadn't had a chance to speak since the shoot-out, an old-West style gunfight of Battle Lake's finest against Hammerhead and Eric. Gary hadn't seemed happy, exactly, when he'd first spotted me stepping outside of the cabin, but at least he hadn't shot me. Eric had taken one in the elbow and another in the shoulder. Hammer had not been so lucky and was now sporting a toe tag. Vienna, using her finely honed hunting instincts, had ducked about the same time as me and gotten away without a scratch.

Once taken into custody, Eric refused to go on record for killing Maurice, though Kennie informed me that Stingray was in the middle of negotiating a deal, narcing on Eric, and admitting to robbing cabins and thrashing Curtis when the old man had caught him and Eric trying to rob the Apothecary. In return, he'd been offered leniency on drug possession charges.

Bill had already been extradited to Chicago for a whole raft of drug-related crimes he'd left behind. For now, the O'Callaghan's brewery was set to re-open once the police were done thoroughly investigating the premises, but it remained to be seen whether anyone in the family knew about the drugs being dealt right under their noses. If O'Callaghan's could be traced back to the influx of OxyContin and fentanyl into Otter Tail County, they would go down hard. I kind of hoped they weren't in on it. The world needed more ice castles and chocolate stout.

"Did too," Mrs. Berns said. "That's why I dumped her. I don't roll with criminals."

"She's not going to be rolling with anyone for a while." Vienna was currently awaiting trial on assisted kidnapping charges. Her ties to the OxyContin trade were not yet clear, but it appeared as though Bill had hired her to be his eyes in the woods, keeping track of anyone who wandered the property. She may have done some dealing, too.

"Shh."

I glanced down at Timothy, who was standing at the pew next to me, and I blushed. There's something about having to be shushed by a toddler that truly mortifies, especially since we were likely at the funeral of his great-great-great-great-grandfather. It took Barnaby Offerdahl's notarized will—retrieved from the hanged man's fife and naming Orpheus Jackson executor of his estate should anything happen to Barnaby and heir to the estate should anything happen to Barnaby's daughter—to convince the county coroner to exhume the hanged man's grave. It would take weeks to verify through DNA that he was indeed Orpheus Jackson, and that Timothy and Alessa were direct descendants of his. My money was on a happy ending.

If all went as planned, the children stood to inherit the land surrounding the Prospect House. Given that most of it was lakefront property, it was worth at least half a million. At least that's what Chuck Litchfield told me when I spilled the whole story. Turns out he'd hired me to find Eric because Eric's father, Gregory, had been hospitalized for a stroke the previous week. Gregory was still hanging on but looked like he wouldn't last through the month. As per his will, which Chuck Litchfield had drawn up, Eric was to be contacted and informed if his inheritance became imminent. Litchfield had kept his motives on the down-low because Gregory had stipulated that no one would know of the land changing hands except Chuck and Eric. I guess old habits die hard.

Because the Prospect House had been rightfully bought and sold at least four times since Gregory's ancestors killed Orpheus to obtain it, it was unclear what would happen to the structure, though Taunita said she and the kids had no interest in it. If lineage was established, she would now be executor of the estate for her children, until they were old enough to decide if they wanted to sell the land or keep it in the family. In the meanwhile, Chuck Litchfield was able to uncover some liquid assets of the Offerdahl estate. He promised to work on obtaining a loan for Taunita with the assets as collateral so she had money to raise the kids until all the legal aspects were worked out. He was also the one who helped her to organize today's funeral for Orpheus, and tomorrow's for Maurice, both at the Battle Lake Lutheran Church. He said it was the least the town could do for the two men. I might have pegged Chuck wrong.

In the meanwhile, Sid and Nancy had offered Taunita and the babies the apartment over the coffee shop rent free and given her a temp job as a barista. She paid back the forty bucks she'd borrowed from me after her first shift. As a bonus, I'd agreed to watch the babies at night until she could make other arrangements. I sincerely hoped she would not be able to.

Taunita stood on the other side of Timothy during Orpheus's service, bright tears streaming down her face, Alessa in her arms. She'd lost Maurice. He'd been her whole family, other than her kids. She didn't have anywhere to go and I'm sure had mixed feelings about staying here until everything was straightened out. I wished I could ease her loss, but only time has that power.

At least there had been a good turnout for today's funeral, and I knew there'd be even more tomorrow. A few of the attendees were ambulance-chasers, but most came because it was the right thing to do. Barnaby Offerdahl's brother had stolen Orpheus's inheritance and likely his life. His brother's ancestor had then done the same to Orpheus's ancestor, and very nearly gotten away with it. Justice had finally been done, possibly with the help of Elizabeth Offerdahl's spirit. Carter and I had spoken about the opening attic door and the falling papers since Eric had been arrested. Neither of us had actually seen a ghost, but we weren't willing to write off the possibility that the Prospect House had an otherworldly protector.

As my eyes took in the full pews, I couldn't help but notice how ridiculously glossy and gorgeous the plants lining the window wells were looking. I felt the familiar jealousy burn. *Kennie.*

When the service was over, we filed toward the basement for the funeral meal and I passed Kennie talking to a particularly perky-looking fern in the hallway. She was wearing all black, but Kennie-style: leather pants and a fur coat, plus sky-high stilettos. Atop her head rested a demure hat with netting and sleek black feathers.

"What're you saying to that plant?" I demanded.

She turned, a guilty expression on her face. She quickly wiped it off. "Why, Mira! You just can't accept that you're not the only one in town with a green thumb."

For some reason, her comment made me glance at her thumb, which was presently blue. I grabbed her wrist and yanked back the loose sleeve of her fur coat. There it was. A catheter bag strapped to her arm, the hose leading to her wrist. It was filled with a Smurf-blue liquid. I sniffed it.

"Miracle Gro! I knew you were up to no good."

She put her hand over my mouth and dragged me into a corner, making smiling "everything is fine here" faces to the people walking past. "I am a plant healer," she hissed into my ear.

"You're a plant liar," I squeaked through her fingers.

She pressed me against the wall, glancing right and left. Her expression grew calculated. "Have it your way. But if I'm not doing my plant and animal psychology, I might go back to renegade makeovers. Or home bikini waxes." She glanced at my crotch area, her eyebrows raised. "You'll never know when I might drop by."

"Fine," I said, exasperated. I didn't want her to know I was actually happy. In fact, I was thrilled to find out she was not an actual plant whisperer. I still wore a smile on my face as I stepped down the church basement steps and smack into Johnny. And his blonde girlfriend. My heart cracked.

I glanced from one to the other, for some strange reason feeling guilty even though he was the one who'd technically cheated. Johnny was as gorgeous as ever, wearing a light green button-up shirt and dark tie. The woman I'd seen him embracing in Bonnie & Clyde's alley was as strikingly blonde as him, her features carved out of ivory. Probably they were perfect for each other. I turned, ready to head back up the stairs. I'd taken about as much pain as I was willing to for the month. I didn't want to be broken up with in a church basement.

I felt a gentle hand at my wrist.

"Mira, have you met my cousin Corinne? She was at my practice last week."

Something in his voice made me turn. "She's your cousin?" Up close, I could see the resemblance: the same hair, stunning blue eyes, and plump curving lips. She was a knock-out.

He nodded. I couldn't read his expression. Was he mad? Disappointed? And why was he getting on one knee?

Before my thoughts could organize, he gently leaned his shoulder into my stomach and stood, hoisting me over his shoulders in a fireman's carry. He began walking up the steps, and the entire basement erupted in a cheer. He kept walking, opening the door, stepping outside into the ice crystal-perfect day, away from the church, and toward his house. The smell of winter air filled my nostrils, and the cool lemon sun glowed overhead. People were staring, some of them laughing and pointing, others looking at me with something like admiration, still others acting like it was just another day in the life.

"I imagine you've guessed that Mrs. Berns told me what you thought you saw, and why you haven't been returning my calls," he finally said, only a little winded. "I'll make a deal with you."

I didn't say anything, just enjoying the ride on his shoulders. It had been that sort of week.

"If one of us wants out of this relationship, we tell the other. No cheating. No lying. No drama. Because you know what? I'm always going to treat you well. But so help me, if you take me for granted, or assume the worst about me, I don't know if we can make this work. Understood?"

He set me down on his front stoop two blocks from the church. Before I could answer, I felt his mouth on mine, hot and seeking. His hands followed, and then his hips pressed into me, pinning me against the door. He kissed me deeply, and then pulled back abruptly to open the door, throw me back over his shoulder, lock the door behind us, and carry me to the bedroom. His house was strong and neat, with guitars leaning against the wall and books lining the shelves. It smelled like vanilla.

Johnny threw me onto the bed. The down comforter held me like a cloud, and sparkling sunlight filtered in through the curtains. I'd been to his house a handful of times, but never in his bed. He tore off his jacket, and then stripped off his tie and shirt. He never dragged his eyes off of me except for the brief moments when cloth separated our gazes.

"I love you. I want to be with you. I want you always. Nod if you understand."

I nodded. At least I think I did. My whole body had been taken over by a buzzing sound that started between my thighs but had since spread to every centimeter of my body, a warm, honey-liquid feeling that warned me I was about to have a really, really good time.

He kneeled on the bed. The sun shone behind him, lighting up his curly blonde hair like a halo, perfectly outlining his sculpted shoulders and arms. His hands were gripped into fists. He had been worried, angry even. But he hadn't left me.

In fact, he'd come after me.

I sat up and yanked him on top of me, both of us falling back into the covers in a passionate, laughing, hopeful pile.

In that moment, I vowed to reconsider how much better it was on top of the bed than under it. And with Johnny than without.

Jane Bailey Photography, Inc.

ABOUT THE AUTHOR

Jess Lourey spent her formative years in Paynesville, Minnesota, a small town not unlike the Murder-by-Month series' Battle Lake. She teaches English and sociology full time at a two-year college. When not raising her wonderful kids, teaching, or writing, you can find her gardening and navigating the niceties and meanities of small-town life. She is a member of Mystery Writers of America, Sisters in Crime, the Loft, and Lake Superior Writers.

ACKNOWLEDGMENTS

Terri Bischoff, this series would have ended at *September Fair* if not for you. Thank you for being an intuitive, kind acquisitions editor and a genius friend. Cheers to many shared projects in our future. Thank you also for lining me up with Nicole Nugent, an editor whose eye for detail is only surpassed by her organizational skills. In other words, she's the Type-A kinda editor this writer needs. Courtney Colton, I'll miss your publicity skills, but I appreciate all the help you've given my writing career. Victoria Skurnick, thank you for being my agent and my friend, and for taking me out for the best octopus of my life. Barbara Moore, thank you for giving me my first break.

Jessica Morrell, I've said it before, and I'll say it again: you make me a better writer every time I work with you. May you live a long and healthy life. Christine Hollermann, your support and friendship mean the world to me. Same to you Dana Fredsti, Linda Joffe "We'll Always Have the Metro" Hull, Aimee Hix, Catriona McPherson, Cindy Pederson, Shannon Baker, Reed Farrel Coleman, Hank Phillippi Ryan, Margery Flax, Kellie Tatge, Stacy Emerson, Jim Pohl, Angie Trulson, and Tony Van Den Einde.

Zoë and Xander, none of it would matter without the two of you. Mom, Dad, and Jen, thanks for consistently helping out so I can still feel like a good mom while following my dreams, and for making convincing me I'm capable of anything.

www.MidnightInkBooks.com

From the gritty streets of New York City to sacred tombs in the Middle East, it's always midnight somewhere. Join us online at any hour for fresh new voices in mystery fiction.

At midnightinkbooks.com you'll also find our author blog, new and upcoming books, events, book club questions, excerpts, mystery resources, and more.

MIDNIGHT INK ORDERING INFORMATION

Order Online:
- Visit our website www.midnightinkbooks.com, select your books, and order them on our secure server.

Order by Phone:
- Call toll-free within the U.S. and Canada at 1-888-NITE-INK (1-888-648-3465)
- We accept VISA, MasterCard, and American Express

Order by Mail:
Send the full price of your order (MN residents add 6.5% sales tax) in U.S. funds, plus postage & handling to:

> Midnight Ink
> 2143 Wooddale Drive
> Woodbury, MN 55125-2989

Postage & Handling:
Standard (U.S. & Canada). If your order is:
> $24.99 and under, add $4.00
> $25.00 and over, FREE STANDARD SHIPPING

AK, HI, PR: $16.00 for one book plus $2.00 for each additional book.

International Orders (airmail only):
> $16.00 for one book plus $3.00 for each additional book